ACCIDENTAL
PROPHET

By the Author

Elf Gift

Butterfly Dream (cowritten with Dave Lara)

Somewhere Over Lorain Road

Accidental Prophet

Visit us at www.boldstrokesbooks.com

ACCIDENTAL PROPHET

by
Bud Gundy

2019

ACCIDENTAL PROPHET

ISBN 13: 978-1-63555-452-6

THIS TRADE PAPERBACK ORIGINAL IS PUBLISHED BY
BOLD STROKES BOOKS, INC.
P.O. BOX 249
VALLEY FALLS, NY 12185

FIRST EDITION: JUNE 2019

CREDITS
EDITORS: JERRY L. WHEELER AND STACIA SEAMAN
PRODUCTION DESIGN: STACIA SEAMAN
COVER CONCEPT: ZALDY SERRANO
COVER DESIGN BY MELODY POND

Acknowledgments

Thanks to the members of my writing groups, whose insights and critiques are essential for me: Scott Boswell, James Warren Boyd, Barbara Brunetti, Christopher Calix, Cole Dennis, Shoshana Dembitz, Susan Domingos, Pat Elmore, Gabriel Lampert, and Tyler Patton. Thanks also to Jerry Wheeler, who amazes me with his precision edits, and to Bold Strokes Books for deciding this quirky story had promise. And to Elaine Eichman for her suggestions and input. There are many others to thank for their help and support while writing this book, but I feel especially grateful for everything I learned from my mom as well as my friend Marion, both of whom I lost while working on this story.

One more time, for Chris

1

Drew Morten's grandmother revealed a number of startling things the night before she died, starting with: "I uncovered what would have been the biggest news story of all time, something terrifying that's still out there waiting to be told," and, "I kept silent about a killing I witnessed, except that it wasn't really a killing. Sort of. It's hard to explain."

Drew struggled to respond.

"And there's a lot more you don't know, Drew."

The lace sheers at her bedroom window misted the room with the amber light of sunset, touched by rose. Grandma's eyes glowed like candlelight above her gently sagging skin, her tight curls in disarrayed bouquets. She smiled, and the yellowing stumps of her teeth softened and warmed her gaze. He was glad she never had them fixed.

"You also need to be on the lookout for a man named Victor."

He drew back. "Why?"

She shook her head, raising her hands. "I don't know."

"Who is he?"

She sighed. "Drew, I've seen much more than you'll ever know, and I kept diaries for years. I guess they call them journals now. About five years ago, I organized them into a memoir. It explains everything, or at least as much as I can explain." Respect and admiration radiated in her eyes, for which he felt wholly undeserving. "Every word I wrote, I thought of you. It's very important that you read it."

She pointed to her bedside table, strewn with medicine bottles. Arthritis inflated her joints like marbles stuffed into her skin. "In the top drawer. There's a card in there somewhere. It looks like a business card, but it only has a printed passcode."

He opened the drawer and rummaged through a clinking assortment of small, long forgotten things. He found the card in back, blank save for a centered line of random, jumbled text.

"That's the code that will open my safe deposit box at Security National Bank in Santa Rosa. You already have my power of attorney, so you won't have a problem."

"Safe deposit box?"

"Don't get all greedy," she teased. "All you'll find is my manuscript. It's about my first year at the network when amazing things happened. I used real names, but most of them are probably dead."

"What do you want me to do with it?"

"Promise to read it. Some of it will sound crazy but I told the truth as best as I could. There are a few surprises in there for you as well. When you're done, you can do what you like with it. Publish it or burn it. It doesn't matter because I told the truth." She sighed as if exhausted from sharing wisdom in such an irrational world. "Just be aware most people don't want the truth. It's one of the things I learned as a television reporter. You have to promise me you'll read it."

"Try to stop me."

"There's one more thing." She pointed to the dresser at the foot of the bed. "There's an old necklace in the bottom drawer. I saw your Aunt Viv looking at it last week, wondering how much it's worth. An old friend left it to me in her will. I want you to have it for helping me all these months, so take it to your room and hide it really well. Viv'll turn the house upside down if she thinks it's worth something."

"Grandma, we don't have to do this now. It's not like you're going to drop dead tomorrow."

"I've been waiting for the right time to tell you these things. I'm certain that time is now. I can feel I'm near the end. I can't explain it. It's not a darkness, and it isn't frightening. It feels like a destination."

"You're tougher than I am, and I'm not dying any time soon."

"Dearest Drew." She stroked his hand. "You're one of the strongest people I know. You'll realize it soon enough."

The next morning, the hospice nurse Tisha knocked and opened Drew's door. A beautiful African American who wore her hair in tight braids, Tisha was just as dedicated to her patients as to her pursuit of a physics degree at Sonoma State. Drew trusted her judgment, and if she interrupted a private moment, it damn well needed to be interrupted. Already awake, he shot up, quickly arranging the tangled sheets to cover his nudity.

"I'm sorry to barge in like this, but your grandma took a turn for the worse overnight. Based on my experience, you should tell your family to get here as soon as they can."

Uncle Dennis and his wife Jean arrived first, hugs all around, Tisha included. Aunt Viv and her a daughter arrived a few minutes later, their heads capped with peroxide puffs.

Drew sat next to Grandma's bed, holding her hand. It looked blue and felt cold. They shared a loving smile. Standing next to him, Tisha put a hand on his shoulder.

"Victor," Grandma said, so softly that if he hadn't recognized it from last night's warning, he'd never have been sure of her final word.

The others looked at him for an explanation, but he focused on Grandma. She rubbed and pinched the bedspread until her eyelids drooped and her head slumped. A death rattle gurgled softly, like a forgotten pot set to simmer.

Drew took a deep breath, overwhelmed by being present at the end of Grandma's life. She was born as World War Two raged. Every moment she'd lived, many as a famous national news anchor, brought her here in this room with these few people, and he was one of them. It was as much an honor as an unfathomable loss.

"Well, that's it," Aunt Viv said quietly, giving her mother a quick kiss on the forehead. "We need to find the stock certificates."

The comment jolted Uncle Dennis. "Viv, Mom told me the stocks were going to be divided between you, me, and Drew. She said she put it in her will."

Drew's cousin Regina looked scandalized. "Why does Drew get a third, but there's nothing for the other grandchildren?"

Uncle Dennis raised his voice. "Because Drew's mother was our sister and she died. If your mom wants to give you some of her share, that's her business, but Drew's parents are dead, so he inherits that third."

Regina started to argue, but Aunt Viv stopped her. "I'll call the lawyer in a few minutes and ask when we can see the will. Right now, let's just find and protect all the valuables." She nodded at the dresser.

"There's an old necklace in there. It's in a purple pouch. I've never seen it before, and my mom couldn't remember where she got it. It wouldn't surprise me if we could get a pretty penny for it."

"Why don't you see if she has some gold fillings to dig out before the people from the funeral home come?" Drew said.

Aunt Viv lifted her chin. "My mother wasn't sentimental. She'd want me to secure the family heirlooms."

Tisha said softly, "Drew, venting your anger at her death won't bring her back."

His anger was bigger than that, but Tisha was otherwise correct, so he turned away and trundled downstairs. Uncle Dennis and Aunt Viv started arguing.

For the past five months, Drew had lived in the tiny pantry/sun room next to the kitchen, the only available room in Grandma's small house with a door that closed. He'd cleared away the dollhouse dining set, inflated an air mattress, and covered the windows with sheets. He'd borrowed a rolling coat rack to use as a closet, and it just barely fit.

He sat on the bed and flipped up the blanket, lifting the purple velveteen pouch Aunt Viv and Regina were searching for upstairs. From its weight, the silver was real, formed into a choker of twisted ropes. He examined the large, tear-drop pendant. Despite a shade of ruby as deep as a royal cape, the flawless crystal was clear enough to read through.

He luxuriated in the gem's hypnotic gleam before pulling the safe deposit box passcode from the pouch. He returned the necklace to the pouch and looked for a less obvious hiding spot, which he found behind a shelving unit displaying decorative but unused kitchen supplies like a fancy porcelain tea service and platters. He gave his beard and buzzed hair a quick brush, grabbed his car fob, and set out.

Grandma's cottage nestled on a hillside among soaring redwoods, ancient giants that ignored the humans living out their brief lives at their roots. Once the masters of forests across the earth, the trees survived in only a few spots of Northern California, with distant relatives huddled in a valley in the misty wilds of China. Limbs shot from the trunks in horizontal precision, softened by the pine-like needles that fuzzed their branches and covered the ground with spongy carpeting.

Across the lane, a light snapped on deep inside another small house hunched in the eternal shade of the redwoods. A friendly widow named

Althea Miller lived there, and if he told her Grandma had died, she'd spread the news across the hillside, sparing him the task. He started across to knock on Althea's door but changed his mind and climbed into his car.

Scattered homes lined the narrow roads that twisted along the hills above the Russian River. He wound slowly downhill, alert to the possibility of an opposing car suddenly appearing around the next curve that would require a clumsy dance of backing up and pulling over. Often one could do nothing but ease aside and let the other car crunch past with a friendly wave.

At the bottom of the hill, he waited at a stop sign for a break in the heavy traffic along River Road. Trucks, RVs, and other vehicles roared past. Merging required gunning the pedal and holding your breath.

He peeled out at a spot between a pickup and a big rig and survived one more time. About ten years ago, late one night after spending the day with Grandma, his parents hadn't. The CHP officer had assured him they didn't see the truck and died blissfully unawares, but Drew never believed her. He knew they saw the headlights, the lightning streaks on chrome moving much too fast and much too close, their screams drowned out by a blasting horn. He never crossed the spot without thinking of their last terrifying moments.

River Road slalomed along, flattening to a straight line only when passing through Guerneville, the once-posh resort town for San Francisco's elite, now a roughened but popular vacation spot for a mix of people casual about being openly gay and startled straight tourists casting surreptitious glances. Restaurants, bars, and tchotchke shops ran for several sunny blocks before the road plunged back into redwood shade.

Forty-five minutes later, he pulled into the parking lot of Security First Bank in downtown Santa Rosa. Inside, an efficient woman confirmed his power of attorney before leading him into a room with an empty table and chair.

She tapped the code into a glowing pad. Soft machinery whirred behind a wall patterned in beige and black. She pointed to an empty recess. "Just enter the passcode on the front. When you're through, put the box back in the slot, hit the return button, and the system will automatically refile it."

A moment after she left, a box rolled forward like an offering.

After he punched in the passcode, the front popped open, and Drew removed a jumbo manila envelope with his grandmother's manuscript.

He returned to Grandma's house, where only Tisha's car remained. She came outside as he parked.

They hugged. "I'm sorry for your loss, Drew. I'll stop by tomorrow morning with the final hospice forms. I'll also have to do an inventory on the remaining supplies."

"Sorry for your loss, too. I know you were fond of my grandma."

"I was." Her eyes glinted. "Your family went to see the lawyer in San Francisco. Oh, and Althea across the way saw the funeral home's van and came over, so she knows, too."

That settled his obligations to the neighborhood.

"They took her?"

Tisha nodded and rubbed his arm. "How are you doing? Do you want to talk?"

"Thanks, but I'm not in the mood. I'm not sure how I feel yet."

"That's perfectly normal. Do you want me to call someone for you? Like a boyfriend or something?"

"I'm not seeing anyone, and I'll be fine. Why don't you take off? I can handle anything that comes up here."

She studied his face. "Okay, then. I'll see you tomorrow morning at the usual time."

She drove off and sounds rose all around. Chattering birds, a barking dog, a distant chainsaw, and the hollow, deliberative *thunk thunk thunk* of woodpeckers.

He couldn't go inside just yet. In the comfortable shade of ancient redwoods, he eased himself into a metallic rocking chair on the porch. He slipped the manuscript from the envelope.

2

Requiem for a Girl Reporter

1943–1975

My name is Claudia Trenton. For fifteen years, from 1965 until 1980, I was a famous television journalist. I was born in Vermont in 1943, and I have no siblings. My father was a soldier killed in the recapture of Guam in 1944, and I have no memories of him.

I've kept meticulous journals all my life and I can report with confidence about a transformative year when I enjoyed a string of triumphs as a television journalist. When the cameras were off, however, my world cracked open and I glimpsed a reality that left me breathless with wonder and fright.

After my father died, my mother moved us to Cleveland to live with her older sister in a brick duplex that overlooked a valley filled with clanking steel mills belching fire and smoke. I attended St. Mark's parochial school where one of my friends referred to my aunt Lydia as a spinster. I took great umbrage because it sounded like a terrible accusation, and my aunt was a kind and sensible woman. I shared my anger with my mother. To my horror, she told Aunt Lydia, and I was mystified when they both laughed uproariously. I'd never seen my aunt more sincerely delighted.

Unlike my schoolmates, I found television shows like *The Mickey Mouse Club* embarrassingly childish and all those westerns excruciatingly dull. Mom and Aunt Lydia loved watching *The Honeymooners* and *I Love Lucy*. I enjoyed those too, but I was transfixed by a mythical being on the local news, a creature so rare and magical all of America knew about Cleveland's *girl reporter*.

Her name was Delilah Fuller, and she was in her forties when she made her television debut, but everyone called her the girl reporter. Her popularity spurred other stations to hire women, which made me anxious. I wanted to be a girl reporter, and I worried I'd never find a job if every station in the country already had one.

I studied the way Delilah looked into the camera, the way she spoke and nodded during interviews. The girl reporters who appeared on the other stations were much more attractive than Delilah. They smiled while interviewing cooks and singers and puppets, while Delilah angrily tapped the table when the mayor or a congressman avoided her question.

I worshiped her.

I started reading both the morning and afternoon newspapers. I studied the weekly magazines at the library and almost never missed a political press conference, State of the Union speech, or special coverage of major events.

I graduated from high school in 1960. My grades weren't exceptional enough for a scholarship, and both my mother and aunt toiled for small wages in the cafeteria of a steel mill, so college was out of the question. I held on to my dreams but couldn't fathom how to fashion such a glamorous and demanding career.

With a plan to save money for college, I became a secretary at an insurance company downtown. Since I was often still on the bus at six o'clock, I missed many of Delilah's newscasts, but I continued to read the papers and magazines and watch as much television news as I could.

For five years, I filled out insurance forms, typed letters, transcribed memos, answered phones, and ordered lunch for executives who didn't seem half as bright as Delilah. I saved money by skimping on clothes and eating only at home. Raising enough for college proved more challenging than I expected, and I felt my hopes fading.

A cultural revolution was brewing. The Beats and the Beatles cleared a path to hippies at Woodstock, protests of every sort, and women's libbers without bras, but Delilah was my role model. While she didn't seem unsympathetic to these changes, by now she was a fussy old woman. In stores, color TV showed her bright red hair and she wore a lot of makeup.

One of my shabby younger bosses who fancied himself quite the lady-killer said, "You could be really pretty if you started wearing nice clothes and had your hair fixed up. I'll bet you could be on television. You're way foxier than that old hag Delilah Fuller."

Maybe that's what television needed: a foxy Delilah Fuller.

That weekend I spent a fortune on a hair stylist and a fancy outfit from an upscale department store. On Monday, I called in sick and arrived at the television station first thing in the morning. I summoned the courage to march inside and ask to meet with the news director.

"What's this about?" the receptionist asked. She was prettier than I was, and I stuttered until I said, "I'm here about a job."

Amazingly, he agreed to meet with me. I perched nervously in a chair facing his desk. He wore a rumpled brown suit and was almost completely bald. He gave me a friendly smile.

"What can I do for you, Miss Trenton?"

I took a deep breath. "I've studied Delilah Fuller for years. I know every move, every look. I've even practiced how she holds a microphone. I've been studying politics since I was a little girl. I gave up my social life to read and watch the news, and I was born to be a television reporter. If you give me a chance, I'll bring something just as fresh to your station as Delilah did."

His smile grew. "Did you know that I hired Delilah?" I gave him a startled, spontaneous look of admiration that, in retrospect, was the perfect response. "You think you can replace her?"

I was mortified. "No, but I can bring a new style to what she does."

"You mean you want to be a pretty Delilah Fuller?"

I felt my face burn. "I mean I can be the voice of a new outlook in Cleveland. We're much more reserved than San Francisco or New York or Los Angeles, but the young generation here is just as restless for something new. I have the talent and the skills to bring those viewers to you, people who appreciate an intelligent woman who understands them." I worried I'd gone too far.

He cupped his hand over his chin, ready to order me out.

"Can you start today?"

Two hours later, I stood in front of a burning tool and die plant in far-off Elyria. I interviewed the manager and shop steward about the loss of revenue and jobs while a scornful cameraman and audio tech rolled their eyes. We rushed back to the station and a sympathetic editor helped me record the voice-over and pull the piece together, peering at the film through an eyepiece while swiveling the hand cranks. My story led the six o'clock news and Delilah Fuller, by now a bona fide journalism star, read the intro copy that I wrote.

After that first newscast, I eagerly waited to introduce myself to Delilah, but she gave me a slight smile and walked past. She rarely took notice of me. My idol tottered around the station like an aging queen who expected scraping subservience. Although she was always regally polite, she rebuffed every attempt to get personal. Now and then, she complimented one of my stories. When the ratings rose because of me, she even seemed tender.

For three years, I worked as a general assignment reporter covering crime scenes, fires, storms, labor disputes, train derailments, and car crashes. I made my mistakes, I learned my lessons, and I was thankful for every moment. I had to prove myself before I could sit down with a congressman and demand answers, and I wasn't interviewing puppets. I made good money, people recognized me everywhere, and my mother and aunt grew giddy with pride. I moved into my own apartment.

I'd never been asked on a date, but soon every kind of man approached me, from the attractive and successful to the slovenly joes I interviewed in sketchy neighborhoods. I cautiously accepted a few invitations to dinner, but only with the handsome and better-off sort. When a date suggested an intimate night at his place, I smiled and said I had commitments the next morning. When he grew more insistent, I truthfully told him my career came first. I got used to being called a stuck-up bitch.

As Delilah's stardom faded, the ratings stalled and began to sink despite our hard work.

In 1968, the old news director retired, replaced by a restless go-getter named Barry with lots of bushy hair and muttonchops. He wore mod, psychedelic fashions and spoke in a rapid patter. Soon after he started, he asked me to lunch at a fancy restaurant. The other diners recognized me and stared.

"Delilah is ancient," he said, sipping whisky and water. "She's also an icon, and you can't buy that for a million bucks, so I'll keep her on the air for as long as she can breathe. But she's a square, and she's getting senile. We have to jazz things up, so here's the nitty-gritty. We need a new girl co-anchor to replace Delilah on the six and eleven o'clock news. Pronto."

I concealed a surge of excitement and hope.

"Check out these numbers." He handed me a sheet of paper. "You're the most popular chick in the market. You're gorgeous and you're smart, but you don't act like some stuck-up bitch. I'm offering you Delilah's spot." He smiled like he'd just suggested something indecent, a proposal that felt inevitable.

I pretended to study the numbers while I considered my options. I was on the verge of a rocketing career ascent, but I couldn't imagine knocking my childhood hero from her co-anchor chair.

I forced the words out. "If you think I'm going to betray Delilah Fuller, you don't know me at all."

"Don't sweat it. We're starting a newscast at noon. We'll park Delilah there for the old people and housewives and cripples. They'll love it, she'll love it. She's a childless spinster, so she can deal with a new schedule. It's mint."

I'd heard Delilah grouch about her late hours, so I knew he was right. She would love it. I accepted the offer. I also turned down his predictable advances. "I dig it," he said. "Don't shit where you eat."

Barry introduced a slew of production gimmicks. For example, the newscast now opened with a wide shot from an overhead camera bolted to the lighting grid, just behind a waffled prop tile only a few feet across. The shot gave the illusion that the small prop was a massive ceiling with a bright, modern, beeswax pattern, an impossibility in a television studio. And just before each show, the anchors did our audio checks on-set before grouping off camera to wait for our cue. As the music and voice-over rolled, we hurried back to our chairs as if we were just rushing in with the very latest news.

Our ratings stabilized before climbing steadily.

Delilah's growing senility became difficult to hide. At noon, she walked on-set alone, looking achingly lonely in the huge overhead shot with the fantasy ceiling. Her ordinary clothes evolved into increasingly elaborate outfits until she shuffled along in floor-length evening gowns, feather boas, and glittering jewelry. The music often ended before she reached the chair, so all was silent until she plonked down and squinted.

As she read, she impatiently swatted at stray feathers, barking for the prompter to scroll back because she'd lost her place.

Her ratings soared.

"Barry's exploiting her!" I said to my mom and aunt. "She wants to be on TV, but people are tuning in just to laugh. It's disgraceful."

"Don't complain," my mom said. "They'll think you're ungrateful."

"Or difficult," Aunt Lydia added.

For five years, I kept silent. Our newscasts led their time slots, and Delilah went along with whatever Barry wanted. As she slowly deteriorated, anchoring solo became too challenging, so an older man was hired to read the news while she waited for her diminishing number of cues.

Around this time, my mother died suddenly at work from an undiagnosed heart condition, a call I took only fifteen minutes before the six o'clock news, requiring a scramble to replace me because I couldn't go on that night. After the funeral, I learned my aunt Lydia had cancer. She died a few months later.

Nobody warned me to brace for the overwhelming dislocation of losing my family. I took vacation time from work to marinate in emotion while clearing out the old apartment where I'd grown up. I was filled with an existential pain most of us feel but few dare mention, a hopelessness as you examine the trinkets of an extinguished life. Jewelry, books, even old pots and pans detach and float away without identity. After several more decades, anyone with even a fleeting memory of that person will also be gone. If a photo survives, it might draw a curious glance every so often, but otherwise that life sinks away.

Underneath my mother's bed, I found a veritable closet of linens in zippered plastic bags. When I removed the last one, I spotted an object strapped to the bottom of the box frame with rope, wrapped in a towel. I shoved the mattress aside and untied the knot. Back under the bed, I gently pulled the rope for just enough slack, easing the object into my hand.

The box was about the size and weight of a paperback book, and as I unwrapped it, I felt its sculptural features and heard fragile clinks. With great care, I turned aside the last fold and inhaled with wonder.

The box gleamed with rich rosewood in meticulous floral designs.

Cabochon gemstones studded tight bouquets of silver rosettes with delicate golden leaves and stems framing inlaid mother-of-pearl hearts. I traced a stem with misty-eyed joy that my mother had kept such a private, magnificent secret all these years.

The lid lifted as if new, and blue velvet lined the inside. On a sturdy card affixed to the top, a note read, *For a priceless heart* in my father's hand. With gingerly pinches, I undid a pretty red lace bow securing a bundle of cream silk, revealing a nest of four pieces of jewelry.

The first one was a plain gold wedding band, which I knew instantly had been sent back from Guam in 1944 when my father had been buried at sea. My mother would never tell me where she kept his wedding ring, and I vowed to reunite it with hers. The rest of the jewelry was a complete surprise, including a necklace with a crystal pendant holding a snip of my father's dark hair. I also found a small brooch with an ancient Egyptian design in what looked like real jet, diamonds, emeralds, and rubies.

The last piece bewildered me, a golden pin shaped like a column atop a curly base, capped with a sort of lamp fashioned from translucent yellow gemstones, probably sapphires. I studied the distinctive form before deciding it was a lighthouse rising above stylized crashing waves. The engraving on the reverse read, *To my dearest* followed by a date that meant nothing to me.

I kept the jewelry box, of course, but got rid of almost everything else. When I returned to work, the everyday demands of the newsroom soon blasted away the fog of my melancholy.

After a while, Delilah was reduced to commentaries she scripted in her office, a space strictly off-limits to everyone. Her popular, daily three minutes on camera rarely rose above cranky pet peeves like the noisy kids on her block, substandard chocolates, and her maid's shortcomings, a recurring favorite. "Well, Harriett's done it again," she'd start with indignation. The air for miles around seemed to fill with raucous laughter.

Inevitably, Delilah found reading the prompter too difficult. I was hopeful she'd retire, but Barry rejiggered her daily segment into an ad-lib feature called, *Ask Delilah!*, where she answered live telephone questions. Snickering teens often hijacked the calls with sexual innuendo, which her co-anchor deflected. Legitimate questions earned grumpy and long-winded replies, frequently cut short.

Soon, she began crying whenever her co-anchor gently informed her they'd run out of time. Public laughter faded, and outraged viewers flooded the station with complaints. Barry ended her live segments but kept her on the air for prerecorded fluff interviews edited to remove her wandering attention and painfully long lapses.

One day in the newsroom, I looked up at the monitors and froze to see Delilah interviewing a puppet.

I worked diligently the rest of the day because anchoring two nightly newscasts requires preparation and concentration. Alone in my apartment the next morning, I rehearsed an angry speech for Barry, demanding he force Delilah to retire while the public still remembered her as a serious journalist. As I formulated my rant, the phone rang, and a man with a posh voice asked for me. Cautious because creepy men sometimes got my unlisted number, I asked who was calling.

He introduced himself as Loren Sanderson, executive producer of the network news in New York. "I had a layover in Cleveland last week and caught your eleven o'clock newscast. You're sensational. How do you feel about moving to New York to be a general assignment correspondent for the national news?"

I moved to New York within the month, in March of 1975. I was thirty-two years old.

Delilah died ten months later, in January of 1976. By then, my life had changed in inconceivable ways, and I'd learned things I longed to hack from my mind.

The night Delilah died, I was in my apartment in Manhattan's cosmopolitan but shady Lower West Side. My still-unnamed infant girl was asleep when my phone rang. I shrieked when it went off, for I had turned off the lights and lowered all the blinds. I was curled on the floor, terrified. Gingerly, I lifted the handset and whispered, "Hello?" My voice shook.

"Claudia?" a woman asked, sounding alarmed by my greeting. "This is Betty from Cleveland. Remember me? The associate producer?"

"Betty," I croaked, wishing, not for the first time, I'd never left Cleveland.

"You don't sound so good, Claudia."

"Don't worry about me, Betty. How is everything at the station?"

"I'm really sorry to tell you, Delilah died today. She was taping. She started rambling some crazy stuff and then she just drifted away. We thought she'd fallen asleep again."

Through everything else, I thought of how happy it would make Delilah to know she would die on camera.

"Barry's planning a big announcement tomorrow. All the bells and whistles." She ticked her tongue. "They're going to exploit her to the very end."

I gently sobbed, and Betty tried to comfort me. "She always thought so highly of you."

"She did? She never told me."

"Well, that's the other reason I called." Her voice went dubious. "I'm not sure how you're going to take this. Are you sitting down?"

I was on the floor. "Yes."

"Well, I'm sure you remember how Delilah never let anyone but the cleaning crew into her office. We called it the royal privy chamber, remember?"

"Yeah."

"As soon as she died I made a beeline for her office. I wanted to get my hands on anything personal before Barry ransacked it. She has no family, so he'd publish her private diaries if he thought they could make a buck. They've been sucking her blood long enough." She dropped her voice. "Claudia, Delilah was in love with you. I found letters she wrote but never gave to you dating back to 1965. She wrote poems about you and little comments about your clothes or a story you worked on. She had all of your publicity stills, and she saved your newspaper clippings."

When I didn't reply, she said, "I just thought you'd want to know." She gave me another moment. "Would you like me to send them to you?"

"Of course," I said in a tiny whisper. "I'll cherish them forever."

Betty gave a nervous little laugh, and I realized what my answer implied. Being thought of as a lesbian seemed comically trivial compared to the knowledge that, at the moment, had me cowering. The world needed as much love as possible, yet people seemed so determined to stamp it out. I felt an ache that Delilah needed to be so secretive, so silent.

I let out a whimper.

"Look, Claudia you sound like you're in a terrible state. Are you sure you're okay?"

"I have to go," I said and hung up. I gasped in surprise when a police siren blasted on the street far below.

3

Drew reached behind the shelving unit to pull the purple pouch from its hiding spot but felt only grit and cobwebs. He used the flashlight app on his phone. The necklace was gone. Stunned, he checked under the blanket, his first hiding spot, although he knew he wouldn't find it.

Five people were inside when he left to retrieve Grandma's memoir: Tisha, Aunt Viv and her daughter, and Uncle Dennis and his wife. One of them had swiped it.

Or it could have been a conspiracy of two people who'd treated Grandma's death like the starting gun of a treasure hunt. As irritating as he found Aunt Viv and her daughter, he never suspected them of such lurid greed.

He let it sink in that this was his house now. Uncle Dennis had called earlier to tell him Grandma left the house and everything within to Drew. He worried Aunt Viv might put up a fight for the rickety cottage in spite of the bonanza from the stocks, which was bigger than anyone expected.

As he searched for the necklace, he also kept his eye out for the beautiful little jewelry box Grandma described finding tied beneath her mother's bed, but it was nowhere to be found.

When the shock of the theft wore off, he stopped looking and sat at the small kitchen table, room for two. How many meals had they shared there?

The sky grew dark. He turned on the light, a bulb in a pink-frosted globe that usually cozied the kitchen with blushing light. Not tonight. She'd been alive at dawn, and now the sun was setting on her final day.

When his parents died in the car crash, Drew felt the dislocation Grandma described in her memoir, the profound shock that the first voices he'd heard, the first faces he'd seen, the people who'd welcomed him to life, were gone. Grandma had been right about the flailing sensation of losing parental figures, stumbling about to find a new, firm foundation with a need that overwhelmed even grief. He'd latched on to her, and to his surprise she clutched back with equal desperation, driven, he later realized, by losing her first child.

Images of Grandma's face over the years drifted in his mind, dissolving into one other like spots of light. As the memories floated, her smile remained tender even as her skin and hair went crinkly and frail. Snatches of sentences came, bright and happy in the early years, deepening to encouragement, and ultimately brimming with intellectual respect: "Grandma loves you more than anyone." "You don't have to be the best at everything." "Didn't you know that people who call you names are just insecure about themselves?" "I miss your mother more than I can say, but I'm grateful her death brought us together."

He'd known about his grandmother's glamorous career for as long as he remembered, but the allure of fame finally came one day in third grade. During a writing lesson, his teacher mentioned his grandmother as a way of illustrating that grammar skills are essential for success. Grandma had walked away from her career twenty years before, and the other students had never heard of her. Nonetheless, after learning she'd been a regular face on national television they turned to him, star-struck, eyes and mouths agape. It felt as if a shower of rhinestones and glitter had burst above his head.

The next time he saw her, he eagerly asked what it was like to be famous. Her reply was among the most useful insights of his life. "You can be happy with or without fame if you figure out how to juggle the things you already have. Most people never figure it out, and I've known many unhappy famous people."

In the years after the accident, Drew typically drove up twice a month to spend the weekend with Grandma. They talked late into the night, watched movies, or played board games, especially backgammon. In rainy winter weather, they frequently spent whole weekends on challenging jigsaw puzzles. He slept on the sofa and woke early to make coffee and breakfast, carrying it on trays to her room where they chatted, ate, and laughed. They caught plays at the homey local theater or crammed into the oversized Quonset hut that showed first-run movies. They attended openings at the local art galleries and read the same books, leading to hours of discussion and analysis. Almost every night, they tried exciting recipes and savored the delicious results. Or found humor in the disasters.

He already knew he'd look back on those weekends as among the happiest days of his life.

He hadn't eaten anything since last night, and hunger suddenly seized him. Leftovers from yesterday's sautéed chicken and mushroom dinner, were in the refrigerator. She'd loved it. He couldn't imagine eating it.

Beneath the windowsill, he saw a bowl of apples he'd bought the other day. She'd found them a bit too mealy.

He plunked a cutting board on the counter, grabbed an apple and a knife, and promptly sliced his index finger. The pain was insignificant but a neat, bright red line slashed his skin and soon gushed. He tried to contain it, but a few drops plinked on the counter.

"Shit," he said, flipping on the faucet and holding the cut under running water. It looked deep but not serious enough for stitches. He pinched it tight and grabbed a towel on the table, getting blood on the manuscript. He swore softly and headed upstairs for a bandage, but someone knocked on the front door just as he passed. He stuck his finger in his mouth and answered.

Althea Miller, Grandma's neighbor across the street, stood on the porch, holding a pie. She was strikingly handsome with grayish-blond hair and a refined but friendly face, twilight washing her in a bluish glow. She smiled sadly and held up the pie.

"I baked it especially for you," she said, with a fleeting trace of an English accent. "I hope you like peach."

He checked his finger and was mildly surprised the bleeding had stopped. The watery distortion must have made it look deeper than it was, and his tight pinch had done the trick.

He thanked her for the pie and invited her inside for a slice.

"I've no wish to intrude."

"You're not intruding. I feel like talking with someone who knew her."

He led her to the kitchen and she put the pie on the table. The crust billowed and cracked with golden perfection and it smelled delicious.

He wiped the blood off the counter and assembled plates and forks, careful not to reopen the wound.

"Is everything all right?" she said, alarm in her voice. He saw a surprising number of bright, ghastly red splashes on the top page of the memoir. It looked like the grisly aftermath of a violent episode, not a little cut. He explained what happened and said the bleeding had stopped.

She read a few words. "Did your grandmother write this?"

"Yeah. She told me last night she'd written a memoir. I only read the first chapter, but I've already learned a lot of things I never knew. The most important is that she named my mom after an old friend. Delilah. Grandma never talked about her friend, so this was the first I'd heard about her."

"What a lovely thing to learn. Now remind me, your mother passed away, isn't that right?"

"Both of my parents. A car accident at the bottom of the hill."

"Yes, I recall that now."

Drew served two slices and they dug in. "Althea, how much do you know about dementia?"

"As much as anyone, I suppose."

The pie was just the right mix of tart and sweet, and he wondered what Grandma would say about it before he remembered he couldn't ask her. His voice caught as he said, "Delilah had dementia. My grandma wrote a really interesting story about it. I wonder if my grandma might have been suffering from it, too. She said a few things last night…"

"What sort of things?"

"Just weird things. She also said some weird things in her memoir, but she told me she wrote this about five years ago. Even up until last night, she was never anything less than one hundred percent lucid, but based on what she wrote, I'm wondering if she'd been losing her mind for a while, but I never noticed."

"It's certainly not uncommon to learn that what seems like old age forgetfulness is, in fact, early-stage dementia."

"I'm talking about delusions, not forgetfulness. Strange stories in her head."

"Drew, it's ended. Don't trouble yourself over things that no longer matter. If I may, how old are you?"

"Thirty."

"And you live in San Francisco?"

"I rent an apartment with a roommate. I've been keeping up with the rent, but now that I own this place, I'm not sure what I'll do."

"The roommate…is he a romantic partner?"

He snorted. "Not a chance. He's fine, but he's just a friend. I'm not seeing anybody."

He didn't remember telling Althea he was gay. Maybe Grandma did. Her question surprised him because he assumed his aversion to romance was as obvious as a facial tattoo. His sole long-term relationship had ended five years before, after a slog of eight months with a moody guy he came to actively dislike. Eventually the dread of spending more time with him outweighed that of a dramatic breakup scene. Despite all the stern lectures about the importance of breaking up face-to-face, Drew stopped calling or texting with no explanation. After a few weeks of return silence, he indulged a transitory indignation that the guy hadn't put up a fight.

He found solace in dating apps, the polite name for sites gay men use on their phones to find quick and easy sex. The photos and profiles offered efficient shopping, the sexual dos and don'ts listed like product features. Despite lamenting about the clinical nature of the process, he found the intimate details and photos highly erotic.

And far from being sterile, the impersonal nature of the sex was a huge turn-on, a knock on the door and almost no conversation before getting started, both guys only concerned with raw sex. The fantasy often collapsed at that point, exposing the digital world, yet again, as people's best disguises. Drew liked to think of himself as honest about such things, but he knew he was as prone to self-delusion as anyone else.

Althea said, "You have friends in Guerneville, yes?" He shrugged even though he didn't. "Why not head out tonight and be with people who understand you? It's usually an effective tonic."

He checked his finger. No blood, and the wound looked almost healed. "I'm not sure I'm ready to be around a bunch of people in a loud bar."

She patted his arm. "You quit your job and moved here to the countryside to help your grandmother, and that's as much as anyone can expect from a young man in the prime of his life. You're quite attractive, a catch, as we used to say. Don't allow grief to upset your equilibrium. I'm certain your grandmother would agree." She cleared her throat uncertainly. "I was here when the funeral director removed her today. I assure you she looked quite serene, which means she was at peace. Let that be your comfort and your guide."

He appreciated her compliments but focused on the more salient issue. Since she'd been in the house earlier, the list of suspects for the missing necklace was now six. It was difficult to imagine Althea rummaging around and clutching it furtively as she scurried home.

"I want you to call on me, Drew. If you find yourself confused or in need of a sympathetic ear. I'll be free at any time. Agreed?"

"Yeah," he replied, surprised.

Later, he realized she was talking about much more than that moment. She meant everything to come.

4

The Warrior Returns

March 1975

The first time I saw Manhattan with my own eyes, I scarcely believed it was the work of humans. Surely, men had merely carved corners and shapes into an existing mountain range of solid silver. It looked top-heavy, resting on an almost imperceptible island so that it seemed in danger of tilting off-balance and crashing into the water.

Once across the East River via the Queensboro Bridge, the illusion of fragility vanished, replaced by one of immortality. Block after block of huge buildings rooted to the land with titanic self-regard, ancient gods who didn't live on Olympus because they *were* Olympus.

The network building rose sixty stories in cream limestone, a stately beaux art symbol of confidence, sporting pillars and medallions. When it opened in 1920, it housed mostly insurance companies and law firms until the plucky radio station on the top floors became a massive television network that absorbed the entire building.

On my first day, I walked off the elevator and stopped in amazement. The newsroom filled the twelfth floor, with executive offices on one side but the other walls knocked out to create a vast open space strewn with desks. Phones rang unceasingly, people rushing and typing and shouting to each other. A glass-encased assignment desk where editors yelled orders into phones and walkie-talkies was on a raised platform in the center. A long row of wire machines clattered and clanged and tapped as they delivered news from around the globe. Paper and pens littered the floor, which was also scattered with huge pods of open boxes overflowing with empty script sheets.

I looked at my watch. Although I was a few minutes early, nobody was on hand to greet me and tell me where to go and what to do. I checked a huge assignment board to confirm I'd arrived on the correct date, afraid that Loren Sanderson had changed his mind about hiring me.

I went to the assignment desk and leaned around the glass corner. A man muttered to himself as he typed.

"Hello," I said. When he didn't respond, I spoke louder. He jerked up. His eyes narrowed. "I'm Claudia Trenton, the new general assignment correspondent."

He gave me the once-over and looked about my feet. "Are you packed?"

"Excuse me?"

"Do you have a travel bag?" His tone implied I was stupid.

"My luggage is at the hotel. I didn't know I was supposed to bring it."

"Jesus Christ." He ripped the paper free, and the typewriter screeched with objection. "Can you get on a plane to Oklahoma in the hour?"

My voice went high. "Oklahoma?"

"Tornado damage. We need a story for the six thirty show. The crew's already there and shot a ton of B-roll. Can you take it?"

I stammered. "I suppose. How long will I be there?"

"Until we need you somewhere else." He seemed to take pity on me and handed me a stuffed envelope. "Two days, probably. These are your travel vouchers. Planes and taxis and hotels. Keep track of your expenses and save every receipt. Just don't eat at the Ritz. The worst damage is outside of Tulsa. Get there by noon and find the crew. I don't know their exact location, so ask around. Shoot your stand-up first, then get whatever interviews you can, and we'll cut them into the package. The satellite's booked for four thirty. You can record the V.O. by phone later."

I felt dizzy. "I have to be in Tulsa, Oklahoma in three hours?"

"You'll gain an hour in the air because they're on Central Time. Look, princess, this is the big leagues. You gotta hustle. Plenty of other pretty faces would be halfway to the airport already."

"Claudia?"

I turned and a wiry man with a thin mustache and a well-tailored suit extended his hand. "I'm Jeff Richardson, assistant news director for domestic affairs. Loren told me to keep an eye out for you. Let me show you the ropes."

Flustered, I looked back and forth. "But this man assigned me to cover the tornado damage in Oklahoma."

"Jesus, Kenny, give her a break. She just walked in. Find somebody else. Come on, Claudia."

Relieved, I returned the envelope to Kenny, who growled, "Have a travel bag ready at all times in the future."

As Jeff led me downstairs, he said, "Loren wants you join him for lunch in his conference room at noon." After signing a blizzard of forms, we returned to the newsroom where he took me to an empty desk with a battered typewriter overlooking the street far below. He told me how to order desk supplies and said he'd see me soon.

I organized my desk, sharing brief and friendly conversations with my busy coworkers. Just before noon I walked to the offices along the far wall. Secretaries in a long row each served two of the various news directors and producers. As the executive producer, Loren Sanderson had the corner office and his own assistant, an older lady in a trim suit and a classic swept-back hairdo. She greeted me with a professional smile. "You must be Claudia. He's expecting you."

She led me to a fancy, paneled conference room with tasteful furniture, glossy plants, and an elegantly prepared, intimate dining table. A moment later, Loren entered. I'd met him only once, at my clandestine lunch interview in Cleveland a few weeks back. I was struck again by his good looks, with a cleft chin and waves of salt-and-pepper hair.

We exchanged pleasantries and sat. A hidden door opened, and a waiter rattled in with a cart holding plates with silver covers. Salad, steak, and potatoes, with wine to boot. We dug in as the waiter left.

"How are things so far?" he asked.

"Just fine. Jeff was a big help."

"Good. He's ostensibly your boss, so I'm glad you got along."

"Ostensibly?"

"He'll have you rushing off to big disasters, but that will come in time." He paused mid-cut to give me an intense look. "I have something I want you to investigate."

"I've never been an investigative reporter." But I was intrigued.

"I know." He shoved a piece of steak in his mouth and chewed aggressively, forcing it down. "I have an entire investigative reporting unit, but I'm uneasy handing this story to them until I know more. There's a personal element to it, so I wish to keep it quiet for now. You'd be doing me a tremendous favor."

I tensed at the mention of a personal element. It felt dangerous to shadow his cheating wife or a son with drug problems. I'd hate it, and my colleagues would never take me seriously.

"Loren, I'm very excited to be here. I promise to give you everything I have, but I'm not cut out to be a private investigator."

"It's nothing like that. It's one of my prep school teachers. His name is Harrison Wheeler. I attended Wallace Lake Academy in Connecticut. Very exclusive. Harrison Wheeler was a teacher my first few years, one of the best I ever had, and he made an indelible mark. He joined the service, as all fit men did after Pearl Harbor, but he never returned from the European theater. Everyone assumed he ended in an unmarked grave outside of Rome. Soldiers vanished with some frequency back then, much more than people your age realize." He put his utensils down and looked out the window. "I saw him last week, at a fundraising gala for the Met."

"That must have been a special reunion for you."

He didn't react for several moments. "Do you believe in the paranormal?"

Alarmed, I straightened. "Loren, I'm here to report the news, not chase ghosts. If you want me on the Bigfoot detail, you should have warned me, and I would have stayed in Cleveland." My words came out more forcefully than I intended, and I braced for his reaction.

He searched my face. "I don't intimidate you. That's good. After I saw Mr. Wheeler at the gala, I thought of asking for your help because you have no friends here yet, nobody who can persuade you to swap secrets. I'll make it known you're working on an important story for me, and everyone will give you plenty of space. But I require your utter discretion before I say more. Do I have it?"

I chose my words carefully. "I can promise you my silence, but I can't promise I'll take the assignment."

"Miss Trenton, either I'm losing my mind or I've found a major story that will electrify the world. If it's the former, I'd rather you tell me quietly. If it's the latter, you'll be a superstar. Bigger than Walter Cronkite and Barbara Walters combined."

I felt a chill of excitement. "Go on."

"Harrison Wheeler had a very distinctive accent. Elusive. We boys argued over whether he was from Britain or some other European country. He never told us, but it gave his voice an arresting effect. He could make anyone understand anything, and we boys hung on his every word. He was a master communicator."

He pushed himself to his feet so swiftly the table rocked. He stared out the window. "That's what stopped me cold at the gala, as I was threading through the tables. That face, that voice. They transported me to my freshmen year in an instant. I could smell the damp rot of our woolen vests."

"What did he say when you told him you remembered him?"

"I never introduced myself."

"But I'm sure an elderly man would be thrilled to know he had such a positive influence on a former pupil."

"Claudia." He faced me. "He hasn't aged a day."

5

Drew helped Tisha load her trunk with the unused hospice supplies, such as the nutritional drinks and adult diapers Grandma never needed. Lastly, he relinquished a locked tin with unopened narcotics and sleeping aids, which she locked into a black metal box secured to the trunk well.

"I still have some time before my next client," Tisha said. "How about taking a walk? We can discuss the memorial service."

"Want to sit by the creek a while?"

"Sure." She smiled and took his hand. "Don't worry, I'm not trying to convert you to our side. Let's just have a little human connection."

Compared to the roughness of male hands, hers felt pillowed and strange but undeniably comforting. They headed downhill, and even though he knew Tisha couldn't have taken the necklace, he needed to ask her about it.

"How's school going?" he said.

"Challenging, but I'll get my PhD. I love being a nurse, but I'm doing the right thing."

"Why are you making such a drastic change?"

"I started reading about particle physics, geometrical space-time, eleven-dimensional hyperspace. I couldn't get it out of my head. I look at all those complex equations that used to frighten me, and it's like I'm looking at the architectural plan for something we can't even imagine yet, like a Cro-Magnon trying to understand the schematics of a space probe. We have no way to see it, to feel it, to sense it because we're trapped in three dimensions. Only physics gets us close. There's something in those equations, Drew. Something big. I want to find it."

"Wow," he replied softly. "I spend my days doing whatever job will pay me enough to afford rent in San Francisco."

"You spent the last five months caring for your grandmother, and nothing is more important than that." She squeezed his hand. "Comforting someone in need, my friend, is the only truly sacred thing in this world."

They stepped onto a faint path in the undergrowth, reaching the narrow, lively creek in moments. It trickled down the steep slope, sounding like a cheerful conversation in a foreign tongue.

They sat on a large rock, and Tisha burst out with a triumphant laugh at something high above. He looked up at tree limbs breaking the empty sky like cracks in glass. "What are you looking at?" he said.

She shook her head with a radiant smile. "Oh, Drew. I feel so hopeful about the world. Everyone is worried about all the terrible things that might happen, that *are* happening, but so many good things are on the way."

"I wish I felt that way."

"You will, when the time is right. Now, how about we discuss the memorial? Do you think your grandma would want us to show clips from her television days?"

"She'd hate that."

"We could get her obituary on the front pages of a ton of websites. People would remember her."

"She'd hate that, too."

She punched his shoulder playfully. "It's for your sake. You've been stuck out in these woods much too long for someone our age. I know what it's like to go without male companionship for a stretch. How about we hit Guerneville tonight?"

He rubbed his knees. "I don't feel like socializing."

"If you're not careful, you're going to end up living alone for years, like some of the men in these hills. Coming to town only for food and whisky. Nobody to tell you you're walking around the store with your fly open."

"That doesn't sound so bad."

"We're going out tonight. That's an order."

Time to change the topic. "Did you see anybody in my room yesterday after I left?"

"I wasn't paying attention. Why?"

"Something's missing. Grandma gave it to me the other night. It's probably pretty valuable."

"Was it the necklace?"

"How did you know?"

"Your grandma showed it to me months ago. She told me she was giving it to you for all the help you gave her. Are you sure you didn't misplace it?"

"Pretty sure."

"Let me know if I can do anything." She stood. "I have to get to my next appointment. And nice try at changing the topic, but I'll pick you up at eight."

It was eight thirty and dark by the time they took their seats at a small plastic table beside the pool at the Guerneville Resort. Low rooms encircled the cement patio, karaoke singers butchering their favorite songs in a lively bar nearby.

A good-sized crowd mingled on the patio, a mix of men and women, gay and straight. Tisha said, "I feel reckless," and ordered two Long Island Iced Teas from a server with rainbow-colored hair.

When the drinks arrived, Tisha took a long sip and touched her head when the buzz hit. "Good thing I live two blocks away and can walk home. I think you're going to have to hoof it back, too. After one of these, I'm going to call nine-one-one on myself if I get anywhere close to a car."

"Hey, Tish." "Tisha!" "Hey girl!" The unending greetings came from people of every kind. At first, Drew tried to follow Tisha's conversations, but he gave up when they focused on people and local gossip he knew nothing about.

"Do you know everyone here?" he said during a rare lull.

"It's a small town. Everyone knows everyone else's business. It's the nice thing about village life. It's also the worst." She ordered another round of Long Island Iced Teas even though Drew hadn't finished his first one. Her voice grew louder and happier in that way of people who rarely get drunk.

"Drew!" a man said.

A good-looking acquaintance from San Francisco named Broderick was smiling down on him. Broderick was a bit older, and they'd gone out a few times and had a few tumbles in the hay. Drew stood, and they gave each other a quick kiss.

"Where the hell have you been?" Broderick said. "I haven't seen you in ages."

Drew explained about taking care of Grandma. Fearing tears, he didn't mention her death. "You're up here for the weekend?" Drew said. Long weekends in Guerneville were a favorite getaway for gay San Franciscans, an affordable way to leave the city for a few rugged days.

"Yeah, I'm with my buddy, Tom." He nodded to a hot guy sitting alone across the patio, wearing a plain T-shirt, shorts, and boots. His dark hair and beard were trimmed to a no-fuss length. "He's cute as hell, and he's never been to Guerneville before. He's ripe for the picking. I'd get a piece of that if I were you."

A couple of guys appeared, surrounded Broderick, and just before they whisked him away, Broderick said, "Seriously. I know Tom's ready to burst, but he's a little shy. Go for it."

As Drew sat, he looked over and met Tom's eyes. Tom smiled just before someone took a spot between them, blocking their view.

For the next few minutes Drew struggled to catch more than a glimpse through the crowd, and Tom seemed to be doing the same. Frustration threatened to swamp Drew's excitement, and his mind started on a prissy lecture about the propriety of a sleazy night with a hot trick so soon after Grandma's death. He felt the moment slipping away.

As if choreographed by an understanding gay god, people shifted in just the right way, clearing a line of sight that brought both men to rigid attention, clamping a look as firmly as steel bolts. Drew chased off the lecture with an urgent vow to give this handsome dude whatever he wanted. The impulse felt as obvious as a hard-on in white pants, and he didn't care where it came from or why. He gave a slight nod of hello that, for gay men on the hunt, also signals a willingness to consider, and probably grant, almost any sexual desire.

Tom returned the nod. Sharing secret, raunchy intimacy with

another man in full view of an oblivious crowd fueled a life-affirming euphoria Drew hadn't felt in a while.

He glanced at Tisha, who was too involved in a conversation to notice he'd slipped away.

He felt his dick responding as he stood, keeping eye contact on his way over. Drew adjusted it without embarrassment. Tom pulled out the adjacent chair in welcome, groping a quick fix between his own legs, also without shame.

His hair was as rich as dark chocolate, a thrilling contrast to his pale skin, and he was as handsome as an erotic sketch. Drew's heart hammered.

They shook hands. Drew told him he'd run into Broderick. Tom nodded. "A bunch of us came up, but I got my own room." He said he was having fun so far, and that was plenty of talk.

Tom hooked a thumb back. "My room's right here."

"Let's go."

The Guerneville Resort wasn't fancy, but the bland rooms served their purpose. Inside, Tom locked the door and yanked the blinds down. Free at last to let rip, they grabbed and grunted through breakneck, sloppy kisses as they unbuttoned, unbelted, and unzipped each other. Tom's torso was thick with hair that fuzzed even the casual muscles of his shoulders and his slightly rounded belly.

Drew moaned in a way that an untrained ear might mistake as menacing. But when he saw the slight smile on Tom's face, he knew they were feeling the same intoxication.

He caught a whiff of Tom's heavy man smell, untainted by cologne. Drew took a deep sniff, and they shared a knowing, smutty, and fraternal smile. The mood deepened, and their eyes filled with a wholly unexpected but clear understanding of what this moment demanded, as binding as any loyalty oath between men, maybe more.

Gay men put as much blind faith in the brotherhood of testosterone as other guys do, often stupidly, but this felt solid and true. Drew thought of the Sacred Band of Thebes, the ancient world's fearsome, elite army that marched into battle as pairs of grimy, sweaty, and devoted male lovers, providing the setting for most of his early jack-off fantasies. War drums filled his ears.

Tom kicked off his shorts, and his dick reared up from a tangle of dark hair. Stunted but thick, it looked like a gay heraldic symbol: a rigid curve tipped with a glistening bubble, the *homo rampant*. Tom stood wide and gave it a slap, and after a few tight bounces it settled, the bubble now hanging as a silky thread.

Drew tore off the rest of his clothes to show Tom his dick, which was longer but less hefty. They gripped each other by the shoulders, looking down as they batted their boys around. With a muted roar, Drew brought them together, stroking both as one.

Tom grunted before impatiently jerking away and dropping to his knees. Drew took charge by cupping the back of Tom's head. He surrendered this round by going still. Drew beat off the powerful urge to ram his authority home, but his pace signaled the drilling to come. He closed his eyes to focus on the jolts streaking from his crotch and exploding in fizzy bursts.

Without warning, Drew's mind filled with a bizarre image of a huge, misshapen tornado churning around a skyscraper in downtown San Francisco, rising to a breathtaking height. Emergency sirens, screeching tires, and thousands of terrorized screams filled the air. Formed by millions of tiny fragments circling at the same speed, the terrifying funnel moved as one, all-knowing and apocalyptic. A woman screamed, "Victor!"

Startled, he opened his eyes. The sight fled, and the screams went quiet.

Thrown off-balance, he looked around, as if the reason for the inexplicable vision was among the plain furniture or the clothes spilling from Tom's duffel bag beside the bed.

He still had time to revive himself before the softening became a problem, so he gripped Tom's head with both hands and pounded. It violated the pacing rules for even the ruthless escalation he knew Tom would accept, but he couldn't think of another way. Tom responded enthusiastically, but it failed to reignite Drew's lust. His concern mounted as he felt himself deflating. His thrusts went tentative.

Tom took confident control by grabbing Drew's ass, a stern order Drew obeyed by going still. Tom powered like a pro, twisting his hand for constant movement, but with the situation deteriorating, Drew worried Tom was only trying to reverse a disappointing turn. Not sexy.

The funnel. The sirens. The screams. "Victor!"

Drew scrunched his face and gave his best effort, but the truth arrived with a limp. After gaming it out for a bit longer, Tom sat back, panting, and wiped his mouth.

"Am I doing something wrong?"

"Sorry," Drew said, blushing. He stepped back and pulled on his pants. He shook his head, trying to scatter the vivid image of the weird tornado and silence the disquieting screams.

Tom stood, visibly worried and shrinking. "What's wrong?"

If he explained about the vision, he'd sound insane. His mind raced for a believable lie. He muttered a lame excuse about Long Island Iced Teas, but he knew Tom wouldn't buy it.

Tom offered a cautious suggestion. "Some guys think my dick is out of proportion."

Drew gasped. "Dude, your dick looks like it just conquered Scotland!"

Tom huffed a grateful laugh, but it bothered Drew. It wasn't the first time he'd assured a man about his dick. He always respected a guy with the frankness and courage to ask, but Tom wouldn't have worried if he'd felt the unshakable allegiance of the warrior code.

"My grandma died yesterday. I guess I wasn't ready for this."

Tom's face creased with sympathy. "I'm sorry. You should have said something." He gripped Drew's shoulder, and it filled him with unexpected strength. "Were you close?"

"She was my best friend." Gratitude pooled in his eyes, and he pretended to focus on pulling his clothes back together, blinking rapidly to drive the tears off. A drop leaked on his face and he swiped it away, a move too obvious to disguise. He wondered why he didn't hesitate to show his erection to a stranger while concealing his tears felt imperative.

"How about a walk?" Tom suggested. "Weather's nice."

"That sounds good."

After Tom threw on his clothes, they went outside. Tisha had moved to the table just outside Tom's door. "I had to get away from all that attention," she explained, her voice fuzzy. "I saw you boys over here, but I looked away for a second and you were gone."

Drew introduced them. "Are you okay? You look a little out of it."

"I had way too much to drink." She rubbed her forehead. "My

head is spinning like a tornado. I was hoping you'd make sure I got home."

Unsteadily, Tisha took the middle spot, sliding her arms into theirs as they walked. As they left the resort, a warm fog was dampening the night. Small, rickety homes on stilts to limit river flood damage lined the streets.

"I can't remember the last time I was this drunk. I think it was my graduation from nursing school. I always forget alcohol makes me pensive. Not pensive, really. More introspective. Reflective. Everyone else is jamming to the groove, and I'm off in the corner wondering what will become of the world."

"Do you ever get an answer?" Tom asked.

She giggled. "I was telling Drew earlier the future won't be nearly as grim as everyone assumes." She looked about. "Take Guerneville. This will be a bustling town in the coming decades. Silver roads, gleaming little cars gliding above, probably some form of magnetic levitation. We'll even start fixing the climate. Flying machines sucking the poison from the air, pumping it back in the ground right where it came from. And oh, those will be some beautiful machines."

Drew thought of the way she laughed earlier at the creek, while staring into the empty sky.

They reached her house in minutes, and she gave them a quick kiss. "Be kind to each other," she said, holding firmly to the railing as she ascended the outside stairs to her door. They waited until she was inside before turning away.

"She's something," Tom said. "You wanna take a walk down to the river?"

"Sure."

Taking each other's hands, they crossed the deserted main street and descended to the riverbank.

Moonlight glowed behind the fog, turning the water into a cottony path through a forest of overhanging trees. They sat at the edge of a cement dock surrounded by inflatable boats and toys, gently bumping in the lazy current.

Tom disentangled his hand and gripped Drew's shoulder, whispering, "I think you're an incredibly handsome guy, and I'd like to get to know you. But I saw you fight off tears earlier. You don't have to do that for me. I'm not afraid to see you cry."

Drew dropped his head and leaned in, grasping Tom's arm. The sobs came instantaneously, his first since her death. The loss was too deep to express in words.

He ached for the sensation of being grateful for the time he'd shared with Grandma, the kind of glib advice popular on websites with peppy headlines like *Top Ten Ways to Overcome Grief*, next to a post about planting a vegetable garden. You can't overcome loss, he realized. The most you can hope for is acceptance, but right now that felt impossible. He'd feel her loss for the rest of his life, always wondering what she'd say about something, something like Tom, who was stroking his head.

Drew cried himself out and they sat in silence for a long while, watching the flowing, moon-frosted water snaking with inky rivulets. In just the past hour or so, he felt better about Tom than any man he'd ever met. Was it too soon to call it love? He didn't think so. Maybe they were incompatible in many ways. Maybe Tom didn't want a relationship. Maybe he whined when he was sick, a major irritation for Drew. And maybe Tom would hate any number of things about Drew. They might annoy each other in a million ways, but tonight, staring at the river, it was love.

Time passed, and Tom yawned.

"I'm keeping you up," Drew said. "I'm beat, too. The last two days have been surreal. I need some sleep."

"Want a ride?"

"Thanks, but I need the walk." He started to pull away, but Tom gripped the back of his head without warning and brought his lips down on his, releasing bolts that tore through him. Drew responded in kind, surrendering to Tom's scratchy facial hair, the fullness of his chest, and the beefy wrap of his arms and shoulders.

They pulled back. "Can I see you tomorrow?" Tom said.

"Yeah, of course." He gave him the address, and they exchanged phone numbers.

They adjusted their crotches and returned to the resort where they shared another lingering kiss before Tom gave a dirty look, biting his lip, and went inside.

Drew walked slowly, thinking about Grandma, her memoir, and how much he wished he could get her impression of Tom. It was late, only the occasional car swishing past on River Road. The buzz of insects filled the air like the whirring of a UFO and, high above, the fog curled and crept.

At the bottom of Grandma's street, he paused near the spot where his parents had died.

Unaccountably, the trill of insects faded. In a blink, a bright daylight scene replaced the night, under an amazingly rich blue sky. A subtle but distinct change in the patterns of the trees and branches struck him. The roads shone as seamless silver planes. A diamond-shaped vehicle zoomed out from Grandma's street, merging effortlessly between similar vehicles zipping around the curves, all sailing a few feet above the mirroring road with effortless grace. He glimpsed people inside who were indifferent to the movements of the—what were they? Cars?

In a flash, the daylight scene vanished, replaced by the night and the concrete road. He cried out when the cacophony of insects burst out in mid-trill.

6

The End of War

April 1975

I spent my first week at the network trying to track down executive producer Loren Sanderson's old prep school teacher.

I discovered that Harrison Wheeler vanished in the fall of 1943, just after the battle of Salerno. He marched north with his unit, but after the Germans fled Rome without firing a shot, he appeared as MIA with no explanation.

"That's the end of his records," I said to Loren in his well-appointed office. "The National Archives said he was probably ambushed and buried by German soldiers outside of Rome. As you said, it happened more than people realize."

I waited for him to respond, but he gestured for me to continue.

"I checked with your prep school. He was entitled to a limited pension from Wallace Lake Academy beginning in 1965, but he's never filed a claim. They couldn't find any records that listed an old address. I contacted several retired teachers who remembered him. To a man, they described him as cordial but very remote."

"Don't his military records list his hometown?"

"He gave Wallace Lake as his address and the superintendent as his next of kin. And I checked the guest list for the gala at the Met. His name isn't listed. I cajoled the publicist for photos. Maybe you can recognize someone nearby who might have exchanged a few words with him."

I handed over a manila envelope that he snatched away. I noticed he wasn't wearing his wedding ring.

He flipped through the photos until he sagged with relief. Triumphant, he slapped the picture. "That's him," he said, showing me a handsome man seated between two society ladies giving faint, phony smiles. "I've been wondering if I imagined seeing him. But if this isn't Harrison Wheeler, he's an identical twin."

In his crisp tuxedo, the man exuded rugged charm and I felt a stir of intrigue. He grinned flirtatiously with a square jaw and friendly eyes.

"He's certainly not elderly," I noted. "He can't be older than thirty-five. Do you know the women in this photo?"

"No, but perhaps my wife—" He stopped, as if surprised. "Well, never mind that. Can you find out who they are?"

I promised to do my best. "But there's another issue I want to discuss. I've been here at the network for a week now, and people are starting to ask me who I am and what I'm doing. The secrecy must be making them paranoid. I'm getting suspicious looks."

"Tell them you're working on a project for me."

"I've done that, and I wish I hadn't. They think I'm your spy, and I don't blame them. Can't you allow Jeff to give me an assignment?" I held up the photo. "I'll go back to the publicist this afternoon and learn everything I can about the people in this picture, but let me prove myself as a reporter. I don't want to start off on the wrong foot with my colleagues."

"It never occurred to me that I was creating such difficulties for you. I know our Senate correspondent in DC had some sort of family emergency and we need a temporary replacement." He hit an intercom on his desk and ordered Jeff to his office. I felt a swirl of excitement. *The Senate!*

Jeff charged in and froze when he saw me. He was one of the many who'd given me strange, worried looks the past few days.

When Loren explained his plan, Jeff looked confused. "The Senate is one of the toughest beats in the country. The intrigues put the Kremlin to shame."

"You told me you needed someone for a few weeks to count votes and be on hand in case anything happens." Loren gestured to me. "She's an intelligent woman, and she can hold down the fort as well as anyone. She's going to spend the rest of the day working on that project of mine, but she can head out in the morning. Now, I have other matters that require my attention, so both of you please give me some peace. Thank you."

I slipped the photos into the envelope and followed Jeff out. He asked me to his office, which was far smaller than Loren's. "Close the door," he said.

Slowly, he took his seat. I remained standing. "You have to tell me what you're working on for Loren."

"I'm sorry, I wish I could."

He raised his voice. "I'm the assistant news director for domestic affairs. It's my right to know how one of my reporters is spending her time."

"And I'm the new general assignment correspondent, and the executive producer has asked me to remain silent."

He glanced at the envelope. "I saw you put some photos in there. A high-society shindig. What's that about?"

I clutched the envelope tighter. "When Loren gives me permission to say something, I will. I promise."

"Is Loren going to shuffle the New York and DC offices? Because if he is, I need to know, and he has no right to keep it from me."

I shook my head with a sigh. I longed to tell him Loren was merely spooked by a ridiculous coincidence, but I couldn't. "He hasn't shared any plans with me. He asked me to investigate a private matter." I grimaced, regretting my choice of words, "Believe me, it's trivial, but he's the boss."

He drummed his fingers against his lips with a malevolent sneer. "The Senate is an old boys' club. You get the best scoops at the urinals. It's not a job for a woman."

I felt my face burn. "I'll do my best, Jeff. I've interviewed Ohio's senators many times."

"A couple of hayseed Democrats. Big whoop."

I went to the door, grasped the doorknob but turned back. "Actually, Senator Taft is a Republican, and nobody's ever called a space hero like John Glenn a hayseed."

"One more question!" he bellowed, rising, his fists planted on the desk like a gorilla. "Are you fucking Loren Sanderson?"

"No. I'm fucking Claudia Trenton. I was the most popular anchor in Cleveland, and tomorrow I'm going to be covering the Senate for the network news." I slipped out, glancing around. If anyone heard Jeff, they didn't show it.

At the assignment desk, Kenny noted my shaking hands and voice as I told him about my new assignment. In a businesslike manner, he gave me train schedules and hotel details. After he handed over the vouchers, his voice dropped. "Don't let Jeff get your goat. He's an asshole, and everyone hates him. He probably won't be in this job much longer anyway. Fuck him. You're a better person than he is."

Grateful for his unexpected support, I gave a short nod and rushed off with my head down to hide my struggle with my tears.

A few hours later, I met with the publicist for the Met. Her name was Beth, and she led me into Central Park to a serene grove of trees in spring bud, where we sat on a concrete bench. As we unwrapped our sandwiches, she said, "Why does the executive producer of the news want to know who was at that particular table?"

"I really can't say anything other than it would be very helpful if you could identify at least one of them, especially the man."

She squinted at the photo. "I don't know him." She pointed to the frosty society woman to the right, "but that's Bebe Bellingham. She lives in Georgetown, but she's a lavish New York patron."

"Oh, good," I said, sitting up. "I'm going to DC to cover the Senate, so I'll be able to look her up."

Beth looked impressed. "Have you covered the Senate for long?"

"Never. I'm going to fill in for a few weeks."

"Are you nervous?"

I forced a thin smile. "I've been told it's a difficult environment for women."

"My sister Mary Ellen is a deputy parliamentarian at the Senate. They enforce all the rules. You should get in touch as soon as you get there. I'll tell her to look out for you. Mary Ellen knows everything there is to know." I thanked her profusely.

The next morning, I rushed out of my new apartment on the Lower West Side and caught the seven o'clock train to DC, reading wire copy about the important business before the Senate.

At the beginning of 1975, it was widely assumed the South Vietnamese government would stave off collapse through the end of the year. But beginning on March tenth, the North Vietnamese army launched a new initiative and steamrolled south. The Ford administration wanted a huge infusion of money to stabilize the South's regime, but the Senate didn't seem agreeable. I hoped something would break while I was there, but I couldn't have imagined my luck.

Modern Brutalism stunted the network building in the nation's capital. Beyond a glass entrance, its hallways ran industrial carpeting into a warren of offices. The newsroom sat at the end. It was just as hectic as any other, but with a low ceiling that made the energy feel compressed and explosive.

I checked in with the Capitol Hill producer, who told me the vote for South Vietnamese aid was the most pressing issue to watch. "Money isn't the real issue. A no vote will signal the Congress is going to wash their hands of this mess, and then Vietnam really will be over. So, get over there and keep your ear to the ground. We have crews on standby all over Capitol Hill, so if you need one, just give me a call."

I arrived at the Capitol mid-afternoon and, after showing my credentials, I walked into the stately Senate chamber, taking a moment to be impressed with the red drapery and gold trim. Except for tour groups in the upper gallery, it was mostly empty. I was the only reporter. I spotted a young aide hurrying off after removing paper from a Senator's desk. I wasn't sure he'd be eager to help a reporter, so I unclipped my credentials and intercepted him just as he was about to leave.

I smiled sweetly. "I'm supposed to meet someone from *The New York Times*, but I can't find him. Do you happen to know where the reporters assemble?"

"He might be in one of the Senate office buildings."

"Where are they?"

"Come on," he said, leading me out a set of wide doors to a utilitarian stairwell that opened into a long, underground corridor. Although well-lighted, it was sparsely populated, and I had the uneasy feeling of exploring a subway tunnel.

From the outside, the distance from the domed Capitol to the various Senate office buildings seems no more than a pleasant, easy stroll. In a claustrophobic underground hallway, it feels like an arduous expedition.

I kept pace with the hurried aide until we reached another hallway. "You can usually find reporters in that building. It holds the press and parliamentarian offices. I'm going the other way, so I'll leave you here."

I thanked him and reached a staircase leading to a suitably marbled and imposing building. I passed the press rooms, which were as empty as the chamber, and found the parliamentarian offices.

I asked for Mary Ellen and, after giving my name, I was led into a small, stuffed office that overlooked a sweeping lawn. In the distance, the Capitol Building looked like a Greek temple.

Mary Ellen resembled her older sister, although her hair was blond and loose about her shoulders. "Beth told me to expect you. How can I help?"

"I'm not really sure. It's my first day, and I'm just wondering if I'm missing something. The Senate chamber is empty, and all the reporters seem to be missing."

"Claudia, the Senate works hours that would shame a banker."

"But the appropriation bills for Vietnam are coming up for votes. The administration wants nearly a billion dollars, and everyone is waiting to see what will happen in the Senate. How come nobody is around?"

She gave me a long, silent look. "If you pretend you don't know me, you can follow me. But keep a few steps behind."

I felt a tingle. "Where are we going?"

"There's a meeting of the Armed Services Committee. It's not exactly a secret, but it wasn't announced, and the media doesn't know about it. Do you know any senators on the committee?"

"I know Senator Taft and a lot of his staffers. I've interviewed him many times in Cleveland."

She lifted a folder. "I have to deliver this to the committee room." She looked hesitant. "I know from my sources the bills won't make it out of committee. They're one vote shy, so none of the funding will reach the Senate floor."

I drew in a breath at the enormity of her words. In a near whisper, I said, "It's the end of American involvement in Vietnam."

She gave a firm nod. "The collapse of South Vietnam is unstoppable. Saigon will fall before the end of the month. Except for emergency airlift funding, nobody wants to spend another penny." Her eyes went steely. "You can't use me as a source, understand?" I nodded. "The latest count is eight to seven against, but they probably won't announce anything until Secretary Kissinger and the White House have been notified."

Cautious disbelief dampened my excitement. Was it possible to break such a huge story my first day on Capitol Hill?

After she warned me again to keep well behind and I wasn't allowed to use her as a source, I followed her to a marble hallway lined with grand double doors. I loitered while she marched into a committee room. A small group had assembled in the hallway outside.

I glanced at my watch. I had enough time to call the newsroom and arrange a crew for a live feed at six thirty if I confirmed the vote tally in the next few minutes.

Just then, I spotted Senator Taft's chief of staff and one of his administrative assistants waiting in the hall. The chief was an older, distinguished man, the aide a younger and somber woman. They paced with their faces down and their arms folded.

They recognized me instantly as the anchor from Cleveland, and after explaining I'd moved to the network, I asked in a soft voice, "I've heard the vote is eight to seven against, and the bills won't make it out of committee. Is it true?"

The chief of staff confirmed it. "Those tallies haven't been made public yet. But we want to inform the relevant administration sources first, and we'd appreciate your discretion."

The aide added, "Consider it classified."

I gave her my best awed innocent look, but I knew such a vote would only be officially classified under the most extreme circumstances. Temporary political inconvenience didn't count.

"Thanks so much," I replied. As I left, my legs shook as I restrained an impulse to run. Once in the stairwell, I rushed down and found an empty office. I picked up the phone, called the Capitol Hill producer, and explained what I knew.

"Anyone on the record?" he asked, sounding excited.

"No."

"Then you need three sources. Do you have them?"

The chief of staff counted for one, the senator's aide as another. Even though Mary Ellen had forbidden me to use her as a source, I decided to gamble. "Yes." We arranged a live shot for the lawn out front. "You'll probably be the lead," he said.

I raced off to meet the crew, calculating the risks. Unless I was dragged into court, I'd never be compelled to reveal my sources, so none of them would know. And the vote tallies would be made public soon anyway, so there were no diplomatic or military concerns. All I was doing was reporting a scoop I'd managed to get without even seeing a urinal.

If the scoop was real, that is. I still had trouble believing I'd stumbled upon such a major story.

I dashed into a restroom and slapped on some makeup before rushing outside. The crew was frantically setting up, trailing heavy cables from a microwave truck. The audio tech handed me a microphone and an IFB earpiece. "Loren Sanderson wants to speak with you."

"Loren?" I said into the mic, pushing the IFB into my ear.

"Claudia," he said from the control room in New York, "there's nothing on the wires about the bills failing in committee. Are you sure about the story?"

I'd gone too far to back down. "Yes. The vote against was eight to seven. I don't know who voted for or against, but I'm sure of the totals."

"You have three sources?"

I nodded, but when I remembered he couldn't see me yet, I said, "Yes."

After a slight hesitation, he said, "Okay, let's go with it. You're the lead. Bill will introduce you. Can you handle two or three questions after your report?"

I grimaced. "I only know that funding for more airlifts will probably be approved, but I don't know any numbers."

"Okay. I'll tell Bill to be brief with a follow-up. You're on in ninety seconds."

The crew scrambled to attach the camera to a tripod, all of them pitching in. They screwed it into place and aimed it at me.

Other news crews trotted over to find out what was so urgent, worried they'd missed a big story.

I tried to screen out my concerns: that I was the only one with the news; the risks of claiming three sources I didn't have; the ruination of my career if I was wrong about the basics. I took a deep breath and released it slowly.

"One minute!" the assistant director yelled into my ear. It seemed hardly a moment had passed before he announced, "thirty seconds!"

"Still nothing on the wires, Claudia," Loren said. "Are you certain?"

By now, he was watching me on the monitors in New York, so I nodded. "Let's go."

The distinctive music of the open played in my ear. I heard the voiceover introduction and the anchor said, "Good evening. US involvement in Vietnam came to end today, when the Armed Services Committee of the United States Senate rejected requests for additional military aid for the beleaguered South Vietnamese government. Reporting live from Capitol Hill, here is Claudia Trenton."

"Thank you, Bill. By a vote of eight to seven, the Armed Services Committee declined to forward spending bills to the full Senate for more than seven hundred million dollars in additional funding for the South Vietnamese military. While the spending was expected to fail in the full chamber, the surprise move by the committee is a clear rebuke to the Ford administration and Secretary of State Henry Kissinger, who argued the money was crucial to reverse the unexpected military developments of the past month. Funding for additional airlifts of refugees is expected to proceed, but these committee votes bring the involvement of the United States in the Vietnam conflict to a close. Bill?"

"Claudia, North Vietnamese troops are advancing on Saigon with a speed nobody anticipated. Is anyone predicting how long the South's government can stand?"

I pushed aside my promise to Mary Ellen. "Nobody wants to go on the record, but there is speculation Saigon will fall before the end of the month."

Bill thanked me and moved on to the next item. I took a deep breath. "I hope you're right," Loren said. "There's still nothing on the wires."

I lowered the mic and twisted the IFB from my ear. Having heard my report, the other network crews were scattering across the lawn, but they wouldn't make it on the air before the top of the hour. I'd scooped them all.

Unless I was wrong, in which case those were probably my last moments on live television, ever.

I had no way to know that at almost that exact moment, the AP wire machines started to clang their alerts for an important, imminent announcement.

The crew started to pack up, and I relinquished the mic and IFB. I felt aimless, unsure of what to do, consumed by doubts and regrets. Had I gone too far to make an impact my first day in the field? Would I come to regret using Mary Ellen as a source after being expressly forbidden? Even if no harm came of that, she'd know I was repeating her gossip about the fall of Saigon, and I'd probably burned an excellent background source. Plus, I was still to learn political gossip is the most unreliable on earth.

With no other plans, I decided to head back to the newsroom when the cameraman shouted, "Claudia!" He held up a walkie-talkie. "Congratulations! The AP just confirmed the news. We scooped everyone!"

7

Troubled by his strange visions the night before, Drew read a few articles online about vivid dreams and hallucinations. After an avalanche of words and phrases such as "anxiety disorder," "PTSD," "bipolar," and "psychotic," he changed his search for advice about how to stop worrying about having vivid dreams. The most popular articles on that topic were as unique as paper plates, differing mostly by the order they listed the same obvious tips, like meditation and daily affirmations. When he came across a list that suggested making a list, he closed his laptop.

Maybe someone slipped drugs into the Long Island Iced Teas. The idea became more plausible when he remembered Tisha's woozy walk home, but he hadn't felt drugged, and he'd been in top form with Tom until he saw the tornado and heard those chilling screams.

He grimaced whenever he thought about ruining such a hot scene. He was almost convinced he wouldn't hear from him again when Tom texted to ask how he was feeling. Drew invited him over for dinner.

With hours to fill before Tom arrived, he started straightening out the garage. He pulled cardboard boxes of Christmas decorations, old kitchen utensils, and dusty bedspreads from their shelves and slid them across the concrete, sorting them into things to keep, things to throw away, and things he'd couldn't decide what to do with.

On the bottom shelf of a metal unit, he found a sealed box with "Delilah" written in black marker in Grandma's hand. He kneeled and sliced the tape with scissors, lifting the flaps reverently. On top was a publicity still of an older woman with dramatic waves of red hair, the name "Delilah Fuller" printed in bold font at the bottom. She cupped her chin reflectively, with the barest hint of a smile. She wore a beautiful cream dress with a large collar of fluffy white fur.

She also wore the silver necklace with the ruby pendant Grandma gave him two nights ago.

"Drew?"

Althea walked in, and he replaced the photo and closed the flaps, as guiltily as a boy caught looking at porn. She noted his reaction and paused. "Am I interrupting you?"

He wiped his knees. "No, you just startled me."

She looked about. "It's a baffling experience to clean up after someone dies. What was the significance of a little doodle they kept in a wallet? Did they cherish and hide this book away for some reason, or did they just forget about it in the back of the closet? I'd imagine you have a million such thoughts, especially while reading her memoir. Are you learning a great deal?"

"You have no idea."

She smiled. "I came 'round to ask a favor. I've a spiced berry compote stewing on the stove, an old English recipe. It needs hours to bubble gently, and I must run errands. If it's no trouble, can you set your alarm for two hours and turn off the stovetop? I'll leave the door unlocked."

"You're going to leave your stove on?" He didn't like the sound of that.

"No harm will come from a low flame for a few hours. And the recipe calls for the compote to be a bit crispy. Burnt, in other words. If you turn off the burner and give it a good stir, I'd be most grateful."

"A guy is coming over later, but I should be able to get away."

She cocked her head. "A friend?"

"I met him last night."

"Wonderful!" She squeezed his arm, and her clear delight made him wonder just how pathetic other people found him. "I hope to meet him soon." After reminding him to set his alarm, she left.

Drew set the timer on his phone. All of a sudden, he couldn't stand being in the garage for another moment, and decided to sort her clothes instead. He slid the box with the Delilah stuff into the "save" section, pulled the garage door shut, and went upstairs.

In the middle of sorting her closet into different piles, Drew heard someone unlock the front door. He was halfway down the stairs when Aunt Viv stepped inside, putting her keys in her purse.

"I'd really appreciate if you knocked," he said, annoyed. "Grandma left the house to me, and I don't want people barging in unannounced."

She wore a comfortable track suit and an icy grin. "I'm so sorry." Her voice rode the razor between genuine remorse and sarcastic insincerity. "I just stopped by to see if I can help with anything. We have to start planning the memorial. I have the videos of her television years, even the time she scooped everyone about the end of Vietnam. It made her a star. We should honor that part of her life."

"Aunt Viv, she never wanted to talk about those years and you know it."

"I want to be sure we give a full picture of her life and who she was. It's not your place to tell me what to prepare for my mother's memorial."

"I won't stop you from showing videos, but it's disrespectful to her memory."

Satisfied with her win, Aunt Viv looked around the small living room, plucking a beautifully painted, wooden bird knickknack from an end table to study the base. She wiped away some dust. "Are you going to keep this old furniture?"

"I haven't thought that far. I'm still going through her closet to see what to donate and what to throw out."

Her face went reproachful. "Did it occur to you I might want to have a say?"

"Why would you want her old clothes?"

"She dressed very stylishly for television. Halston, Saint Laurent, even Vivian Westwood for evening wear. They display those outfits in museums these days."

He gestured. "Take whatever you want."

Upstairs, she tore apart his piles and created her own, explaining her reasoning even though she undoubtedly knew he didn't care. "By the way," she said, "My mother had a necklace in her dresser that isn't mentioned in the will. The gem looked like a real ruby, and it was heavy enough to be silver or platinum. We didn't find it the other day. I'm wondering if you know where it might be."

"I have no idea."

"Did she show it to you before she died?"

"Yes."

She went suspicious. "And you don't know where it is?"

"I was going to ask you. Or your daughter."

Anger crinkled her face. "That's a terrible accusation."

"Spare me the indignation. You just accused me of the same thing."

Her self-realization seemed genuine. "Where did you last see it?"

"Grandma gave it to me a few days ago. It was mine, so I hid it in my room, but it was gone when I got back from opening her safe deposit box."

Her eyes got big and he silently berated himself for letting that secret slip. "Safe deposit box? Why didn't you tell us about that? What on earth was in there?"

"Just a manuscript. Grandma wrote a memoir and asked me to read it after she died, so that's what I'm doing."

"Where is this memoir?"

It was sitting on the kitchen table, and he realized he'd have to be more careful with it. "You don't need to worry about it."

"She was my mother, and you can't keep that from me!"

"Aunt Viv, she said she wrote it for me. She asked me to read it and do what I want with it, and that's what I intend to do. Now, I have a friend coming over soon. This is *my* house, and I want some privacy. I promise not to discard anything without telling you, but for now I'm going to have to ask you to leave."

She held up a finger. "Drew, these situations can be very treacherous for families. If everyone isn't honest and up front, it can lead to years of trouble. You'd best think about your actions and realize the world doesn't revolve around you."

"Point taken. Now once again, I need you to leave. Please don't come unannounced again. Just to be sure about it, I'd like to have your keys to the door and garage." He held out his hand. She hesitated. "You need to think about your actions, too. I can have the locks changed, but I'd rather handle it like adults."

She sighed and removed the key ring from her purse. As she twisted them free with a rattle, she said, "We aren't done with this discussion about the necklace and that memoir. I'll swing by tomorrow to finish with the clothes, and we can finalize the details of the memorial." She plinked the keys into his hand. "What time is good for you?"

"I'm spending the weekend with a friend. I'm not sure of my schedule yet, so let's connect in a few days and set a time."

She reluctantly agreed, and he escorted her out. "Let's try to keep this as civil as possible," she said. "I'll do my part if you do yours."

"It's a deal."

Before he shut the door, he glanced at Althea's house, still worried about open flames on her stovetop.

Tom wasn't due for a few hours, and Drew suddenly couldn't face separating any more things into piles.

He plopped into a low, wooden chair with a deep slope and heavy cushions. It sat next to a built-in bookcase stuffed with a jumbled assortment of both hardcovers and paperbacks, most showing their age.

The bottom shelf was stuffed with at least fifteen of her journals, hardbound and thin. She wrote about consulting them to write her memoir. Drew scanned them every so often, but the notes and lists made little sense without context.

He scanned the titles on the upper shelves. Grandma had loved history and had been especially fascinated with the English monarchy. Even with all the years and all the thousands of opportunities to talk about it, he'd never asked more than a few questions. He felt a reproachful ache of regret. Grandma lingered for months. He knew time had been running out, and yet he still hadn't asked. Stupid. Maybe he'd find the answer by leafing through some of her books.

His eyes landed on a thick volume entitled *The Royal Lineage*, an obvious place to start. The leather-bound book was tooled with a sumptuously gilded cover. He checked the title page and sat up at the date 1560.

A thin, modern receipt from the Antiquarian Shoppe in New York City fluttered to his lap. An unfamiliar hand had written: "The Plantagenets. 1154–1485." He set it aside.

The antique paper felt as sturdy as cardboard, the pages filled with arresting, lavish illustrations in brilliant colors. Hand-painted names, the letters formed by fantasy beasts and lush foliage in the style of the Irish illuminated manuscripts, connected the earliest known hereditary dynasties. The lines of descent sailed across the pages until around the year 900 when faces started to appear. The artist arranged the royal families in a cartoony, medieval style.

He drank in the masterful depictions, studying the weapons, the scepters, and the clothes. The kings sat on their thrones with their legs wide, staring confidently at the reader. The others gazed serenely off page. Queens wore modest versions of their husbands' commanding crowns, the daughters in elaborate veils and headdresses. The princes went bareheaded or made do with a simple cap.

The lineages tangled without logic. The ornate names and dates were difficult to read, but he thrilled at studying an unknown medieval masterpiece probably only seen by a handful of people over the centuries. He sank into the book until his phone alarm went off.

He smelled smoke and heard a massive roar. The room filled with a crazed reflection of fire dancing with shadow. With just enough presence of mind to set aside the book with care, he leaped up and raced to the living room window.

He staggered back in mortal terror.

Flames engulfed the hillside, ferociously devouring the plentiful fuel. A cliff of violent, undulating fire consumed the ancient redwoods, with twisting and shrieking pillars leading the advance. Althea's house looked tiny in the massive sweep of the inferno, still bravely standing as an empty frame but fully encased in translucent flames.

He cried out. A multitude of racing thoughts logjammed, until an overwhelming, instinctive imperative to run burst free.

He rushed to the door, bracing against what was sure to be a blast so brutal it might instantaneously set him aflame. He shielded his face with his arm, closing his eyes, frantically trying to work out which direction provided the best escape options. With his head lowered, he flung the door open and crept outside, daring a glance.

A happy golden retriever watched from the end of the driveway, his tail wagging as if hopeful Drew's crouch was an invitation to play. The dog's owner, an older hippie lady, walked up behind and gave Drew a friendly wave. The dog lost interest and loped off to sniff a bush. Althea's house slumbered in redwood shadows.

Drew began to tremble, his heart still pumping like pistons at full throttle. He sank into the rocking chair, gripping tightly to keep balanced. Exhaling heavily, he put his face in his hands and took measured, steady breaths.

What is happening to me?

When he felt steady, he crossed the lane. Inside Althea's house, the spiced scent of cloves, cinnamon, and nutmeg instantly calmed him. It reminded him of sipping Grandma's holiday mulled wine while wrapped in snug comforters at each end of the sofa watching corny Christmas movies.

In the kitchen, a small blue flame burned steadily under a pot filled with a thick, bubbling liquid. He turned it off and gave it a stir.

He turned to leave and froze at seeing the purple pouch in full view on Althea's kitchen table.

No way. Not Althea.

Disbelieving, he picked it up, the necklace still inside. The discovery felt planned, deliberate. Even as he held the evidence of her theft, he thrashed his mind for an innocent explanation.

There wasn't one. He returned home with the necklace.

8

Rose Kennedy's Revenge

April 1975

In the public mind, the fact that I scooped everyone about the end of U.S. involvement in Vietnam passed like a vapor. I was just a face on television nobody outside of Cleveland recognized.

In political and media circles, the response was electrifying.

The regular Senate correspondent I'd temporarily replaced suddenly announced his family emergency miraculously resolved itself, and he rushed back to his beat the next morning. Loren called and offered me the assignment, but it felt obligatory on his part. I didn't want the job anyway. He sounded relieved when I said I'd rather return to New York.

"But you're not coming back just yet," he said. "We want you to be one of the panelists this Sunday on *The Press Report*."

Writing this more than forty-five years later, it's difficult to remember the prestige and influence of the Sunday morning news discussion programs. Skilled partisans gave their points of view, but policy details dominated in the most informative shows on television. If a conspiracy theorist or an obvious liar got past the gates, the producer would have been given a warning and the guest exiled. The decline of these important public service programs into horn-honking, screeching propaganda circuses alarmed me for years, until I realized the situation was hopeless, and I stopped watching.

I told Loren I lacked the detailed policy background to be a sophisticated voice on an important program like *The Press Report*, hosted by journalism grandee Parker Elston, who'd been on television for as long as I remembered.

"Just relate your experience in getting the information first. We don't want to bang our own drum too loudly, but we were the first to have the news and we'd like to make sure our viewers understand that."

I took a deep breath. "Okay, I can handle that."

He chuckled. "If Parker Elston gives you any trouble, just mention the JFK funeral. He spent five minutes going on about the anguish of Rose Kennedy when the camera was showing Queen Frederica of Greece. He goes crazy when anyone mentions it. Besides, he's retiring soon anyway."

"Why would he give me trouble?" I guessed the answer. A veteran journalist like Parker Elston might resent a rookie national correspondent on his panel.

"He's a traditionalist, which is another way of saying he's an old cuss." I felt a tug of alarm. It wouldn't be the first time I'd heard a man who resented professional women described benignly as "traditional." Loren dropped his voice. "And what about that other matter? Were you able to identify anyone in the photo?"

"I have someone in the DC area who might be able to tell me more. I promise to try before I return to New York."

"Thank you," he said with evident relief.

I searched the newsroom background files to study the senators on the Armed Services Committee. When I felt confident about delivering a few insightful points on *The Press Report*, I asked around for Bebe Bellingham's contact information. One of the reporters knew a society editor at *The Washington Post* who gave me her phone number.

Bebe's assistant answered. After I gave my name, I heard a muffled conversation before she returned. "Are you the reporter who broke the story about Vietnam funding?"

I replied with a startled, "Yes," and asked if Bebe was available to discuss a personal matter regarding the gala for the Met. "I'll be returning to New York on Sunday afternoon, which only gives us tonight and tomorrow, but I'd appreciate even just a few minutes of her time."

After another consultation behind her hand, the assistant invited me to visit the next day.

I took a cab to the address in a leafy, tony Georgetown neighborhood.

Stately Federal-style mansions lined the streets, as perfectly presented as gifts from Tiffany's. I could imagine people strolling past these elegant brick homes in the flouncy fashions of the nineteenth century.

Bebe lived in a three-story town house, her front door a few steps up from the sidewalk. Her assistant answered the door. She was a younger, exceedingly polite woman who led me upstairs. "She's very curious about meeting you."

Bebe sat in a front parlor that overlooked the street, and I recognized her from the photo. She wore a flowing pink afternoon gown that draped dramatically about a high-backed chair, her dark hair a curving slope that fell to her shoulders where it swooped into a tight curl. Her makeup looked like it was applied as more of a lifetime habit than an attempt at beauty or to conceal her age. I guessed she was around sixty.

She invited me to sit with a wave of her hand. "My son is a senior manager for one of your rival networks. He told me about you, how an unknown reporter cracked the Senate and broke the week's biggest story. I was very surprised and curious to get your call. You wished to ask about the fundraising gala for the Met?"

"Yes." I removed the photo from the envelope and handed it to her. "I was wondering if you could identify the man next to you in this picture."

"Why?" she said, even before glancing at it.

"There seems to be some confusion about his identity. I know it sounds like an uninspired lie, but I'm asking for a friend who would very much like to know his name."

"I'd never met him before, but he claimed to be a professor of history at Columbia."

"Do you recall his name?"

"Arthur Brittany, as in the French province. Despite his name, he was British. Old school British, it seemed to me."

I scribbled into a narrow reporter's notebook. "What do you mean by old school?"

"He was very cultured, very refined, and extremely well-spoken. I'm certain he has an aristocratic background but has the self-possession to refrain from saying so, which I applaud. There's nothing more tiresome than a duke who won't stop talking about how his grandfather squandered the family fortune on dance hall floozies and racing cars."

"Did he say where in England he came from?"

"No."

"His age?"

She shook her head.

"How about where he lives now?"

"No." She returned the photo to me. "He did say something odd. I asked his favorite historical period, the sort of silly question one asks an historian since there's nothing else to talk about. He replied he was particularly fascinated with the Plantagenet dynasty. When I asked why, he said he'd experienced it for himself." She flipped her hand. "I asked him to clarify, but of course he only gave me an enigmatic smile, as if it were a riddle, which I had no interest in pursuing. It was a momentary thing."

"He'd experienced it for himself?"

"It made no sense to me, either. That's why it stuck with me."

I vaguely remembered the name Plantagenet from grade school history books, mostly for how strange it looked on the page. "Do you know anything about the Plantagenets?"

"Not a thing."

I wrote the name down and made a mental note to go to the library.

The next morning after the makeup artist finished with me, I arrived on the set of *The Press Report*. You might imagine the host sat down with the media panel before the show to go over the topics and hash out important details. You might imagine we compared notes, identified conflicting accounts, and anticipated areas of disagreement. You'd be wrong. I arrived on set without the slightest idea of what we were going to discuss in front of millions of Americans.

I took my spot in a modish red chair, shaped like something out of *The Jetsons*. The other two panelists, both men, worked for *The New York Times* and *U.S. News & World Report*. We faced Parker Elston himself, who looked much older in person. He gave me a skeptical look as the others congratulated me on my scoop.

"I'm afraid I'm no expert on the Senate," I explained to Parker. "I got lucky my first day, but I've studied a lot about this issue and the senators involved, so I think I can manage a few insightful remarks."

"You're here for your tits, honey," Parker said. The other panelists laughed with the nervous quality I recognized from interviewing countless people after tragedies. Tornado victims especially can't seem to stop giggling.

I froze, resisting an urge to flee. I studied Parker's face, the one I'd trusted for so many years to analyze the news from DC. I never imagined such grotesque comments delivered with his gravelly, melodic voice.

As the show began, I felt my anger rise in equal measure with my resolve. Parker introduced us to the audience. I looked into my camera, smiling and nodding when he said my name. We were off.

Parker spent the first fifteen minutes discussing the Armed Services votes with the men. I listened, feeling like a decoration, adding an occasional comment greeted with polite nods. I felt useless, and no matter how much I distrusted Parker, I worried he was disappointed with my contributions.

During the commercial break, he said, "Don't interrupt the discussion. I'll mention your scoop near the end of the show and give you a minute to talk about it. By your own admission, you know nothing about the Senate, so leave it to people who do." The other panelists squirmed.

I kept my anger in check. "I didn't say I don't know anything. I have some insights to share."

"Just show your legs." Soon we were back on the air.

Another seven minutes passed, and the stage manager gave us the three-minute signal. Parker was deep into a talk with the others about the impending fall of Saigon, and I felt my one minute at the end of the show slipping away. Parker avoided my eyes, and a sense of disgust and contempt overtook me.

I thought of the girls watching, eager to hear from the woman on the panel. They'd be bitterly frustrated I had so little to say.

Parker said to the men, "I'd imagine that Senator Glenn on the Armed Services Committee would be anxious to help the South Vietnamese forces."

I saw my chance. "Actually, it's the other Ohio senator, Robert Taft, who sits on the committee. He voted in favor of the funding."

"I see." He gave a grim smile. "Well, I apologize for getting Ohio's senators confused."

I laughed as if he'd said something witty. "It's a bit like mixing up Rose Kennedy and," I pretended to pick a name at random, "Queen

Frederica of Greece." Parker's face went a disbelieving ashen. The other panelists froze. "But I've known Senator Taft for years, and I'm not surprised by his vote." I went on to explain the senator's long history of supporting military operations, moving right into the story of how I rushed outside to share the news with the public, filling the final two minutes.

The print journalists listened politely, and when I finished, the reporter from *The New York Times* said, "You were way ahead of all of us," with a note of admiration.

"Well, that's all the time we have for today," Parker said into his camera and closed the show.

The key lights in the studio went dark, turning us into shadows as the credits rolled and we pretended to talk.

As soon as the stage manager gave the all clear, Parker rose and stalked off in a huff. He announced his retirement a short time later, but for years, women at the network told me how they cheered.

9

After dinner, Drew drove Tom to Armstrong Woods, a redwood grove of startling beauty and serenity, preserved as a state park. Tom had never seen it, and Drew promised he'd be awed.

After the fiery hallucination and discovering Althea's theft, he'd considered canceling with Tom, but a surprising and welcome sense of calm soon overtook him. In an unexpected way, the afternoon's events smoothed his mental turbulence. It confirmed the existence of a strange reality into which he could slot the visions, diminishing his concerns about psychosis. It gave him space.

With the park closing in a few hours, the parking lot was almost empty. As they set out on the path beneath the towering redwoods, dusk claimed the sky. The dirt trails skirted massive trunks and climbed the slopes, and a hush blanketed the forest.

"Redwood forests are always quiet," said Drew. "Almost nothing can grow in the shade, except for a few ferns, so you don't get much wildlife."

"It feels like we have the place all to ourselves."

Tom reached out with a grin, and Drew took his hand. They walked until they came across a toppled redwood trunk carved into a bench in the spot where it fell, worn to a smooth, inviting gloss.

As they sat, Tom said, "How are you doing, by the way? Don't take this the wrong way, but you seemed really distracted when I got to your house, and it still feels like your mind is somewhere else."

Your house. Drew pondered the merciless flow of life. Tom only ever knew Grandma's house as belonging to Drew. It was surreal that something as substantial as a house could morph so quickly with a new identity.

"I have a million things on my mind."

Tom seemed like an honest and sincere man, and Drew counted his casual disregard for things like fancy clothes as among the most desirable masculine traits, especially since it matched his own. They could focus their attention on supporting each other, building a life, planning for the future, things that mattered. Drew warned himself to be cautious, but he could still dream.

Yet Tom had come along at exactly the wrong time. Drew needed to discuss the strange events since Grandma's death, and he wasn't comfortable sharing with anyone, least of all on the second date with a guy he barely knew. The only person who would give him a fair hearing died two days ago. Why start a relationship with so much to conceal?

"I remember when my parents died," Tom said softly. "It was a few years apart, but both times, it was weeks before my emotions started feeling normal again, like a haze lifting. I didn't realize I'd been in shock. I think you're in shock and you don't know it."

"That's a rough story," Drew said. "Who raised you after your parents died?"

"A whole lot of people."

A shaft of rose-colored sunset speared the branches and deepened to a rich caramel glow on Tom's face. Drew held back an urge to surprise him with a kiss as Tom said, "I grew up outside of Detroit. Went to Michigan State, both for undergrad and my master's."

"Did you say you work in marketing?"

Tom nodded but averted his eyes in a guilty way that raised Drew's suspicions. "Got an offer in San Francisco, and I've lived here ever since, for two years. My career's pretty standard. I work for a tech firm that's beyond the start-up stage but still struggling. My love life is pretty standard, too, what there is of it. I've never dated a guy for longer than a couple of weeks, and before you ask why not, it's because I'm an all-at-once guy."

"All at once?"

"Rip the bandage off. Yank the sliver out. Jump into the freezing water. Get it over with all at once. Life's just too short to drag things out, right? The hard stuff, I mean."

Drew noted the unguarded hope and trust glinting in the deep green of Tom's eyes. He felt an orbital pull intensified by a giddy optimism. All too soon, he felt the familiar grip of certainty that a man like Tom could only desire him at the initial, superficial stage of physical attraction.

Regardless of sexuality, most men measure other men by their visible accumulations: money, status, possessions. Drew knew when he'd hit thirty years a few months ago, the standards instantly became more demanding and would increase exponentially in the coming years. By the time a man hits forty, he'd best have something to show for his life if he values the respect of other men. Drew always felt immune to that game, both in judging men and caring for the approval of those who do, no matter their numbers.

Right up until that moment. The opinion of a man he could imagine sharing his life with was substantially different.

By San Francisco's standards, Drew was clinging to the middle class. He could only afford to rent an apartment with a roommate, and he'd severely depleted his savings to care for Grandma. Thanks to her, he now owned a small house, and the stocks amounted to a hefty chunk of cash. And while the method of acquiring things was regarded as inconsequential, an intellectually honest man could never see it that way. Inheriting from Grandma didn't demonstrate his worth to a romantic interest. He was suddenly convinced what he saw in Tom's eyes wasn't real.

Tom wasn't the fittest of men, nor the best looking, but he carried himself in a way that suggested firm purpose, solid character, just-the-facts. He was math and science instead of drama, and in recent years Drew had discovered the value of facts and figures.

The sun dipped behind the hills. They locked eyes, their breath going shallow and hard. In a replay of last night, their faces marbled with lust in an instant, no need for words. Drew's heart pounded, and his throat tightened. A primal pulse burst into shivers in his chest and shoulders. His dick kicked and swelled, and they gripped each other and leaned in, mouth-to-mouth.

With the first sloppy, sensual kisses, Drew understood last night hadn't been a rare moment of passion but a glimpse of possibility. He explored Tom's lips with his own, running his tongue along his gums and stabbing deep into his mouth. Tom groaned with a dizzying tonal balance of approval and rage, and his tongue responded with the demand to explore where it willed, as deep as it wanted.

Drew felt Tom searching for and finding the steel in his crotch. He felt around between Tom's legs until he found the concrete-hard shape.

Piercing feminine shrieks filled his mind. Drew gasped and pulled back. Out on a street, a row of uniformed men pointing rifles descended on a young man. Even from behind, Drew knew it was Tom in the crosshairs, wearing a suit. With his hands high in surrender, Tom went facedown on the ground.

Drew disentangled from Tom and shot off the bench. The dusk in the forest descended with a swift chill, the temperature seeming to drop by the second.

"What's wrong?"

Drew turned away, his heavy breaths going ragged.

"Hey." From behind, Tom gently caressed Drew's shoulders and arms. "Is it still too soon after losing your Grandma?"

Seizing the excuse, he nodded.

"I get it." Tom gave a grunt of frustration and leaned back, pressing his crotch against Drew's ass, releasing his unspent lust into the trees with a roar, after which he molded to Drew's back, embracing him around the chest while resting his head on his shoulder. "Can I spend the night? I promise to behave."

Misbehave all you want. "Can we give it a little more time?" he said.

Tom kissed his neck. "Yeah, okay, if you insist. Broderick has our entire day planned tomorrow. How about I come over on Monday morning before I go back to San Francisco? I know a great spot for a breakfast picnic."

Drew nodded. "That sounds good. I'd like that a lot."

Back at the house, they shared another kiss before Tom drove off. Drew trudged inside. In the living room, a gleam of a light from somewhere outside reflected off the gilt highlights on the cover of *The Royal Lineage*.

Instantly inflamed, and dimly aware his anger was misdirected, he stormed outside. Althea's lights were on, and he trotted across the lane and banged on the door. She answered, looking serene.

"What can I do for you, Drew?"

"I want to know why you stole my grandmother's necklace."

Her smile remained steady. "In truth, it belongs to me. It's a very long story."

"Why are you lying to me?"

She invited him inside, where the scent of spiced berries still lingered. He followed her to the kitchen where she'd been making tarts.

As she went back to work, Drew said, "One of my grandmother's old friends gave her that necklace, Delilah." He raised his voice. "There's a picture in my grandma's garage of Delilah wearing that necklace decades ago."

She nodded. "Delilah Fuller left it to your grandmother in her will. Back in 1970, I gave it to Delilah myself, a token of regard from an ardent fan."

He was insulted and amazed she'd concocted such a fable to get her hands on the necklace. She didn't seem the type to crave fancy jewelry, let alone pursue it with such blatant dishonesty. "That was more than fifty years ago. You would have been a little girl. A teenager at most."

"Obviously, I wasn't." She gave him a brief glance. "I detected Delilah's devotion to your grandmother, and it felt like the safest, most natural way for it to come into Claudia's possession one day, which was essential. I've learned to trust my instincts. They've never led me astray. I admit it's a weakness, but I can't help but feel pleased my plan worked."

He tried to make sense of her words.

She worked away, filling little pockets of dough with the compote. "Your agitation is revealing, Drew. It means you've had your first vision already."

Vision?

"Don't ask me to explain what you saw. You must trust your ability to understand the visions for yourself. All the information will be at your command when you need it most. And I'm very pleased to say you'll get help soon enough."

He groped for a plausible explanation.

"One more thing," she said, looking into his eyes. "You've acquired a rare and special gift. You may already have a faint inkling about it. Think back on the other night, when I brought the peach pie. As I walked in, what were you doing?"

He couldn't remember.

"You opened the door in the midst of an emergency."

"I cut myself." He flashed on the scramble to wash out the wound, the way it dripped on the counter and the manuscript, his relief that it wasn't as deep as it looked.

"It healed rather quickly, wouldn't you say?" When he didn't reply, she went on. "You've acquired the power to heal yourself. It requires no effort on your part. It will happen naturally, but you must keep cautious. You aren't immortal. You won't grow a new head if you are guillotined, and you'll die if you are burned at the stake. But you can survive even serious trauma, and ordinary aches and pains are in your past."

He looked at the finger. No trace of the cut remained.

She went back to work. "I know from long experience your thoughts are scrambled right now. After you've had a while to think, please ask what you like, and I'll do my best to answer. Do you have any questions now?"

"What do you know about a man named Victor?"

"Only that he plays a crucial role. Soon enough, you'll know everything you need to know about him without a word from me."

She returned to her work, chattering about the tarts and her favorite old English recipes.

10

The Last Prince

April 1975

When I returned to New York and stepped into the newsroom, people erupted in cheers, forming a ragged half circle that opened like I was a rogue sun clearing everything in my path. I smiled and nodded and waved, stopping just in front of the assignment desk where Loren Sanderson approached, beaming as he clapped.

He raised his hand, and the room went silent, save for the ringing of phones and the clacking of the wires. "One week on the job, and she broke the biggest story of the month. And in the spirit of first-rate, professional journalism, it's with great feeling that I say," he turned to me, "Claudia, and everyone else, get back to work!"

After a burst of laughter, people resumed their day, and Loren took my elbow and led me to his office. As we sat, he said, "Well, you certainly made an impression with only one day's work at the Senate."

"Thanks, it was a thrilling experience."

He chuckled. "You obliterated Parker Elston with that reference to Queen Frederica and Rose Kennedy. I'm surprised he didn't have a stroke right on set."

I was relieved to see he was on my side. I'd been worried I'd pay a price for tormenting a big personality like Parker Elston on the air, but I had no respect for him any longer.

I told Loren about my meeting with Bebe Bellingham. Excited, he asked me to look up Arthur Brittany at Columbia University.

As tactfully as I could manage, I told him I didn't see the point.

"Loren, the man in that photo is far too young to be your old teacher. He may bear a striking resemblance, but he's not the same man. It's impossible."

"Please." His voice caught, and his expression went pained. I looked down in embarrassment to see such an impressive man crumble. "My wife has left me and filed for divorce. My children are barely speaking to me. I made some regrettable mistakes, and I'm paying a terrible price. Claudia, please look at me."

I raised my eyes and he went on. "If that man only *looked* like Harrison Wheeler, I would agree with you. But I'm as certain as I've ever been about anything that he's the same person. I know it's impossible. I know he'd be an elderly man. And yet I also know they're one and the same."

Arguing was pointless, so instead of getting another assignment, I set off for Columbia University the next morning. Walking on the Ivy League campus on the Upper West Side, I felt as if I'd passed through a portal. The frenzy of the city faded into the intellectual hum of stately academia. Even though I'd come much farther in my career than I'd ever imagined possible, I felt a tug of regret for never attending college.

I asked around and was directed to Fayerweather Hall, a handsome building of red brick and contrasting cream stones. Inside a small office, a young assistant told me Professor Brittany was teaching a class, but he'd be free soon.

I gave my name and said I'd be waiting in the square. She smiled and replied she'd be happy to give him the message, and she hoped I enjoyed the scenery. Meeting strangers came so much more easily back in 1975.

Fayerweather Hall blocked New York's busy Amsterdam Avenue, and trees and manicured hedges softened the delightful square out front. Chattering birds darted about, and tulips and daffodils ached to bloom, their green buds slashed with brilliant colors. I took a bench to enjoy the Italianate beauty of St. Paul's chapel bordering one side of the square. A green copper dome and lantern topped the church, as tidy as an heirloom Christmas ornament, reminding me a bit of my mother's lighthouse pin. I thrilled to the students walking past, laden with books, deep in serious conversations. After a while, a deep voice asked, "Miss Trenton?"

I instantly recognized him from the photo. He was craggier than

I'd expected, with a firm chin and thick brown hair as sturdy as thatch. His gray eyes gave me a penetrating but curious and not unfriendly look. Even in the frumpy, forgettable clothes of a professor, he possessed an overwhelmingly masculine air.

"I'm Arthur Brittany. I understand you were looking for me." He spoke with a faint accent Bebe Bellingham identified as British, but I wasn't so sure. And his voice had a crisp distinction, as Loren said.

As he sat, I told him I'd only take a few minutes of his time. He nodded and said, "But before we begin, may I ask if you're the same Claudia Trenton who I saw on the news last week? You look like her."

"That was me, but I'm not here about a story. I'm doing a favor for a friend."

He gave a devastatingly handsome smile, crooked and warm. "I'm happy to help, if I can."

My heart pattered. "I'm not sure how to ask this, but this person I know…he's convinced he knew you a long time ago. Does the name Harrison Wheeler mean anything to you?"

I expected a shake of the head, after which I'd ask a few biographical questions to satisfy Loren that Arthur Brittany and Harrison Wheeler were not the same man, and that would be the end of it.

Instead, Arthur said, "Why is your friend curious about my connection to Harrison Wheeler?"

I pulled back. "Are you saying there *is* a connection?"

That heart-melting smile again. "It's a complicated question."

"Are you his son?"

"Would that it was that simple." He checked his watch. "I have a department meeting in a few minutes." He cleared his throat as if working up his courage, which gave me an unexpected jolt of hope. "May I ask you to dinner tonight? We can discuss your questions in more detail and perhaps get to know each other a bit."

I hadn't been asked out by such a handsome man in several years. I was also intrigued by the idea of dating an intellectual. He asked me to meet him at eight at his favorite restaurant, which was within walking distance of my apartment. I quickly agreed.

Setting out on foot for such things was still a novelty, and I enjoyed it immensely. Except for delivery people and the extremely wealthy with their own drivers, everybody walked or took the subway and cabs. I was a tad nervous, given that there was a well-publicized mugging over the weekend that ended with a gunshot and an advertising intern in the morgue, but I reasoned that it was still early, and the crowds would keep me safe.

When I moved into my high-rise, the broker warned me that the area was home to many "self-avowed" gay people. "They usually keep to themselves," he said to placate my fears. In truth, I was apprehensive. Several neighborhoods in Cleveland were said to be popular with gays, but I never saw any homosexuals when I drove through.

Yes, that's how we thought.

A bar at the end of my block catered to men dressed head to toe in black leather. At another bar around the corner, it took me a while to realize the glamorous women in glittering outfits were men. The drag queens often greeted me and complimented my hair and clothes. I sometimes took extra care with my hairstyle and makeup, relishing an enthusiastic response from one of the regulars. As my national fame grew, they offered tips for improving my look. Every woman could do with a drag queen looking out for her.

Years later when I lived in San Francisco and my grandson came out of the closet, I was grateful for these first brushes with gay culture.

Arthur Brittany's favorite restaurant was called Coach House, an intimate place with an eighteenth-century pub façade. Small buildings of brick and stone lined the street, one of the oldest surviving neighborhoods in the city. Well-to-do couples clustered outside, waiting to fill any cancelled reservations.

Inside the dark and cozy restaurant, a waiter led me to a table where Arthur greeted me with a smile and a respectful handshake.

"This looks like a popular spot," I said, mentioning the people waiting out front.

"One must usually make reservations weeks in advance. But I'm old friends with the owner. He always keeps a table or two open for his favorites."

He suggested the black bean soup with corn sticks to start, followed by a chicken dish that, rumor had it, Warren Beatty paid couriers to fly nonstop to Los Angeles.

"Did you know that Carly Simon's song 'You're So Vain' is about Warren Beatty?" I said.

"Of course, but you needn't go to Hollywood for examples of

unwarranted vanity. Manhattan is filled with people who did little but inherit fortunes. Many aren't bright enough to understand their money draws flattery and acclaim, not their brilliance. It's no better in England, where people delude themselves family lines make them superior. One encounter with the aristocracy is more than enough to demolish such illusions."

Our wine came, and I took a sip. "I know nothing about any of that. I grew up in Cleveland which, despite its reputation, is not a hick little backwater. But I feel like a mouse scurrying around here in New York." I told him about the gay bars in my neighborhood. "It's a world I know nothing about."

"A person with your intellect is never unprepared to deal with new sights and sounds." He swirled his wine and studied it. "Tell me about your background."

In my experience, first dates were dreary affairs where I listened to monologues from men who thought they were dazzling the girl from television with their triumphs. I'd never met a man who let me detail my accomplishments first, and my attraction grew as I shared my life story.

We finished eating, and he asked my impression of the restaurant.

"I'll dream about those corn sticks," I said with absolute honesty. I felt fuzzy from the delicious food and wine, and Arthur's many appealing qualities. He smiled, and I saw he was pleased with my satisfaction, not smug about his choice of restaurant.

The modest chill of early spring freshened the night. I slipped my arm into his as we sauntered down the leafy street. It felt natural to connect with him, and he patted my arm with an affectionate grin.

He invited me to see his home, which was just around the corner.

"That would be wonderful." I made an instant decision to trust him, unleashing a hot recklessness.

Within minutes, we reached a brownstone that reminded me a bit of Bebe Bellingham's Georgetown home, although much smaller. Books crammed everywhere in the front room filled the air with the dusty smell of old paper.

"Can you handle another glass of wine? I have a Sonoma Pinot Noir, 1958. I've been saving it for a special occasion."

"Is this a special occasion?"

He winked and left, returning a few minutes later with two glasses half-filled with a velveteen, ruby liquid. We clinked and took a sip. The wine filled me with a decadent warmth.

He leaned in to kiss me. I pulled back. "I've never slept with a man on the first date."

His voice rumbled. "Does that mean you never will?"

My mind ran a muddled race until it reached the only honest answer anyone can give. With a smile, I shook my head.

He leaned in again, and this time I didn't pull away. When his lips met mine, a delicious happiness knocked me out of gravity, and I soared. I was certain this was my first experience of romantic love's whirling happiness, followed by a sense of safety so enveloping I felt like a pet melting into the arms of a kind owner.

The next morning, I woke in Arthur's bed with just enough time to get home and get ready for work. I threw aside the covers and got dressed.

He stirred, rumpled yet still arrestingly attractive. I gave him a light kiss on the cheek, both of us turning away to spare the other our morning breath. "When can I see you again?" he said, his eyes bleary.

"Let me check in to see if I have a new assignment. I could end up anywhere, and I won't have any idea how long I'll be gone."

He grasped my arm. "We need to see each other again."

I smiled. "I know."

I hurried home. After spending the entire evening with Arthur, I still knew nothing that could erase Loren Sanderson's insane suspicion he was the same man who'd taught at his prep school. I saw this as a regrettable but understandable failure on my part, for who wouldn't prefer to coast on romantic currents? Much later, I recognized it as the first clue that Arthur Brittany was a man skillful at concealing his past.

Two hours later in the newsroom, I learned Jeff had quit. Loren himself would be passing out assignments until the position was filled.

In his office, I told Loren I'd met the man at the Met gala, but I didn't have the chance to ask him about his past. He didn't look happy, but after I assured him I'd see Arthur Brittany again, he handed me a stack of papers. "These are the latest wire reports on the recession. They think unemployment will hit ten percent in the next few months. We need you to report from at least three cities where people are feeling the worst of it and have a report in a week. Can you handle that?"

"Of course."

Television journalism differs from print reporting in significant ways. Television reporters need the same level of confidence in sources but also require visuals to make the information accessible to viewers. It's not a question of culling a few statistics to share on the air. It's a difficult challenge to make complicated information understandable in the sparse time we are given for our reports, which are called "packages."

I chose Detroit, Chicago, and St. Louis to illustrate the grim unemployment predictions. I hopscotched these cities, recording at least a dozen interviews informed by extensive reading. Only a few would end up in my package, and I worked diligently on a script that would tie the sound bites together.

Once my report was ready, I was scheduled to lead the evening newscast again, a rare opportunity. With the Gateway Arch behind me, I read my introductory script live: "The industrial heart of America's Midwest is bracing for the worst employment numbers in years. Manufacturing is expected to slow as imports replace American-made products."

The next day, the Labor Secretary and the White House issued a sneering dismissal of my story, which only elevated my prestige among my colleagues.

I wasn't back in New York for half a day before Loren sent me out again to cover one natural disaster after another. I was gone nearly a month before I was back long enough to make plans with Arthur, which we arranged for the coming Saturday night.

In the meantime, Loren took me to a posh restaurant for dinner where he told me viewers were calling to share their enthusiasm about me, and a focus group gave me stellar marks.

"You're fresh and smart and beautiful. I knew you'd be a winner. I'm so happy you're on our team."

He asked about Arthur Brittany, and I told him I hadn't seen him again. I didn't mention our upcoming date, which I eagerly anticipated. I didn't want to get Loren's hopes up, but I also wanted to relish a secret as delicious as a budding romance.

On Saturday, I set out to meet Arthur for an invitation-only opening at an art gallery owned by one of his friends. There'd been another mugging a block from my building, but it was still early, and I felt safe on the bustling sidewalks in full daylight.

The artist was an up-and-comer who used the unforgettable moniker Gina Ginger Soda, suggesting a sheen of Warhol pop glamour sandpapered by working-class fury. Her arresting gaze on the invitation unsettled me, as if she found me wanting. She looked hardly more than a teenager, extremely pale with a helmet of dark hair. She wore a plain T-shirt and jeans, both far too big and cinched with a long belt hanging to her knees that looked, deliberately I'm sure, like a useless phallus.

Arthur warned me to arrive early because Manhattan's elite were expected to attend in large numbers. "There's a lot of talk about Gina Ginger Soda. If she becomes big, every snob in town will get bragging rights for discovering her early. John Lennon might put in an appearance. Even Jackie O. If she does, it'll be worth a year of dinner party invitations for everyone in the room."

I bubbled with excitement. Even a few months ago, I wouldn't have believed I'd be heading out from my New York apartment to attend an exclusive art opening with glitterati like the recently re-widowed Jackie O.

I was also thrilled to spend more time with Arthur.

I was again struck by his rugged bearing as he waited in front of the gallery. We broke into wide smiles and greeted each other with a tender kiss.

"I've been looking forward to this," he said.

"Me, too. I missed you while I was on the road."

Obviously pleased, he bent and touched his forehead to mine. We giggled to share our delight at being with each other again.

"I'm sorry to let you down," he said with a smile that didn't look at all apologetic, "but no Jackie O. No John Lennon. Gina Ginger Soda is angry about the mayor's plans to freeze city hiring, so she's not coming as a protest."

"How does sabotaging her own art opening help city workers?"

"Creative people make connections we mere mortals can't understand." He offered his arm. "But let's view the art anyway."

The crowd was small, which pleased me because it gave us time to explore an interesting collection of paintings. Minimalist and bold, they radiated the confidence of primary colors.

"I'm not usually a fan of this kind of art, but this is really stunning," I said.

He agreed. "I'd advise you to make a purchase if you can afford it. Gina Ginger Soda is going to skyrocket."

Over the years, I've often wished I'd taken Arthur's advice. Any piece from Gina Ginger Soda's first major gallery exhibit is worth a fortune. In the decades since, I've seen her name quite often, and she's been to San Francisco for a number of shows.

Even with such sparse attendance, three people recognized me and shook my hand. After sipping a cloying white wine for a bit, Arthur said he knew of an off-Broadway production at a nearby theater he'd been meaning to attend.

"The reviews haven't been good, so we'll have no trouble getting last-minute tickets. But it was written by a former student, and I promised to attend. If we leave now, we'll just be able to make it."

I hooked my arm into his as we strolled to the theater, a ramshackle affair set in the back of an old brick warehouse. Despite the uncomfortable seats, I was perfectly content.

A woman came onstage to announce that some technical difficulties meant the show would start a few minutes late.

"I'm sorry," Arthur said. "These small productions do the best they can, but this sort of thing is very typical."

"I'm happy. It gives me a chance to hear a bit more about you."

"What would you like to know?"

"Where you come from, for starters. You have a faint accent, but I can't place it."

"It's my own personal accent, formed by living in various places across the world for many years."

"Many years?" I gave what I hoped was a lighthearted smile. "You aren't old enough to make that claim."

"Are you trying to ask my age?" he said in a tone that perfectly matched the mood I'd hoped to set.

"I'd be lying if I said I wasn't curious."

"I'm thirty-five years old."

I was three years younger, so our age gap was perfectly acceptable. Also, it was final confirmation he wasn't Harrison Wheeler.

"And what made you so interested in history?"

"I was born in Brittany in the north of France, where I spent my most of my youth. Hence my last name. I grew up among remnants of medieval life. I can still close my eyes and be at the keep of Rouen Castle. Only the tower remains, but it's a very significant tower indeed. It's where Joan of Arc was imprisoned for her trial."

This must explain his odd statement to Bebe Bellingham that he'd experienced the Plantagenet years for himself. I hadn't been able to get to the library, so I still didn't know who the Plantagenets were. "Doesn't that place also have a connection to the Plantagenets?" I said casually.

His face went cool, his suspicion alerted. I wished I could take back my foolish question.

"It does," he said with a touch of frost. "Many."

Just then, the same woman appeared to announce the show was ready to start. The lights dimmed.

The play was a surrealist comedy about talking fruits and vegetables. The woman wearing purple balloons as a bunch of grapes was a hit, but otherwise it bumped along for about an hour and ended with polite applause.

It was raining when we left, a steady downfall that quickens the step. We hurried to a wine bar where he ordered a delicious French apparition, and we snacked on cheese, crackers and prosciutto, discussing the play.

I sensed his guarded reserve, no doubt a result of my stupid mention of the Plantagenets. He was perfectly polite but lacked the easy spontaneity of our earlier exchanges. I decided to confront the situation head-on instead of letting it fester.

"Arthur, when I told you a friend of mine was interested in you, I had to do a little digging around to find you. I spoke to one of your tablemates at the Met gala you attended a few weeks ago."

"Who?"

"Bebe Bellingham. As you know, I was in DC reporting from the Senate. Bebe lives in Georgetown, so I paid her a visit. She told me of your interest in the Plantagenets. When I mentioned them just before the play started, I was trying to explore your interests, the things that fascinate you." I put a hand to my forehead and shook my head. "It was stupid to try to be sly about it. I hope you don't see it as a reason to distrust me."

He looked grateful. "Thank you for being honest. It was much too specific to be coincidental, and I wondered how you knew."

I grasped his hand. "Please tell me all about the Plantagenets. I want to know what fascinates you."

His smile flooded me with relief, and he explained how the Plantagenet dynasty began with the force of nature known as King Henry II, matched in brilliance and strategic thinking only by his wife, the powerhouse Eleanor of Aquitaine. Henry and Eleanor took the throne in the year 1154, and their descendants ruled England until 1485.

"So much happened during those centuries, it would be impossible to explain it to you. But it's the early years that interest me the most."

"Why?"

We'd finished our wine and snacks, and he suggested we continue the discussion at his place.

"I'd like to show you mine instead," I said. "It's not even close to being fully furnished, but I have a wonderful view I haven't been able to share with anyone yet. I'd love for you to be the first."

It was late, but people leaving shows and concerts and parties filled the sidewalks of the main streets. The rain tapered to a steady but refreshing drizzle, and we decided to walk the mile or so from Midtown to my apartment. I asked about his family. His father died while his mother was pregnant with him, and she passed a few years later. He'd had two sisters, both gone, too.

"You're the only one left?" I said. "That seems so sad to me. Not that I have a large family. I have two uncles with kids in New Hampshire, but I've only met my cousins a few times."

"Who is this friend of yours who is interested in Harrison Wheeler?"

No more lies, I decided. I told him Loren Sanderson had seen him at the gala and was amazed at the similarity with his old prep school teacher. "If I'm not mistaken, you recognized the name when I mentioned it. Did you know Mr. Wheeler?"

We turned the corner to a lesser, emptier street that led to my building on the next block. A large truck roared and rattled by, drowning out Arthur's reply. He took my arm and led me to a narrow alley slicing a brick-lined shortcut to my building. As a single woman, I would never walk such a darkened route alone, especially with the recent muggings.

Although I felt safe with Arthur, the alley frightened me. I tightened my grip on his arm as we entered. The truck noise fell by half.

Every shadow slithered, distorted by lights reflecting off rain puddles. I berated myself for being so jumpy and was almost calm when one of the shadows stepped into our path, holding a gun. He was smaller and seemed young, his face covered by a billowing hood, his hand inside a leather glove. I never did get a good look at him.

"Give me your purse and…" His next words were swallowed by the growing din of the truck's approach.

A leaden fear immobilized me. Arthur stepped forward. He shouted something to the youth, who responded with angry words. How they understood each other, I have no idea. The truck had nearly arrived, funneling a cacophony that echoed and intensified in the narrow brick pathway.

Just as the truck reached the head of the alley and the roar became deafening, Arthur grabbed the gun. The kid jerked back, pulling him off balance.

I was terrified, incapable of reacting. They shuffled back and forth. Suddenly, I heard a distinct pop, and Arthur collapsed. The kid ran.

I don't know if I screamed, but I didn't hear it if I did. Nor did anyone else with the truck overpowering all sound.

I stooped over Arthur's body. He was on his side. I tried to roll him on his back, but he was too heavy. I rocked him a few times, but he was a dead weight. Frantic, I grasped him with both hands and yanked with all my might. He flopped face up.

The tricky light obscured his facial details, but his mouth hung open and he stared off into nothing. He looked dead. The truck was now beyond the alley and someone might hear my call for help. I cried out and started to move, intending to run to the street and scream.

Arthur grabbed my arm before I could get to my feet. I stopped in amazement. He focused on me, his hand far too strong to be attached to a man who'd just been shot.

"Arthur!" I cried, kneeling and running my hand across his cheek and forehead. "I thought you were shot." I reached for his hand but drew back, feeling a slick liquid at his stomach. Even in the poor light, I recognized the oily stains on my fingers as his blood. "You *were* shot!"

Again, I moved to flee. He pulled me back.

"Claudia, stay with me." His voice was so clear and lucid, it shocked me into stillness.

"You could die! I need to get help."

He tightened his grip. "I'll be fine." He forced a smile. I glanced at his shirt, and the blood made it look solid black.

"There's too much blood. Please let me get some help."

He groaned and pushed himself into a seated position. I sank back in amazement. He drew his legs to his chest and draped his hands across his knees. "I'll be fine," he repeated. He reached down to his stomach, squinting with effort. He let out a small cry of pain before his face went placid again, and he held a small, blood-covered bullet pinched between his thumb and forefinger, the point sharpened to a pencil tip. He twisted it about. A drop of blood fell away.

"I've been shot before. Much worse than this."

11

Drew tried to sleep but only managed restless bits of unconscious-ness, flopping about on the inflatable mattress. He rose at the first flush of dawn on Sunday morning.

He needed to talk to someone. There was nobody.

He poured a cup of coffee. When he replaced the pot, he had an idea.

If I think about it too long, I won't do it.

He moved the pot to a dish towel, exposing the hot burner. He closed his eyes and pressed his finger to the burning metal. His flesh sizzled, the pain exploded, and his brain demanded he pull away. He fought the instinct with a grimace, holding out for a few more seconds. When he lifted his finger, the metal greedily clung to him before ripping free. The room smelled like a pork roast.

Gasping, he flipped on the cold water, extinguishing the pain. The oblong spot looked like a charred hamburger patty with a ragged border of furious scarlet. He'd done this to himself. On purpose. He heard the crackling of raw meat from the burner, his skin, cooking to ash.

He fixated on his finger. Nothing was happening. He feared Althea left out a warning that intentional self-harm wouldn't heal. He told himself it couldn't work that way. How would the microscopic emergency crew already surging by the millions in a coordinated, frantic response, know the difference? It made no sense.

None of it makes sense. The thought speared him. He'd deliberately caused a third degree burn that looked likely to disfigure him for life, a permanent reminder of self-destructive stupidity.

He removed his finger from the cool flow. The pain flashed to life, and with a gasp he returned it to the water.

Later, he'd berate himself for not timing how long it took until a faint pinkish shade appeared and slowly but relentlessly overpowered the red border. He held his breath as it seeped inward, leaving a healthy, healing expanse in its wake. It slowed as it neared the worst of the damage, separating into tiny rivers of health as if seeking out the easier repairs, forming a pink delta that flooded to cover everything.

He left the water running as he lifted his finger. The fresh skin seemed as fragile as cellophane but thickened. Ridges lifted and restored his fingerprints. A slight discoloration slowly faded.

Suddenly, the kitchen melted away, and he saw a handsome, well-dressed, muscular man leaving a building in the busy chaos of San Francisco's business district. Drew watched the man cross the street and push his way into a coffee shop.

The name Victor was a little uncommon in the United States, but not unusual. Keeping his original name made it easier for the man who was born Viktor Alexeev of Tolyatti, Russia, to move about as Victor Thompson of anywhere in the U.S. that produced a handsome, driven young investor.

Three years before, the main instructor at his branch of Russia's GRU military intelligence agency explained Victor's mission to him and added, "Do not trouble about money. Spend what you will, for men of considerable wealth are financing your mission. We need a detailed understanding of what is happening in Silicon Valley, and all you need to do is keep your eyes and ears open. Nobody will suspect you. Only your fear and your compassion can give you trouble."

Victor had smiled. "Then I won't have trouble."

He walked to the coffee shop across from his Market Street condo. Merely being in this neighborhood was a monumental achievement for someone who'd started life as a ragged and emaciated boy growing up in the gloomy destitution of an old Soviet factory town.

He ordered a latte with four shots of espresso. The dark, attractive girl behind the counter laughed as they chatted about the strength of his drink. She handed over his change with an engaging, willing smile, glancing at his arms and chest.

"Is that a Midwest accent?" she said.

"I'll never get rid of it," he replied with a wink.

She twinkled, a familiar response from a pretty girl, although he almost never followed up. Sexual release was less complicated and easier to manage on his own, and he didn't trust women.

He took the compostable cup to a table where he removed the compostable lid. As he blew on it, he looked about.

After training for twenty years in a secure GRU compound on the vast sloping land mass between the Altai Mountains and the Western Siberian Plain, he had been selected for this, his first mission. It aligned so perfectly with the only goal he'd ever longed for, it felt predestined in some incomprehensibly complex algorithm. Amazing coincidences are just coincidences, but they feel profound when they happen to you, he thought.

From the age of ten, Victor had spoken English as his primary language. By the time he was a teenager, he'd erased every trace of Tolyatti from his tongue. He'd studied Americans and their culture in a way few foreigners ever would, in a way that gave him more insight than the native-born. "Never look at people as your enemies simply because of where they were born," he'd learned as his training intensified. "They are not, and you will be a weaker agent if you can't understand that. Other things make them your enemies."

Looking around the coffee house, he spotted many potential enemies from their carelessly revealing signs: a sticker on the back of an open laptop, easy-to-manage haircuts on young women, difficult hairstyles on young men. And yet Victor hated none of them and was content to leave them unharmed. He marveled at his serenity and control. He hated nobody, except for Jennifer.

And this mission would deliver her to him.

Victor regretted what was to come, but the world would understand if he carefully explained. He'd contemplated leaving a note or video, but nobody would ever see it. Even more, it could never convey the potency of his rage, focused like the energy of a star concentrated into a laser beam.

A little boy and his mother waited in the coffee line, holding hands. They looked like an advertisement for an ideal life, both well-dressed, clean, and in good health. The mother smiled down as the boy earnestly explained something. She asked a few respectful questions and seemed satisfied with his replies. Such scenes still had the power to amaze him.

Growing up in the chaos and wreckage of the Soviet Union's collapse, Viktor never heard a calm word from his parents. When he started school at the age of five, everything he knew about them came from the insults they screamed at each other. His father was a drunken bum with no job and a limp dick. His mother was a junkie and a slut.

His father rarely left their filthy apartment, drinking a caustic, clear liquid from large bottles all day. His mother frequently stormed out for days or weeks at a time. Sometimes after she left, his father turned him facedown and lay on top while covering his mouth, doing something that tore and scrambled his insides. He struggled to breathe through the excruciating pain, and he took to desperately concentrating on his studies, for he enjoyed school.

Viktor's life changed drastically in the middle of his third school year.

He walked home one day among the massive Soviet housing blocs stretching like an endless formation of giant yet shabby prison guards. Inside his building, at the end of a reeking, urine-soaked concrete hallway, he joined a hushed, listening crowd in front of the only elevator clanking around high above. They angrily shushed anyone who broke the intense silence, one person with a finger on the button. The elevator only responded to the first signal after its door shut with a distinctive clunk, so all up and down the building, people waited and listened, their fingers at the ready. When the door closed, everyone rapidly pumped their button, making for long waits and meandering rides. It was still better than using the stairwells where dark anarchy reigned.

Eventually, he reached his floor. The hallway ran the length of the building, lighted by bare bulbs hanging from exposed holes where, according to his mother, chandeliers once dangled. "But not good chandeliers. Just tin and glass. Soviet shit." In many residential buildings of the post-communist world, the lawlessness escalated by floor. Anything of value was long gone, even shit chandeliers.

He unlocked and opened the apartment door carefully so he could skitter unheard past the off-balance sofa his father inhabited, but he wasn't there. Viktor drew back with disbelief when he realized the television was gone. He entered cautiously.

He found his mother at the kitchen table, her head in her hand while her dark hair fell in misshapen clumps. She'd been crying, and black makeup had leaked and dried under her eyes, the shape and color of wall mold. With a scabby arm as thin as gas pipes, she sucked on a half-burned cigarette, long gone cold. Her needle sat on the table. She didn't look up.

"Your father left. He said he got a job. He promised to send money, but I'll be crowned the tsarina first."

"He's not coming back?"

"No."

He knew to consider the potential effect of his words before speaking. Tenderly, he said, "Don't be sad. You always fought with him."

She brought the cigarette to her lips, noticed it was out and mashed it into an ashtray. She fiddled with her needle until, without warning, her face went pointy with rage, and she raised her arm. He ducked, but she was faster, the back of her hand crashing against his cheek. Colorful blobs exploded in his eyes, and he sprawled to the floor, crying out. She threw aside the chair and bent over him, her finger in his face.

"You little shit!" She spritzed him with spit. "He got a bigger pension from his factory days, and now that's gone! How do you think we've been keeping you clothed and fed? What am I supposed to do when they are cutting everyone's pensions?"

Viktor's clothes came free from a local council, where he waited in line without his parents. And other than a bag of something salty now and then, he couldn't remember the last time he ate at home.

In the following days, his new reality dawned, growing brighter and more glorious. He found himself alone night after night, his mother gone more frequently for longer periods. He could study in peace without the drone of the television and the omnipresent threat of the tearing, awkward pain his father inflicted from behind. He liked the solitude, and he passed the next year and a half almost peacefully, reading, studying, and thinking.

At the end of his fourth year, when he was nine, the teacher singled him out to stay behind on the last day of school for a special exam. Indignant, he asked why nobody else had to take it, but she told him to follow instructions without complaint, just as he always did. It was an easy test with word games and little essays. He finished quickly and raced out of the huge, crumbling school complex for the summer.

He'd given his new friends Dmitryo and Misha the key to his apartment so they wouldn't have to wait outside while he took the test. The last few months, the three of them spent all of their free time at Viktor's apartment. With his mother absent so often, the other boys reveled in the novelty of not having adults ordering them around.

A nearly fatal flaw marred this idyllic world, for his mother never replaced the television his father took with him. Dmitryo and Misha complained bitterly and, feeling responsible for their disappointment, Viktor feigned even greater outrage, although he didn't care.

He'd never had friends, and he copied their mannerisms and inflections, using their words whenever possible. One day, Misha said, "I wish we had a tablet or phone to watch videos. Having no TV is like having no eyes."

"It's like having half a tit," Viktor said.

They roared and used the phrase whenever possible for any situation, and they always laughed.

Dmitryo knew all about sex and explained everything, especially how to finger a girl, which he discussed obsessively, claiming he did it all the time. Viktor understood Dmitryo didn't expect them to believe his outlandish tales, which were impossible for many reasons. The point was to have fun with friends, to share fantasies and voice feelings. Sometimes Dmitryo's stories grew so overblown, the boys fell back in scorn, which Dmitryo took in good humor by excitedly adding absurd details that made them laugh until their stomachs hurt.

As the hot summer without television wore on, they grew bored. Viktor loved reading about exciting things and wonderful places around the world, but his friends mocked him as a bookworm until he stopped. With Dmitryo's lead, they invented a game to encourage girls to take off their clothes. They eagerly refined the elaborate rules to the finest point, but it required an enticing prize for the winner. They couldn't afford even a dinky one.

Things got better when Dmitryo began stealing bottles of alcohol from his uncle. The thefts made Viktor uneasy, but he knew better than to say anything. He hated the way the liquid seared his throat, but he luxuriated in its euphoric cleanse. It made everything unimportant, even the knowledge of what his father had done to him all those times, which Dmitryo unknowingly explained.

When year five began, they drank vodka on the way to school every day. About two weeks into the term, a fussy administrator appeared in the classroom and ordered Viktor to come with her. His friends made faces and snickered. He felt good, reckless, the vodka buzz lingering. As he followed the woman, he decided to tell his friends she took him away and begged him to finger her.

In her office, they sat across from each other and Viktor worked the desk into his tale, how she writhed on top with ecstasy.

She smiled pleasantly. "Viktor, you've been drinking. No, I'm not shocked. Many students drink before school, but I have something to tell you I hope will stop you from doing it again."

He doubted it.

"Do you remember taking a special test at the end of last term?"

He shrugged.

"We gave you the test because you are an exceptional student. Did you know you always score at the top of your class, even higher than most older students?"

He stilled.

She went on sympathetically. "No, of course not. How could you know if your mother and father never told you? They never responded to any of our letters or calls. We tried to visit, but they were never home. In the old days, we would inform the Party deputies, and you'd be placed in a special school for advanced students. Do you live with both of your parents?"

He fought against the vodka to push himself up. "My father left a long time ago. I don't know where he is."

"And your mother?"

"She is hardly ever home. She uses a needle."

She frowned. "I see. Well, that is not uncommon in these days without central control. But I hope you never use needles because your mind is very strong, very good. It can take you far." She gave a huge smile. "It can make wonderful things happen for you and take you to exciting places."

His mind raced, his eyes popping. *Wonderful things? Exciting places?!* He scarcely believed she was speaking such words. He longed to live in the foreign cities in books, places far from Tolyatti, but you needed a lot of money to move somewhere nice. He assumed he'd never have enough. Nobody did.

"Your scores on the special test drew the attention of some very powerful men. One of them visited me before this term started. He asked me to keep a watch on you. He was happy to learn all of your teachers say you are an attentive and obedient student, always finishing your assignments on time and eager to learn. He said you will be old enough at the end of this year for a special program. I planned to tell you just before the time came, so you wouldn't grow impatient. But because of your drinking, you have started this year poorly. You still have time to change course, but it must happen immediately. Would you like us to find your father, so you can live with him?"

It felt like a slap. "No!"

"A mother using a needle is a very bad thing. Your father may look after you better."

The vodka proved useful, giving him the strength to reveal the truth about his father.

She sighed heavily. "Then you must stay put. You are the most fortunate boy in Tolyatti, in all of Samara Oblast. Let me tell you the wonderful things waiting for you." She gave a promising smile. "World travel. Beautiful homes. Tropical vacations. Nice cars and boats. Fancy food and good clothes. How do those sound?"

He sat rapt, his jaw slack.

"But it can slip away just like that." She snapped her fingers. "One transgression may be all it takes." She named Dmitryo and Misha, and it stunned him to learn adults had been noticing his life beyond the classroom, taking stock of his friends. "You must stop seeing them. Your friends are not bad, for they are only copying other boys and don't know any better. And that is why the drinking will soon become drugs. Crime. I know you don't want to hurt their feelings, but they will understand in time. You have a chance at a much better life. Do you understand?"

Open-mouthed, he nodded.

For a week, Dmitryo and Misha pounded on his door before giving up. Dmitryo shouted angrily, "Being friends with you is like having half a tit!" At school, they gave him hurt looks that soon morphed to hate and then nothing at all as they made new friends, coming to school increasingly uncoordinated and sloppy, laughing at things that weren't funny.

For the rest of the year, Viktor rushed home to study after school. He never went outside on weekends or state holidays. Learning became a passion, and it was intoxicating to sit in the apartment by himself with books that took him anywhere he wanted to go.

He met regularly with the administrator. She always praised him but said she hadn't heard from the man. As the fifth year neared the end, he grew frantic, worried the man had forgotten about him in this remote, miserable place. He begged the administrator to find him.

"I don't know how to reach him, Viktor. Have patience. He came a long way to ask about you, and he has not forgotten."

School ended. His mother came and left. He sat alone, day after day, listening to the distant sounds of kids playing far below, feeling a new emotion, the crushing, terrible ache of dying hope.

A few days later, someone knocked on the door for the first time since his friends gave up many months ago. "Who is it?"

"My name is Mr. Thompson. I'm the man you've heard about, Viktor."

He opened the door. The man looked so ordinary, balding and not very tall. He wore clean, expensive clothes, and he was younger than Viktor imagined. He looked serious, but a smile glazed his eyes.

"Aren't you going to ask me inside?"

He stepped back as Mr. Thompson entered, his face souring as he looked about. Viktor was glad his mother wasn't home.

"You were very well-behaved this year and kept your grades high."

He fidgeted.

"I saw your mother earlier today. She spends most of her time with a crowd of degenerates in a squalid shack near the old port." He flicked his eyes around. "A place even fouler than this. She willingly signed the papers to make you a ward of the state. A ward of mine. I gave her a good bit of money, but I'm sure it's already been stolen, for others saw the exchange." He bent to look directly into his eyes and dropped his voice. "I told her I want to use you like your father did. She told me she didn't care, to do whatever I like."

Viktor felt his face burn.

"But I lied to her. I won't do that, and I won't let anyone else do that to you ever again." He straightened. "But she was willing to let me, because she wanted the money. Do you want to kill her? Or your father? You can use my pistol. Nothing will happen to you, but you must decide now. Yes or no? Quickly."

He breathed heavily, knowing it was a test. He decided to whisper the reply he would give anyway. "No."

Mr. Thompson smiled. "In addition to being intelligent, that tells me you are very strong, even if you don't know it. You are one of only twelve boys in all of Russia who are qualified for a new project. You will learn a new language and have a better life, but the world will never hear of Viktor Alexeev again. Does that trouble you?"

"No." It thrilled him.

Mr. Thompson looked at him for a long time. "What do you think of my name?"

"It's strange."

"It's a common American name. We will make you and the other boys into Americans. From now on, you will be Victor Thompson. You will think of yourself as my son, and the other boys will be your brothers. If you are agreeable, we can leave right away."

He didn't move.

Mr. Thompson cocked his head. "If you don't want to come, I don't want to take you. I will not be upset with you, but if you wish to have a new life, you must say so. Without delay."

"I want to go. Yes." His heart pounded with wonder and dread, but above all with the exhilaration of restored hope.

He was ten the day he left with Mr. Thompson. After a short train ride followed by a long flight in the small, windowless hold of a plane, they arrived at a remote compound of three rectangular concrete buildings. Hunched in a valley among stark and rocky hills, the compound looked like an attempt to replicate its surroundings. The structures seemed to inflate as he got closer and details resolved. High up on some of the corners, but nowhere else, clusters of windows lining several floors revealed their massive scale. Gated fences and razor wire enclosed the complex, and Mr. Thompson explained how the security kept unworthy people out. "Many important things happen in these buildings, but you boys will have a very nice little corner to yourselves."

Victor's apprehension rose as they drove past the armed guards onto a massive asphalt expanse. They approached one of the looming structures, as forbidding as anything back home, but not as foreboding for a reason he couldn't identify until inside.

Mr. Thompson led him through empty corridors with closed doors to a functional barracks with bunk beds, tucked into a ground floor corner. "You will share it with eleven other boys, all about the same age as you. They are on their way."

In the large opening to the barracks, Victor realized why this utilitarian world didn't seem grim. It hit him like a blast of cool air in the sweltering summer. From the beds to the floors, walls, sinks, toilets, communal showers, and individual lockers, everything was new, clean, and tidy. No mold, grunge, filth, decay, rot, or stink. No broken glass and crushed cigarettes on the floors, the light fixtures were all in place, no filthy bedding or clothes, no kitchens thick with grime. He stared in amazement.

He took his first hot shower with real soap and dried off with a clean beige towel. Afterward, he dressed in simple yet fresh blue coveralls, feeling capable of anything, determined to do whatever was required and most of all, to never be dirty and poor again.

The other boys arrived over the following days, looking as filthy and amazed as he must have looked. Wary at first, they bonded in the high-spirited way most boys do when thrown together as strangers in a new setting.

Mr. Thompson introduced them to their various instructors and left them with, "Your teachers will only speak English. The workers who will fix things and deliver supplies have orders to never speak at all. I will see you again when it becomes necessary."

The boys existed in a tight complex of rooms just outside of their barracks, but never beyond. They ate bland yet satisfying meals, but once a week chowed down on hamburgers and fries, hot dogs, pizza, fried chicken, pies, ice cream, and other American favorites. From the moment they woke, they studied, memorized, practiced, rehearsed, and exercised in the English language, falling into a deep sleep the instant they hit their bunks. On Friday and Saturday nights, they watched American television and movies with no subtitles or translations. Within weeks, most of the boys could roughly follow the stories. They celebrated American holidays, excitedly hanging decorations.

They called each other names like Billy, Todd, and John. Every now and then, one of the boys broke into tears, but he always claimed to miss going outside, not his family or home. When it eventually happened to Victor, he realized his experience was more complicated. He didn't miss anything about Tolyatti, but he didn't exactly long for the outdoors. Even when it happened again, he couldn't put it into words, especially not American words. It was forbidden to share details of their lives when they'd answered to names like Oleg, Aleksei, and Sasha.

One day after lessons concluded in the classroom, the pretty teacher who dressed like the American girls on television told them to remain in their seats. "You have a special visitor." She left and a few minutes later, Mr. Thompson walked in, electrifying the room. They hadn't seen him for a while.

He gave each boy a long look and when it was his turn, Victor realized how it made everyone feel special, noted.

"It was one year ago this week that you came here."

Gasps filled the air as the boys snapped about, sharing disbelieving looks at the speedy passage of a whole year.

"Your transformation is remarkable. I know it has been difficult to remain inside. Even though you have all the exercise equipment you need, you are boys and want to run and play. Find a tree to climb, or a woodland to explore. While we cannot allow that yet, your world will get bigger, for tonight you will move to a new wing built just for you, a place called Maple Grove, Michigan, where you will attend junior high school."

He told them to pack, and they raced to their barracks. When they were ready, Mr. Thompson opened the door, a threshold they hadn't crossed for a year. They followed, bristling with excitement, their sharp whispers echoing in the empty corridors. They took a myriad of turns and walked up two separate staircases until they reached a large metal door.

Mr. Thompson tapped a card to a plate and after a beep the door opened automatically. The boys moved forward, but Mr. Thompson stopped them with a hand, giving each another private look. At last, he waved them inside, where they drew amazed breaths.

Mr. Thompson came up behind. "Welcome to your new home."

It was magical, enthralling.

❖

A sudden waterfall spilled over the counter and Drew jumped back. He'd left the tap running while Victor's story unfolded in his mind. The sink had overflowed while he was in Russia. He turned off the faucet, intending to get a towel to dry the floor.

But he didn't move as he reviewed the details of Victor's story. He was vaguely aware of a constant trickle as the water drained, until the last of it swirled down with a hearty suck.

12

Midnight at Dawn

April 1975

One of the most baffling mysteries about the murders orchestrated by cult leader Charles Manson was answered nearly thirty years after that savagery. The revelation outraged many people, as I'll explain, but after seeing Arthur Brittany survive a point-blank gun shot in a New York alley, I bring a different perspective to the objective facts.

At the secluded home in the Hollywood Hills where Manson's followers slaughtered pregnant movie star Sharon Tate and four others, a young man named Will Garretson survived untouched. He lived in the guesthouse beyond the pool, working as the property's caretaker. The night of the murders, a friend visited Garretson and left around half past midnight. His friend came upon the stealthy cult members in the driveway, just as they arrived to fulfill Manson's orders to shock the world.

The killers rounded up everyone in the house and announced, "You're all going to die." The panicked victims fought for their lives, screamed for help, and begged for mercy. For at least ten minutes, but much longer by some accounts, neighbors along Benedict Canyon froze with alarm when they caught a disquieting snatch of sound in the air—the pop of a gun, a woman shrieking, a frantic man pleading. Shaken, several called the police. At least one man jumped in his car and drove the deserted streets looking for the disturbance. The echoing hillsides made fixing a location impossible.

In the morning, the maid arrived and discovered the bodies strewn from the driveway into the living room and across the lawn. The first police officers on the scene crept among the carnage until they heard a man shushing a barking dog in the guesthouse. They crashed through the door and Garretson cried out, oblivious and confused. As the hired help, he kept his distance from the glamorous residents and couldn't identify the mutilated bodies. Traumatized, he even failed to recognize the corpse of his friend, who had been the first to die. He told detectives he'd heard nothing and was released after passing a polygraph exam.

Three decades later, Garretson confirmed many suspicions by admitting he'd heard everything, or at least enough to understand what was happening. Alerted by the ghastly commotion, he secretly watched as the young coffee heiress Abigail Folger fled the main house, chased by a crazed woman who tackled and repeatedly stabbed her on the lawn. He also heard Folger's soul-wrenching surrender, asking the killers to end her agony and finish her off.

In an existential example of standard cult strategy, the murderers left Garretson isolated and outnumbered by cutting the phone lines. Hiding in the dark during the most infamous murders in living memory surely haunted him until his death in 2016.

After his confession, many people deplored Garretson as cowardly. I don't fault him for not sacrificing his life, the likeliest outcome if he'd intervened. However, I understand the anger about those poor people scattered like party trash left for morning cleanup. In recent years, we've learned when his followers returned and described the murders to Manson, the cult leader drove to the house and prowled the grounds alone in the dark before dawn, savoring the butchery. If Garretson had sought help soon after the killers left, Manson might have been caught, sparing the subsequent victims.

So, I won't defend Garretson. And yet I believe he was sincerely shocked when the police stormed into the guesthouse. I'm also convinced he passed the polygraph by latching on to the silent aftermath of the murders as proof he'd imagined the horror. He drifted into sleep, certain he'd wake to the immense relief of a terrifying dream swept away by the cleansing light of dawn.

On a much less violent scale, I tried something similar, and it didn't work for me, either.

Right after he plucked the bullet from his own abdomen, I helped Arthur to my building. He stooped to hide his bloody shirt from others.

Inside my apartment, he stripped to his waist and examined his torso. Despite a hole in his shirt and gory smears on his skin, his flesh was clear of wounds.

"You were shot," I said. "How is it possible it looks like nothing happened?"

"I can't tell you."

"Do you mean you don't know, or you won't tell me?"

"Claudia…"

Already disoriented, I felt enraged at his attempt to calm me. "And what did you mean by saying you'd been shot before? How does that happen to an Ivy League history professor? Is tenure that competitive these days?"

He chuckled, looking out my wall of windows where the rain turned New York City into a manic abstraction of slashes of light streaking through a thousand glinting eyes. "I don't begrudge your anger. I can only ask for your patience. There's so much I can't explain because you would think me mad."

The truth hit me, and I sat for fear of losing my balance. "You're Harrison Wheeler. You were Loren Sanderson's teacher at Wallace Lake Academy, and you disappeared after the battle of Salerno."

After a beat, he nodded.

"You lied to me about being thirty-five years old."

"It wasn't a lie, but it isn't the truth, either."

"How?"

"I'm not prepared to give you an answer. Not yet."

"If you're Harrison Wheeler, you should be an old man."

He smiled sadly. "You have no idea."

I felt a deep chill of unease. "I keep thinking you're joking or playing with me, but you were shot. You dug the bullet out of your abdomen. If you're crazy, then I'm crazy."

He knelt, taking my hand. The drying blood crusted his brown chest hair, salted with gray. "Claudia, the world is more magical and startling and wondrous than you can imagine. More than most people can imagine. You've had a glimpse, but only a very tiny one."

"I've built a career on asking questions. No matter how good you are at hiding the truth, I'm better at uncovering it."

"Strictly speaking, there are no rules about concealment. No clandestine oaths, secret handshakes, decoder rings."

"Please be serious. I'll figure it out eventually, but it will be much easier on both of us if you come clean with me now."

He looked about my new and chic apartment, barely furnished but obviously expensive. "You're a talented and successful woman. If anyone can get to the bottom of things, I'd certainly place my money on you."

"How old are you really?"

"You won't believe me."

"After the trauma of thinking you'd been killed, at the very least you owe me the truth about your age."

He looked pained. "Is the answer that important to you? It could change everything between us, and you're the most intriguing woman I've ever met. Do you want to destroy what we've been building?"

So, he knew I had feelings for him, just as he clearly had feelings for me. My voice broke. "You're the first man I've ever felt hopeful about. But I can't compromise when it comes to honesty. You lied to me about your age, which isn't usually considered a trick question. Why can't you tell me your birthday?"

"My birthdate is March twenty-ninth."

"Why are you being so evasive about the year, your true age?"

"Beautiful Claudia." Tenderly, he cupped my chin and gave me a soft kiss. "Give me the agency to reveal myself in my own time."

I wiped away a tear. "Your age is such a strange thing to keep secret. I can't understand it."

"Is it too much to ask you to accept that I have my reasons, and I'll tell you when the time is right?"

I sighed, confused and conflicted, the worst possible state to make an important decision. "I don't mean to be rude, but I need to be alone right now. I need time to think."

He stood and slipped on his bloody shirt, pausing to wiggle a finger through the bullet hole. As he put on his coat, I went to the door. I felt sick, and my eyes started to burn.

He gave me another soft kiss at the door. It tore through me. A tear broke free and raced down my cheek. Arthur wiped it away. "I'll see you soon?"

I nodded. After an intense look, he left. I locked my door and slid down the wall until I hunched with my hands in my hair. I felt queasy, fighting a sudden lurch in my stomach. I swallowed hard, but the urge to vomit was too strong, and I made it to the toilet just in time. I stood up and reached for a tissue, but my limbs began to quake. Gripping the vanity, I sank to the tiles, consumed by a blinding impulse to rush home to Cleveland where nobody walked away unscathed after being shot.

Instead, I decided to clear my mind with sleep, convinced I'd spot the logic in the cool pragmatism of dawn.

Like Will Garretson, the bloody truth greeted me in the morning. I leaped out of bed and threw up again.

13

At twilight, Drew was in the kitchen cutting himself when someone knocked on the door.

After deliberately burning his finger in the morning, he'd spent the day testing his new healing power. Injury's initial pain was just as sharp, but many things surprised him: a split to the skin or a burn healed faster than a bruise; the depth of the wound was secondary to the length; he bruised most easily on his upper arm and shoulders. His fingernails and hair could never be trimmed beyond their current length because they grew back, although it took several hours.

The pain also allowed him to drive Victor's story from his mind.

Drew answered the door. Tisha stood on the porch, wearing a striking emerald caftan edged with a bejeweled pattern. She held her arms wide, smiling.

"Move over, Norma Desmond, that's my close-up you're hogging. Drag queen bingo tonight, and you're my guest. Unless you're busy with Tom."

"He already had plans for today. He's coming by in the morning before he drives home to San Francisco."

She motioned him outside. "Then no arguments. You're lucky I always order an extra ticket. Drag queen bingo is the most popular monthly event in Guerneville and it always sells out. People plan for weeks."

He felt giddily euphoric after a day of steady pain. He grabbed his necessities and followed Tisha to her car. As they headed into town, he felt a bold impulse to confront her. "The other night you said something about cars driving around using magnetic levitation. Where did you get that idea?"

"I said that?" She laughed in a studied way. "Some Long Island Iced Teas may have given me that thought."

His endorphin rush fueled a sense of invincibility. "It was too sophisticated to be a drunken thought. Where did it come from?"

"Where'd you learn to be so insistent?"

"It can't be a coincidence."

"A coincidence requires two things that are similar. What's the other thing?"

They passed the bridge into town. He wasn't ready to share his visions. "Never mind."

To his relief, she let it pass and after she parked, they headed for the community lodge, a low, municipal-style building with a dramatic peak on one side. In the dark, it could easily be mistaken for a church. Groups of people came from every direction.

Inside, drag queens glided along, dripping with elaborate costume jewelry, keeping everyone in line with arch instructions that drew laughter and applause.

Drag queen bingo attracted an amazing cross-section of Russian River life, from clutches of little old ladies to straight couples of all ages and groups of gay and lesbian friends. Even the local young glamour girls came to preen, drawing the young straight guys who sprawled with the relaxed, wide limbs of the rodeo.

Drew and Tisha collected their raffle tickets and bingo cards and sat at a long table in the hall with the vaulted ceiling. Although huge, the room was plain and undoubtedly hosted decades of Veteran's Day dinners and other standard civic ceremonies. People settled while others lined up at the snack bar. Music played, indistinct under festive babble and laughter.

Tisha plucked two daubers from a grouping in the center of the table and handed one to Drew. "So, tell me how it's going with Tom."

He thought about the vision of the uniformed men with rifles as Tom dropped to the pavement. "I'm worried the timing is wrong." The dauber left a misshapen splotch of pale purple ink, and he selected another. "My life is too unsettled to add a romance to the mix."

Across the table, three old ladies giggled conspiratorially before counting down from three. They banged the table with both fists, shouting, "Free shit!"

The chant spread across the room, and a drag queen in a sparkly red gown stormed to the stage. "What a greedy crowd you are! Who invited the Trumps?"

After the laughter died down, the emcee announced the beneficiaries for the night, a local senior center and an after-school art program for children with parents who worked late. With everyone volunteering and donations from businesses around the region, every year the drag queens raised tens of thousands of dollars for local charities. "Free shit" was the call for a raffle, so the host selected one of several gift bags and started the night.

After every bingo game, losers wadded up their game sheets and tossed them randomly. Halfway through the night, drifts of crumpled paper lined the rows between the tables like plowed snow. The emcee announced a fifteen-minute break and people lined up for more snacks, headed to the restroom, or ran outside for a quick smoke. Drew and Tisha remained seated as their table emptied.

"Are you still reading your grandma's memoir?"

"Yeah. I'm learning a lot about her life, things I never knew."

"What's the most surprising thing you've learned so far?"

"I don't know where to begin."

Tisha raised an eyebrow. "That must be a hell of a book. People pay good money for juicy memoirs from television personalities."

"My grandma would smite me with a thunderbolt from heaven if I did that. Besides, nobody would believe it."

"Let's test that." She rested her arm on the back of her chair. "Give me a few highlights."

Tisha's eyes had the dimensions of space. Her teeth dazzled, and a dimple on one cheek gave her beauty a rakish dash. She'd pulled her braids tight as wires, and they exploded in a puff behind her head.

Nobody is immune to beauty in any gender, no matter their sexuality, and Drew thought of Tisha as a fine work of art. Sitting in the bingo hall, he felt a tug of chaste desire, the allure of being near something special. Her eyes swept him into a whirlpool, the spirals tightening until, with a breathtaking plunge, he felt like he was falling straight into her soul.

She knew everything, he realized. Althea said someone was coming to help him, and that person was Tisha.

Suddenly, he was looking at the famous view from the Marin Headlands just in front of the Golden Gate Bridge, with the skyline of San Francisco beyond. The tornado towered over downtown. A fearsome shape twisting like a snake, it was little more than a vapor. Another twister formed. Then another. Even miles away, Drew heard the screams and sirens and the chaos filling the unseen streets. Suddenly, buildings started to plunge while the tops of others dissolved into billions of pieces that looked like smoke scattering into the sky.

"Hey, Tisha baby," a drag queen said, slapping her on the shoulder while passing.

"Oh, my God," Drew whispered.

Tisha's smile grew. "No, just me."

"Tell me what you know."

She placed a hand on his arm and leaned in. "You and I have a world to save."

14

We Have the Stars

May 1975

A few mornings after I watched Arthur brush off his gunshot like an insect bite, Loren Sanderson called me to his office. I assumed he wanted to discuss my investigation of Arthur Brittany, but he had a different topic in mind.

"We're planning a big splash for the Apollo-Soyuz mission," he said. "Regular newscast features, wall-to-wall live coverage, a prime-time special on dock day, and a two-hour Sunday night recap afterward."

Excitement for the joint U.S.-Soviet space project was escalating as the July date neared. The American Apollo spacecraft would dock with the Russian Soyuz capsule high in orbit, for two days of handshakes, shared meals, and experiments. Conceived before President Nixon resigned as a way to thaw the Cold War and to demilitarize space, the project inflated hopes of future cooperation between the superpowers.

I was eager to claim even a small part of so consequential an event. "Are you sending me to Florida to cover the launch?"

"We want you to be the main anchor for our special coverage. You'll be the face of Apollo-Soyuz for the network. You'll do feeds to the network's owned and operated stations and affiliates, so in addition to national exposure, local viewers across the country will get used to seeing you."

"Oh, Loren!"

He was clearly tickled by my response. "Your Q-Rating is through the roof, and you've delivered some solid journalism. I think we have a star on our hands, but I don't want to overwhelm you. It's a big assignment, and you need to get up to speed in very short order."

"I never give anything less than my best."

He told me I would leave for Florida in a few days and remain for the duration. "We have a support team in place, so you won't have to start from scratch. Take the next few days off to get your local affairs in order because you're going to be away for two and a half months, and it's going to be a very rigorous assignment. You'll be busy all day, every day. You won't spend your weekends at the beach."

I assured him I understood the importance of the assignment, and I wasn't afraid of hard work. After we discussed logistics and strategy, he settled back in his chair and jammed his fingers together. I wasn't surprised when he changed the topic. "And that other matter..."

Obviously, I couldn't tell him about the surreal experience with the gunshot, and I was tired of constantly bracing against the topic. Now that I needed all my concentration for such a huge assignment, I resolved to rid myself of the stress. "Arthur Brittany is thirty-five years old," I lied. "There's simply nothing there."

Loren nodded sadly. "I suppose you see me as a delusional old man whose personal life has fallen into disrepair. I'm sure there's gossip in the newsroom about my marriage."

A few overheard comments came to mind, but I said, "I've only been here a month. Nobody's going to blab to a newbie about the boss."

"Then newsrooms have changed. In my salad days, a divorce was a topic of endless speculation. It's the nature of the beast. Journalists are insatiable gossips. But in case you hear something, please know I didn't have a conventional affair. It was a moment of weakness my wife learned about long after the fact. She's from a stodgy and very old Boston family. Puritanical stock. They urged her to throw me out, as if thirty-five years of marriage could be discarded like a wrapper in the trash."

In spite of my misgivings about getting too personal, I said, "Is it over for good?"

"Our lawyers are already in touch."

I felt oddly protective. "You don't owe me or anyone in the newsroom an explanation."

"I've been living at a seedy men's rooming house for the past two weeks. It's all I can afford while supporting my wife on the Upper East

Side, plus two children at university and a third at Phillips Andover Academy. I have a private room but share a bath with another man who thinks of hygiene as optional. I was in the service so I'm not squeamish, but don't ask me how one man can make a room smell like it's used by sixty boot camp Marines." A tear fell, and he reacted as if a spider landed on his cheek, swiping it away with horror. "What a disgrace. A grown man weeping like a teenaged girl because of unpleasant smells."

I felt an urge to flee, until I saw a way to wrench the conversation in a positive direction. "You can stay at my place while I'm gone. I don't have much furniture yet, but you'll have privacy."

I expected him to refuse, but he perked up. "That's a very generous offer. Are you certain? I haven't had a decent night's sleep in weeks."

"I wouldn't have made the offer if I wasn't sincere. You can stay in my guest room, but it doesn't have a bed."

"I can pick up a cot for a song, and I'll be as comfortable as a king. Thank you, Claudia. That's a weight off my mind."

We decided he shouldn't move in until after I left for Florida. I regretted making the offer. Loren was right about newsrooms. Rumors spread faster than flames on gasoline, but he seemed so relieved I didn't have the heart to change my mind.

I hadn't seen Arthur since the night of shooting, but I called and asked him to meet me at a tea room in my neighborhood. It seemed only fair to tell him in person I was leaving for ten weeks. He pressed for an invitation to my apartment, but I insisted on a neutral setting.

I arrived at the bustling tea room a little late. Fluffy window treatments gave the room a cozy feel, along with teensy furniture sprightly with curlicues. Arthur waited at a table already set with a pot of tea and a three-tiered serving tray like a Christmas tree with tiny sandwiches, cookies, and cakes.

He wore a stylish gray leisure suit over a dark green turtleneck, a notable change from his standard academic sport coat and tie. I imagined him on a hurried visit to the department store earlier in the day to find hipper clothes, the helpful but jealous salesgirl charmed by his nervous attempt to impress his date.

He gave me a quick peck on the cheek. I smiled at the lovely array on the table. "How did you know what to order?"

"Who doesn't like sandwiches and cakes?" My heart fluttered at his effortless masculinity, the kind that easily navigates the delights of a frilly little meal.

I told him about my new assignment, and he enthusiastically congratulated me. "I'll be watching your every report."

I felt my face go warm. "I arrive in Florida tomorrow afternoon, and I'm heading for a production meeting straight from the airport. I'm going to hit the ground running."

We talked for a few more minutes, exhausting the topic. In our first uncomfortable silence, I gobbled two dainty sandwiches followed by a lemon petit four iced like a wrapped gift. My heart sank, realizing this meeting was a ridiculous fraud, a way for me to fake normality under so many abnormal circumstances.

I decided to make my excuses and leave when he leaned in. "Claudia, we need to talk about what happened that night." I admired his straightforward approach. "I'm sorry for the way I left you with so much unspoken, but I was ashamed."

"Why be ashamed? You obviously have some sort of remarkable gift."

He gave the crooked smile that disarmed me. "More like a curse. It's interfering with my relationship with you, and it's more than a little agonizing. I was very pleased to get your invitation for tonight." My internal heat escalated. "I would love nothing more than to explain everything, but I must be selective. So, I've decided to start by sharing a secret I've kept for many years."

I nodded for him to continue.

"I'm a descendent of the Plantagenet dynasty, the royal lineage that took the English throne in the year 1154."

"You have a royal background?" I asked, my voice rising.

"There's no need to curtsy."

"Good. I've forgotten the courtly etiquette I learned in finishing school." We chuckled. "But seriously, why keep something like that a secret? Most people would brag."

"I'm not interested in attracting the sort of people who would be impressed. I enjoy being an anonymous history professor."

In the primordial soup of what I knew about Arthur's strange story, strands connected like DNA. He told Bebe Bellingham he'd experienced the Plantagenet years for himself, he told me he was far older than thirty-five years, and he'd survived a gunshot, which meant he could survive many other things.

I started to ask a question, but he stopped me with a raised palm. "One step at a time. And I'll understand perfectly if you decide to break up with me before we go deeper."

There was my chance to be sweet but glib, bid him goodbye and end this chapter of my life with the depressing but sensible conviction that steady reason is preferable to zigzagging uncertainty. Life with Arthur Brittany promised rocketing adventures followed by terrifying plunges, endlessly repeating until I went mad.

Get out now! a voice inside my head screamed. I felt disoriented and dizzy. His kind eyes and misshapen smile filled me with an ache of longing so exhilarating and piercing, I nearly burst into tears of joy.

I took his hand. "One step at a time," I agreed, and we returned to my place.

The next day, I reveled in the happiness of Arthur's arms about me, the scratch of his facial stubble, his hot breath on my skin. He possessed an exquisite sense of timing to match my changing passions, intuiting I was ready for more. The few men I'd been intimate with forced instead of guided, grabbed instead of caressed, and went meek instead of tender. He understood a man's sexual power comes from inflaming women, not subjugating them. Other men were taller than Arthur, others more muscular and more conventionally handsome, but his brilliance with sexual interplay made him the most masculine man I'd ever met.

By the time I landed in Florida, I knew I was in love with him.

I felt confident heading into my first Apollo-Soyuz production meeting. A taxi dropped me off at a temporary, sunbaked trailer park just outside the gates of Cape Canaveral. I took a moment to gape at the skyscraper silhouette of the launch pad at the end of a long peninsula.

The trailer park consisted of buildings on wheels emblazoned with media logos and arranged in obvious groupings. Even though liftoff was scheduled for more than two months away, the park hummed with people walking briskly from trailer to trailer, deep in conversations, dressed in slovenly but comfortable-looking clothes.

I struggled with my bags to the network pod of four trailers, two of which swarmed with crews running cables and rolling bulky electronics for the production control room and studio. A handwritten sign taped to another denoted "Makeup and Lounge" while the last was marked "News offices." I threw open the thin door of the office trailer and yanked my bags inside. Three men in shorts and T-shirts looked up from a small round table.

The office was a single large room with a tiny restroom in back. Posters of beautiful women dressed mostly in smiles decorated the walls. Aside from the center table, two long card tables held rows of typewriters and phones.

As I piled my luggage to the side, I said, "I'm Claudia Trenton. I'll be the main anchor."

"Yeah, we know," said the oldest man, stout and bald. "I'm Rick, the lead producer." He nodded to a man who looked similar. "This is Colby, senior producer, and that ugly cuss is Ron, field director." Ron wore his dark hair and beard trimmed close. He gave me a cunning smile, as if he knew everything about me.

They'd scheduled my first interview the next morning with a scientist. "He's one of those humorless types," Rick said scornfully. "He's going to explain some of the experiments the American crew will conduct with those commie bastards." He rolled his eyes. "This mission is a crock of shit. Tricky Dick was a fool to agree to it. Why play patty-cake with the Russkies? We should nuke the shit out of them."

Colby laughed, but Ron gave me a private "oh, brother" smile.

Rick jerked a thumb at Ron. "Gorgeous George here has all the background you need for the interview. Better study up. Right now, me and Colby have a meeting with a six-pack back at the hotel."

"I have to take a dump," Colby added, "but I'll wait until I get back to my room, so I don't stink up the place for the girly here."

My face burned while Colby and Rick left in a cloud of sneering laughter. After they closed the door, Ron lifted his nose and sniffed. "The air does smell fresher without them." I smiled as he went on. "Don't let them get to you. In ten years, their kind will be extinct."

I frowned at yet another lecture about showing patience for boorish men. "We were supposed to have a production meeting."

He asked me to sit, and we went over his research and the questions he'd prepared. I was impressed. "I've never seen a field director take such a direct hand in content."

He ran his hand along his facial hair as he spoke, and I realized it was one of those habitual obsessions. "I was the executive producer of

The Press Report. I'm going to develop another show after this mission ends, but in the meantime they asked if I'd lend a hand for Apollo-Soyuz. I wanted a front-row seat, so here I am."

"I was on *The Press Report* a few weeks ago!"

"I saw." He grinned. "Parker looked like he wanted to throw a chair when you brought up Rose Kennedy and Queen Frederica."

"Why did you walk away from such an influential show?"

"I'm sick of that insider DC culture. All that phony posturing when any two-bit whore has more integrity. People have no idea. My new program will be out of New York. We'll cover politics, but we're not going to trot out the same damn faces every week."

I suddenly understood my starring role as the Apollo-Soyuz lead anchor was an audition for Ron's new show, and that his job as my field director was a way to observe me up close. My competitive juices surged.

"Come on," he said, "let's get out of here." We set off for the hotel, and I felt queasy about such an unstructured beginning.

I checked into my room, a bland but serviceable space with a view of the dumpsters. My stomach did an itty-bitty jig, and I vomited the airplane meal. I wiped my mouth and felt a seizure of fear when thinking about the number of times I'd thrown up recently. I'd slept with Arthur that first night after dinner at Coach House, but I reminded myself flying always unsettled me.

The next morning, a three-man crew picked up Ron and me in a van and drove us to a nondescript set of office buildings several miles away. Unlike the media encampment, the NASA offices bustled with people in professional attire. As the crew unloaded bulky equipment, Ron led me inside to a drab, windowless conference room with only a table and some chairs.

"Damn it," he said, petting his beard. "I asked for some plants. This place has the pizazz of a marshmallow. Dr. Stein should be here soon. You stay here while I scope out some nearby offices to see if I can grab something with some color. Can you believe NASA gave us this boring room?"

He rushed off, and Dr. Stein arrived moments later. He wore black slacks, a white shirt, and a pale blue tie. His dark hair was combed in a conservative, utilitarian style with the sheen of a fur coat. He looked younger than me.

"I've never interviewed an astrophysicist before. My director wrote up some questions, but please feel free to tell me if you think we haven't covered something sufficiently."

"I've seen you on television lately," he said. "Do you have a scientific background?"

"No. I've been getting a crash course the past few days."

"I'd be glad to be your informal scientific advisor. I'm sure you have a million media relations officers at your beck and call, but if you want the true story, you need to talk to a scientist."

"What a generous offer. That would be very helpful."

"Good. After the interview, I can walk you through the outlines of the mission. From a science perspective." He gave a faint smile. "The mission itself is just a glorified publicity stunt but it will yield some amazing insights. Every time we go into space, we learn volumes of things."

Ron returned, carrying a sharp-leafed plant that looked tired of life. A number of large lollipops in transparent wrappings stuck out at crazy angles, and Dr. Stein squinted in disbelief.

"I got the candy from a bowl on someone's desk," Ron said, positioning the plant on a table along the far wall. "We'll set you guys up front, defocus the background elements, and it will look like flowers." On-screen, that sorry little plant with the lollipops looked like gorgeous tropical foliage, and we used it for dozens of interviews.

The crew arrived, pushing two carts rattling with equipment. After they set up, we shot the interview inside of twenty minutes. Ron's questions were perfect, and Dr. Stein was a bit stiff but gifted at making complicated things sound easy. I was struck by the seriousness of the planned experiments, such as measuring the rate of bacterial infection from one capsule to the other, the effects of weightlessness on metal production, that sort of thing.

A question Ron hadn't thought of popped into my mind. "Will the astronauts conduct experiments other than these highly publicized joint efforts?"

Dr. Stein blinked with what looked like admiration, taking me aback since my question didn't seem especially insightful. "Of course," he said. "The Apollo astronauts will remain in orbit for an additional four days after the capsules separate. Any space mission is a rare opportunity for tests, and they'll work nonstop."

"What will they be testing?"

"Let's focus on the joint mission," Ron interrupted. "It's all the public cares about."

Ron brought enormous expertise to our production, but his comment annoyed me. As the lead anchor, I was free to ask what I wanted. I decided to save my fire for something more important.

As the crew started to tear down, I told Ron that Dr. Stein was going to walk me through the project from liftoff to splashdown. "Would you like to tag along?"

I couldn't miss the instantaneous reluctance from both men. Ron said, "I have to go over some schedules back at the trailer camp."

Confused by their strange reactions, I followed Dr. Stein to his office on the second floor. Papers and books teetered on metal filing cabinets, adjustable shelves, and a wooden desk. A large window overlooked a lush, unkempt field.

He gave me a huge block of paper bound with a sturdy spiral, a printed overview of the project from start to finish. "This will give you all the official information at your fingertips. There's even an index to make it easy."

I saw a lot of technical jargon and precise schematics. "This will be invaluable," I said. "I won't have to waste your time if I can just look something up in here."

He went silent, and we stared at each other across his desk until I said, "You look like you want to say something."

"I'm glad that bearded director didn't accompany us. I wanted to be alone with you."

I felt a beat of dread. Reserved men like Dr. Stein often intensify from clumsy to egregious in a matter of seconds, angered by their inability to grasp the nuances of tactful human interactions. I wasn't in the mood to be understanding. "Dr. Stein, I'm sure you're a very nice man, but I am sort of involved with someone right now."

His astonishment was immediate and sincere. "I have no sexual interest in you. I think of myself as asexual."

I squashed my amazed delight at such a surprising announcement delivered without hesitation.

"I'm grateful we're alone for a much different reason. I need to tell you something I haven't been authorized to share." He shook his head in self-reproach. "That's a preposterous understatement. Let me rephrase it this way. There's a secret experiment planned for the Apollo capsule known to just eight people." His eyes locked with mine. "I don't think it should be a secret. Science belongs to everyone, but I don't have any experience dealing with the media."

My pulse quickened. "What's the experiment about?"

"I'll tell you on the understanding this can't be reported. What do you call it? Background? Everything will change if the experiment succeeds, and I'll make sure you have exclusive access for a huge story. I'm taking an enormous risk and putting myself at your mercy."

My aggressive instinct collided with my concern for a naïve scientist. "You can count on my discretion." I thought of Mary Ellen in the Senate Parliamentarian office, but that was a one-time lapse. "However, as a professional courtesy, I need to caution you. What might seem like background to you could look very different to me. I have an obligation to the public, even if the public doesn't always like what they hear."

He flicked his hand, unconcerned. "There are no security implications. And while I sympathize with your dedication, concern for your own reputation will prevent you from being reckless. You're not a tabloid reporter, and at least one trustworthy media personality should be aware of what we're looking for. Science should never be secret, and we shouldn't treat the public like children."

"I agree."

He held out a dark blue folder with a blank cover. "This is a very succinct description of the clandestine experiment developed for the Apollo, which you will not find in the official overview. It piggybacks on an already planned experiment with distant neutron stars, so even the astronauts aren't aware of it. If you wish to read it, this is your only opportunity."

I eagerly grabbed the folder. The summation ran a page and a half, but it read like a standard study of radioactivity from a nearby star.

"This sounds routine."

"It's anything but." He pressed his hands together. "The star is very faint and not visible to the naked eye. It was only discovered three years ago by an astronomer studying our galactic neighborhood. How much do you know about the Doppler effect?"

"A little. It has something to do with detecting the movement of objects in space. If they're moving away from us, the light spectrum shifts to the red, but it's blue if they're approaching."

"Exactly. When this star was discovered, it had an almost imperceptible blue shift. But a few months later, the astronomer took another quick look and, to his amazement, the spectrum had shifted to red. Stars do not suddenly reverse course. He suspected a heliocentric correction accounted for some of it, but he was shocked to find a precise match."

"I didn't follow that last part."

"All by itself, the earth's orbit around the sun caused the spectrum shifts. When the earth was circling toward the star the spectrum was blue, but when it rounded the sun and receded it changed to red. In other words, the star appeared to be motionless, which is impossible and would upend every advancement since Newton uncovered the laws of gravity."

I felt something momentous approaching. "I'm still unclear."

He went grave. "The object was keeping pace with our solar system, as if tracking and observing us. It wasn't a star. And it has disappeared."

15

Drew found nothing online about a secret experiment for the Apollo-Soyuz mission.

He switched gears and typed March 29, Arthur Brittany's birthdate, into a search engine. Flipping the pages of his grandma's memoir, he added key words from Arthur's story, and numerous links popped onscreen. After reading for a few minutes, his brain tipped, a sensation that felt as permanent as the earth's tilted axis.

Duke Arthur of Brittany was born on March twenty-ninth in the year 1187, a prince of the Plantagenet dynasty and heir to the English crown. When he was twelve years old, Arthur was next in line to become king upon the death of his homosexual and childless uncle Richard I. But in his final days, King Richard shuffled the succession by naming his own brother John as his successor. After years of fighting to reclaim his throne from King John, Arthur was captured on the battlefield and imprisoned in the castle at Rouen where he vanished from history.

Grandma's memoir revealed she was already pregnant by Arthur of Brittany when she arrived in Florida to cover the Apollo-Soyuz mission. She gave birth to Drew's mother Delilah in January of 1976.

Drew's grandfather was the usurped king of England, who somehow survived hundreds of years into the modern age.

At the kitchen table, he nudged his laptop aside, anticipating a rush of amused embarrassment for entertaining such supercilious thoughts. Nothing came. Over the past days, every self-inflicted burn, cut, and bruise healed completely. He had never felt better. It wasn't hard to believe his grandfather had the same ability.

Drew barely remembered Loren Sanderson, the distinguished and legendary executive producer of the network news whom he'd always known as his grandfather, and who stood alongside his grandmother in all the photos. At the cusp of her greatest fame, Grandma married him even though she was decades younger. In Drew's earliest memories, Gramps was already ancient. His voice shook, he trembled, and his skin crinkled like bedsheets in the morning. He died when Drew was in first grade.

In the living room, Tisha purred a soft snore. After they returned from drag queen bingo, they talked for a long while. Drew told her about his vision of the flying cars, the freakish tornado, and Victor's astonishing story from Russia.

She explained she'd been having visions too, combined with information implanted in her brain without explanation. "I know there's going to be a terrifying event in San Francisco with the potential to destroy the world. You and I have to help stop it, along with one other person."

"Who?"

"I don't know. I only know that three people will stop it."

After their talk, Tisha decided to crash on the couch since today was President's Day, and she didn't need to get up for work or school. He moved to the door to watch her sleep. She retained her beauty in slumber, a rare gift.

He spotted *The Royal Lineage* on the chair where he'd dropped it two days before when fleeing the phantom inferno. He retrieved it and returned to the kitchen table, carefully turning the heavy yet fragile pages until reaching portraits of the first Plantagenet king, Henry II, and his queen Alinor, encased in red and purple medallions. Thick bands descended to smaller circles bearing images of their nine children, and beneath a prince named Geoffrey more lines connected to his children, daughters Alinor and Matilda, and his son Arthur.

His grandfather's simple line-drawing portrait lacked details since the artist could only imagine what he looked like. Under a tight white cap, Arthur's blondish hair curled out above his forehead and behind his neck. He smiled with princely calm. Drew drove away all thoughts to catch even the faintest spark of familial recognition against the emptiness. Nothing.

He stood. He sat. He made a pot of coffee and forgot about it. He poured a cup and it cooled to lukewarm while the day brightened. He popped it in the microwave and forgot about it again. His mind had the focus of a puppy sniffing in the park.

After a while, Tisha stirred. She padded upstairs to the bathroom and started the shower. A little while later she floated into the kitchen wearing the glittering caftan from the previous night. She'd wrapped her head in an emerald turban fashioned from a scarf he recognized as his grandma's. He felt euphoric, as if it demonstrated that Grandma still mattered.

She gave her head a saucy pat. "I know you don't mind I borrowed this. Us black ladies have hair issues that require advanced strategic thinking and situational resourcefulness. It makes us invincible, but don't you dare say a word about that until after we take over the world."

"Cross my heart."

She headed for the coffeepot. "How are you handling everything we talked about last night?"

"There's a million things I need to know."

She made a cup of coffee with cream and took a sip. With a satisfied sigh she said, "Okay, hit me with your questions."

"Did you know my grandfather was supposed to be the king of England back around the year twelve hundred?"

She raised an eyebrow. "Very impressive, Your Royal Highness."

"I'm not joking."

She took a seat. "I didn't know about your grandfather, but after everything I've learned, nothing will ever surprise me again. Maybe Cleopatra was my grandmother."

"I feel like I'm losing my mind."

Her voice softened. "I know what you're going through. When Althea told me I'd stopped growing older, and my body would heal itself, I must have looked like you do right now."

"How long have you known?"

She exhaled. "Just before you moved in with your grandma full-time. I was leaving after my morning visit and slipped off the porch. I twisted my ankle, went down and bang," she slapped her hands with a loud crack, "right on my forehead. Althea ran over and took me to her house. I said I needed a doctor, but she made some tea and told me to wait. I was in no position to argue, with someone pounding a railroad spike into my head and my ankle throbbing like a bad romance novel.

In thirty minutes, I felt better than I can't remember when, and Althea told me I'd stopped aging and my body would heal itself."

Her voice went reflective. "It was a Thursday morning. I don't know why it struck me as strange to learn something so major on a Thursday morning. It's like those people who find an image of Jesus on a potato chip. The banality alone demands your doubt." She locked eyes with his. "But the truth was too obvious to deny. I had my first vision that night, but I've lost count of how many I've had by now."

"It sounds like my grandfather had the same abilities. If it's a genetic thing, we should have been aware of all of this years ago."

"I've wondered why it started so suddenly, too. I'm nearly thirty years old. I don't know the answer, but it doesn't feel genetic to me."

He poured another cup. "What kind of visions are you having?"

"Nothing as involved as the one you had about Victor's life in Russia. I get glimpses." She unclenched her fingers in quick bursts. "Impressions. Flashes. Amazing things."

"You never saw any tornadoes?"

"No, but I know something bad is going to happen and three people will stop it."

"Who chose us?"

She rested her chin on steepled fingers. "Just one more piece of the mystery. It'll come, piece by piece. Maybe the next one is just about to arrive."

They shot a look at each other when someone knocked at the door, but Drew remembered Tom was coming for a breakfast picnic.

Despite the typical chilly Guerneville morning, Tom wore shorts and a T-shirt. On the porch, he gave a smile that filled Drew with an ache of longing shot through with lust.

"Hey there," Tisha said, coming up behind and draping her arm over Drew's shoulder.

Tom looked surprised and pleased to see her, and he explained about his plans for a breakfast picnic. "Do you want to join us?"

Tisha looked uncertain. "I don't want to get in the way."

"You won't," Drew said. He liked the idea. She'd make him feel like he had an ally.

"In that case, I accept," she said. "There's some fruit salad in the refrigerator, and it won't take fifteen minutes to throw together some toasted egg sandwiches."

Tom offered to help, and Drew went upstairs to shower. His mind spun. Tom appealed to his sense of ideal masculinity. Rational and kind, cute and warm, his manliness seemed unstudied in a way Drew envied. Even growing up in suburban San Francisco, Drew feared a misplaced word or gesture might reveal the hidden homo. The city of gays often seemed light years away, and the anxiety still lingered.

When he returned downstairs, Althea was in the kitchen. "I called her to see if she wanted to join us," Tisha said, "and would you believe she'd just baked?"

Althea pulled aside a gingham towel of the wicker basket in her arm to display a nest of golden muffins studded with blueberries. "Fresh from the oven," she said merrily.

With the others in a cloud of carefree spirits, they set off in Tom's car with the picnic supplies. Within minutes they turned on a narrow asphalt lane that ascended like a meandering old river oxbow to a small parking lot just below the summit of a high hill. Gathering up the food and drinks, they walked single file along a narrow path through waving grasses to a cluster of boulders at the very top.

In every direction, California hills and mountains rolled with their famed golden crests above flows of redwood valleys, dark and deep. In the distance, a hazy blue line marked the start of the Pacific's epic sweep across the globe.

They settled into rocky seats, passing around paper plates and food. Drew pretended to follow the conversation, but he quietly studied the unlikely scene. Three of this group shared astounding secrets about humans that lived for millennia and had visions of the future, while the fourth participated with such innocent trust, Drew felt guilty.

The morning sun picked out silver strands in Tom's brown hair, like tinsel in the carpet months after Christmas. Tom was aging. Drew never would again. How could they have a relationship?

"What kind of work do you do?" Tisha asked Tom.

The other night at Armstrong Woods, Tom turned away guiltily when he claimed to work in marketing at a small start-up. He repeated the same story now with no more confidence. He was a terrible liar.

Drew didn't fault people for telling a few harmless fibs upon meeting others. Untrue alternatives were easier than pointless details. Maybe Tom just left a job or was fired. Why go into all of it?

On the other hand, why lie? Simply say you're between jobs. After a few vague replies, most people will understand you don't want to talk about it. Later, there'd be no need to correct the record.

Drew heard screams and braced for another vision. In the next instant, the vast landscape vanished, replaced by the urban bustle in downtown San Francisco. Tom stood next to Lotta's Fountain, the cast-iron Victorian landmark on Market Street. He looked into the sky, his arms wide, as the tornado swirled above.

Drew jumped off the boulder as images flipped in his mind, like videos as they uploaded, allowing a glimpse of one frozen frame every few seconds: an older woman on the sidewalk in a long, fashionable coat cinched at her waist. A terrified crowd looking skyward. A bearded man with his hand cupping his chin.

Tisha leaped to his side. With one look at Drew's face, she said, "I think we need to get back."

Tom was stunned, his face creased with wary concern.

On the drive back, Tisha and Althea tried to fill the awkward silence with banalities about how Drew still hadn't absorbed Grandma's loss, that he needed time. Tom said nothing, his face expressionless. Drew wished they would stop talking.

When they arrived at the house, after Tisha and Althea got out of the car, Tom said, "I really need to get back to the city."

"I'm sorry," Drew said, his first words since the mountaintop visions. "You must think I'm crazy."

"Don't worry about it." He smiled faintly. "It was strange, but I'm sure you had a good reason to go batshit."

Drew held his breath before chuckling. "It was batshit, wasn't it?"

"Let's forget it. Maybe I can come up after work on Friday?"

Drew felt an overwhelming sense of gratitude, soon poisoned with caution. Tom either possessed an unjudgmental heart or had an agenda. "I'd like that."

They came together in a lingering kiss. Tom carried the stimulating and pleasant whiff of a man baked in the sun for a bit. They drew apart and with a wordless smile, Drew got out and closed the door.

Tom's car rounded a curve out of sight. A gentle breeze blew, and the redwood forest looked lush, green, and fragrant.

The view melted into another of a manicured park, houses in the distance, everything as still as a photograph.

❖

Victor and the other boys stood awestruck, mouths agape.

"Welcome to Maple Grove, Michigan," Mr. Thompson said.

They were inside a massive room the size of an airplane hangar dressed up to look like a park. The padding beneath the fake grass felt springy. Two stunted trees and several bushes gleamed resin perfection. A mini-jogging track, benches, exercise equipment, and even three holes of miniature golf fit nicely. Massive photos printed in minute detail covered the walls, giving distant views of an American community. Above, more intricate photos displayed a blue sky and fluffy clouds. High in the corners, bright spotlights illuminated the dreamlike, indoor scene.

"It looks like a movie," someone said.

Mr. Thompson led them to a wide corridor paved and painted like an American road, complete with a yellow stoplight flashing red, yellow, and green. "You'll become familiar with all the places important to an American teenager."

Large rooms lining the street opened to a variety of full-sized interiors such as a classroom, a gym, a locker room, a church, and a fast-food dining room. It went on with a barber shop, and offices for a dentist and a doctor in one space.

The many rooms of a typical American house followed: a kitchen with a dining area, a garage complete with a car, a living room with an enormous flat-screen television. Instead of barracks, twelve single beds lined two walls of the bedroom. The last room matched the park in size, filled with shopping aisles representing different kinds of stores, the walls covered with photos of a mall food court. Along the far wall, another locked door led to the world beyond.

Even though Maple Grove was sealed off from the world, they felt rich with space, and their excitement fueled their determination and enthusiasm. They settled in, diligently shaving the last rough Russian edges from their words, with varying levels of success. The sudden crying fits ceased, and junior high passed with studying, reading, taking apart and reassembling the car, and watching television and movies.

But most of all, Victor and the others became obsessed with working out. In addition to the gym equipment, they adapted every useful object for exercise. The sturdy resin tree limbs started sagging under the weight of countless pull-ups and nobody used the comically small jogging track ringing the park, opting instead to run the length of Maple Grove.

A man called Coach supervised from Friday afternoon until Monday morning, along with a rotation of assistants. Bald and gruff, Coach's muscles looked massive enough to create gravity. At night, Coach and his assistants watched movies with the boys but spent the bulk of the day on fitness. He never pressured anyone to participate and rarely spoke about anything but exercise.

While Coach and his assistants slept on cots in the gym, cameras supervised on weeknights. The obvious ones sat high on the walls behind dark plastic bubbles, but Victor suspected many more. Once when a chemistry flame tipped and ignited a stack of papers, uniformed men with fire extinguishers appeared in no time at all. The boys managed to smother the flames right away, but the rapid arrival of the outsiders gave rise to disturbing questions about how closely they were being watched.

The fourth year, time started to drag. Although they'd trained in many methods of memory control, Victor let brief vignettes of life in Tolyatti run free, telling himself remembering the poverty and decay helped restore the deep gratitude he felt after that first hot shower. While his parents faded to phantoms, he recalled rolling about the filthy apartment with his friends, convulsed in vodka laughter.

In Maple Grove, they grew muscular and sturdy, and most started shaving several times a week. A full tangle of curly hair grew seemingly overnight on three of the boys, carpeting their bodies from their necks to their feet.

They graduated from junior high in caps and gowns, sitting in metal folding chairs in the gym, eagerly anticipating the announcement of a move to high school, a move to a different set of fake rooms.

When the ceremony concluded, the principal smiled and wished them a happy summer. They craned their necks, waiting for Mr. Thompson to appear.

The principal walked off, trailed by the handful of teachers and Coach. Just before they left, a boy asked loudly, "Aren't we moving to high school?"

"Most American children remain in the same communities until they begin higher education. Your Maple Grove Junior High will be renamed Franklin Delano Roosevelt High School."

Thus, graduation ended with angry breaths, the air thick with betrayal. A new faculty of eight teachers and a principal arrived for the first year of high school. The boys sneered about their choppy English, much coarser than the junior high teachers. Plus, the new instructors were older and rarely smiled.

Looking back, Victor could easily identify the warning signs of restless minds taking sudden, unplanned sprints. They started sophomore year, when one of the hairy boys named Dan woke up one morning, took a shower, and refused to get dressed. The teachers harangued and hectored, Coach tried reason and rage, and the boys whispered urgent warnings. Dan went uncommunicative, his eyes vacant. When the second day began the same way, the other boys dressed only in jock straps, a reluctant solidarity that ended when Coach exploded and military personnel escorted Dan away, never to return.

He'd been witness to smaller rebellions, too. Once in the park, one of the taller boys named Jeff loudly announced, "We're outside, so I can piss where I want." Several others joined him and let loose on a plastic bush. The joke played out so many times, the park developed a distinct urine scent until Coach ordered them to spend an entire weekend scrubbing with soap and mopping with bleach water.

Maple Grove started to fray at the edges. High-definition photos in the windows curled at the edges, and the foam pad under the fake grass lost it sponginess. The tough resin plants snapped in a few places, leaving distinctive white chips. Plastic went dull, paint faded, and the shelves in the mall grew dusty, the empty boxes misshapen from too much handling.

One morning, when they were getting ready for school, one boy named Tom made a swift turn without looking and accidentally knocked another named Phil back to his bed.

"Whoops. Sorry, buddy."

Propped on his elbows, Phil went red. Victor knew they had trouble even before Phil sprang up and clocked the other boy so hard, he went down, out cold.

A doctor rushed in, led by two armed guards. The injuries weren't serious, and the boys apologized to each other. Everyone shrugged it off.

Soon after, the principal announced a Homecoming dance. "You will be decorating the gym like harvest and Halloween, very spooky things." She flushed at the derisive snickers. "You will be choosing one girl, and she will be coming here for the dance, looking very pretty. There are many girls to be choosing, so there is not a reason to fight." She slapped a stack of photos on the desk and walked off.

Stunned, the boys stared at the photos until the first movement set off an explosive dash like a beast of many limbs tearing a path through the classroom. They passed the pictures around, whooping and hollering and arguing. With at least forty smiling girls to choose from, they felt like sultans.

On the floor, Victor saw a photo of a girl with light brown hair spilling about her shoulders, her head dipped shyly. His heart went double-time as he took her picture, his mind electric, touched with dreams. Her tight, nervous smile promised to burst into a radiant glow, and her brown eyes looked directly into his, hoping he would choose her. He gazed a long while before turning the photo about and seeing her name, drums pounding in his ears. "Jennifer," he whispered aloud.

Their suits arrived a few days before the dance, and they excitedly tried them on, strutting and posing, busting moves like rappers. Coach gave a growling lecture with only one side of his mouth, his voice as thick as borscht.

"They are nice girls, not prostitutes." Spit shot from his lips. "You must to be remembering their fathers are Americans with good jobs. Their mothers will be calling your mothers if you are not behaving. You might try what any boy might try, but you must not to be strong, with force." Unsmiling, he pumped a loose fist. "You know how to do with yourself, so I don't listen to bullshit about why you are not keeping inside your zipper."

The night of the dance, the boys became giddy, talking and laughing as they dressed. With time to kill, they primped each other, straightening ties, smoothing lapels, arranging one another just so. When the hour arrived, they sauntered down the street to the gym, where the coach and principal waited. Victor saw affectionate flashes in their eyes, as brief as a quantum particle flaring for just a spark, happy they were so happy, hoping they would have fun.

The principal said, "The girls are soon to be arriving, and me and Coach Kelly will be as your chaperones, but we are not having eyeballs all over our heads and maybe we leave early." The boys exchanged sharp-eyed joy at the possibility of no supervision for the night. "But if angry parents call to the school, your father, Mr. Thompson, will be angrier still. Like volcano." The coach glared and nodded along. "Much care has been taken to make this happy dance for you. Many people working, and the money makes a big commotion. Do not do things that will turn out bad for you, for who is to know what your punishment would be?"

Every boy thought of Dan's unknown fate with dread. Would they be sent back where they grew up, dropped off with nothing to do in a place where nobody remembered them, or just pushed out the gates into the wilderness?

The silent workers who drifted in and out of Maple Grove had set up tables with punch bowls and paper cups, along with sausages, cakes, and other small foods. The refreshments lined a wall beneath the paper decorations the boys put up that morning: autumn leaves, spiders, ghosts, and crepe-paper swags soaring and twisting across the gym.

American pop music started, but it was too loud, and the boys shouted into the air to turn it down. Whoever controlled the volume lowered it to a soft background.

Soon, they heard a tiny beep. The door in the park unlocked and clanged open, followed by the nervous giggle of girls. The titters deepened into feminine oohs and aahs, and Victor recalled the thrill of the first glimpse, the promise of a perfect life. Someone closed and locked the door, and the girls went silent until one called, "Hallo?"

"We are this way," the coach said, waving them forward.

Moments later, the girls floated into view, their dresses flowing, their hair carefully arranged, as ethereal as apprehensive wood nymphs. The principal said, "Girls, here you will see your dates for the prideful Homecoming dance, much school spirit." She urged them in. "The boys know your face already, they choose it, and they will stick flowers on you with pins, as we have said."

Several girls, seeing only nervous boys their own age, lost their hesitation and strode inside with the fearless hips of adventurers, flipping their hair, ready for battle. The others followed. Boys bumped about when spotting their dates, creating a tangle, soured with the unexpected tension of possible disappointment.

Victor saw Jennifer near the back, curious rather than courageous or fearful. She wore a pink and rose dress as light as fog, her hair tied back with ribbons. Their eyes met, he held her gaze, and she brightened. With a jolt of confidence, he stepped forward.

Silently, he held up the corsage and she nodded. He pinned it securely the first time and she took the boutonniere, eventually getting it to stay. They shared a triumphant grin.

He took a deep breath, his nose filling with her honeyed perfume. "Hello, Jennifer. I'm Victor."

Confusion crossed her face until she put an embarrassed hand to her lips. "I forget my name is Jennifer. It sounds so funny. But you have a Russian name!"

"It's an American name, too. Your English is very good."

"No, it is not, but yours is wonderful. You sound just like the Americans in movies."

The principal clapped and instructed them to line up for photos beneath a trestle threaded with silk autumn leaves. The coach snapped the pictures with his phone and gave them a brusque wave to hurry the next couple into place.

When it was their turn, Victor felt Jennifer tittering with joy. Her fluttery trembles filled him with a happiness so complete it extended to all of Maple Grove, even the principal and her foresight in capturing their first moments together, a photo they'd cherish for the rest of their lives. They stepped aside for the next couple and walked to the center of the gym.

"You look beautiful," he said.

She blushed. "They said I can keep the dress. I spent a whole afternoon last week with a lady, and we talked about what would look good on me. And today, we had another lady do our hair and makeup. I'm glad you like it. I try to make everything perfect for you."

They fell in love in that moment, he was certain, and a surge of emotion overcame him just as the music faded up and couples began to dance.

The daring girls whirled and promenaded with hands on their hips. They swiveled and sank, their long hair crashing about with seafaring drama, casting temptress glances from every angle. It inflamed some of the boys and terrified others.

Jennifer danced with bubbly sweetness. He nodded and smiled

as she bounced about, her arms moving like water, spinning only fast enough to lift her skirt into modest, dainty twirls. His pride surged, and he was the happiest boy in the room.

He'd never danced with a girl, but she was so encouraging and spirited, she gave him the strength to imitate what he saw on television and music videos. She applauded at the trickier moves, her laughter like a swag of joyful Christmas bells. He grew bolder, inventing his own styles. He relaxed into the music, punching on the beats, ruffling his fingers on the stings. After a few songs, she said, "You dance good!"

"You, too. Where do you live?

"I'm supposed to say I am living near Lansing, Michigan. I looked it up on a Google map. I would have chosen New York City."

"What did they tell you about us?"

She beamed and wagged a finger, like he was a naughty boy. He longed to kiss her. She was the most beautiful girl he'd ever seen, the most beautiful girl on earth. As a filthy, starving boy on the streets of Tolyatti, he never knew to dream of a night this sublime.

After a few more songs, she fanned her face with her hand. "It's getting so hot. Can we have a rest?"

He tried to remember what to do at a dance if you aren't dancing.

She looked over at the tables, where cheerful couples snacked, and a few unhappy ones nibbled silently, envying other dates. "Can we get some punch?"

"Oh, yeah! Come on!"

He took her arm and they laughed as they trotted across the gym. It felt like they were running in the sky. He filled a paper cup and arranged a little plate, proud to show her he'd always give her whatever she wanted.

"Thank you. Aren't you going to eat anything?"

He shook his head.

She looked around. "It must be fun to live here."

He shrugged.

She craned to look down the street. "Can I see everything?"

"Yes! Let me show you."

They walked along the street and she squealed and raved, stopping to gawk at the perfect little replicas of American life. He wondered if she noticed the tattered edges. When they reached the mall, she ran through the aisles with her arms outstretched, ending in a happy twirl. "I would never want to leave! I am going to America, too. Just like you!"

He pulled back. "How do you know where I'm going?"

"They said we'd meet boys who are studying to work in America."

"What else did they tell you?"

"Hmmm," she said, as if debating to go on before she let loose with, "They told us we had to be nice. They said we shouldn't ask you any questions, and to not answer your questions. We were talking about it at the airport in Moscow. We all flew in there and had hours before we boarded the plane to take us here, so we got to know each other."

He wondered why they took different flights to Moscow. Letting it kick around in his head, he took her hand and they strolled through the mall. She picked a box from a shelf and shook it. "Are they all empty?" He nodded, and she returned it. "After living here, I'll bet you can't wait for the real America. I'm going to be a software engineer or run computers for a company. I already have lots of experience and get very good grades. My cousin said I could live with her in San Francisco while I get my feet to the ground. I'd rather live in New York City, but beggars can't be choosing. I have so many plans." She bounced, clapping lightly. "Tell me your plans so we can see if they match!"

"Why did they send you to Moscow first? Don't you live nearby?"

She blinked. "No, we come from all over Russia." She looked around conspiratorially and lowered her voice. "They said we must not talk about anything but the music and decorations." She slapped her thigh with exasperation. "They go on and on with how we must tell the boy he is a good dancer, to smile all the time. It made me angry. I said that you are a good dancer because you are, and I smile because I like you. I'm nearly seventeen years old. I don't need anyone to tell me how to think." She blushed. "I need to use the room for little girls. They said we should knock on the door at the end of the mall and someone would let us out."

He led her to the metal door that led to the outside world, where another girl waited, perched on the checkout counter smoking a cigarette. "Go on," she told Jennifer with a wave. "I'm waiting for Aniyyan, who is putting on more makeup. There's plenty of room." Jennifer knocked, a guard opened the door, and she slipped to the other side.

Victor felt jealous rage at how casually she left, while he was forbidden.

The girl on the counter had long dark hair and a slinky dress, and he recognized her as one of the sirens of the dance floor. She took a long drag, assessing Victor in a way he found irritating.

"We don't smoke in here," he snapped.

"Thank you for telling me. I wouldn't have known, except for everyone else telling me already."

He softened. "Who is your date?"

"Kenny. He's a very nice boy and attractive. He's had a hard-on all night, but he's embarrassed and keeps trying to hide it. It's cute."

He liked her spirit but was still taken aback.

"How is your date going with Jeneuer?" She rolled her eyes, realizing her mistake. "I mean Jennifer."

He shrugged and nodded.

"I hope so. The people who brought us here told us there were boys living with only boys for years in a special private school, training to go to America. They said you needed to blow steam with some girls and a dance. As soon as we pulled up to this place, all those gates and guards, I think to myself that all you ever see are old potatoes in babushkas." She smiled. "Jeneuer is doing her best."

He knew she was right. "You girls came from all over Russia?"

She dropped her cigarette in a plastic cup where it sizzled. "Yes. We just met yesterday morning."

"Why did they send random girls who don't know each other? Who live all over the country? Why not from the nearest big city?"

She crossed her arms. "What is your name?"

"Victor."

"Victor, I don't lie to people I respect, and I've known you for two minutes and already I respect you more than most boys I've known. I also feel sorry for you, living in this place. How can anyone hope in this place? It's like living inside a child's toy."

A child's toy. The words sliced him. All of the boys assumed they were training and preparing to work as spies in America, but every now and then Victor considered that nobody had ever said so directly. It worried him.

"They have us girls in a dormitory somewhere inside this spaceship, and last night we found the connection." She paused as if it was her last chance to turn back but she forged ahead. "While us girls are strangers to each other, it is our brothers who know each other."

"How?"

"Our brothers are in a special place, but not a good one." Hairline fractures crackled her tough façade. "They do evil things. Murder. Rape. My own brother, who is three years older, he rapes a grandmother and her grandbaby and…" Her voice caught, and her eyes filled with tears. "No, I can't say more. But I remember before it happened, all the times he is sitting with me and all of a sudden, he's gone. Not his body, but his mind," she spiraled a finger away from her head, "into space. After what he did, I talked to doctors so many times I cannot count. My mother, too. Endless hours but I always tell them the signs were all the time, every day. Me and my mother, we didn't know what it meant. Nobody did. We got used to those things. That was just the way he was."

Victor couldn't breathe.

"Victor, I know they will take us to interviews tomorrow and probably days after that, to ask us if we see the same things we saw with our brothers, and I will tell them no. I will say that keeping you locked up here is the evil in this place. I tell them for you."

She slid off the counter and gave him a hug. "I will do something to improve this place. I'm going to give Kenny a blow job. It should take not a minute, so I will soon see you on the dance floor."

Jennifer returned and gave him a bright smile that speared him with a delicious ache. His eyes went misty with gratitude for her kindness.

She asked to dance again, so they locked hands and walked down the street. As they neared the gym, a melody filled a skeleton of repetitive musical beats. She drew a huge, happy breath and said, "I love this song! Come on!"

She deserved a carefree dance to her favorite tune, proclaiming her place on the dance floor with anyone else who ever loved a song, so they raced. He laughed with such abandon he nearly passed the gym, veering inside at the last moment and almost crashing into the wall. He pushed off just in time and she screamed with joy as they skidded and wheeled to the center where the others celebrated the unrestrained moment, singing along at the top of their voices.

The "yeah" hook started high and spiraled down step by step, a catchy tumble of notes that registered so quickly even those hearing it for the first time could join in the middle and finish at least close to the right note. They screamed Miley Cyrus's next line about a party in the U.S.A.

He remembered the first time they saw Coach, striding into this very room to announce he was taking over from the junior high coach. Coach towered over them in shorts that looked like Speedos and a tank top with spaghetti straps, every bulge an implied threat of what they were up against, his biceps as big as an impressive pair of thighs. He wore regular gym clothes most of the time, but every so often he arrived in the skimpy outfit of a go-go dancer. While the boys snickered about it later, the effect was awe and submission, and Victor suddenly realized that was the point.

Jennifer tossed her head, carried off by joy. If the girl on the counter was right, and Victor had no doubt she was, tomorrow Jennifer would go to a doctor's office where she'd recount every detail of her night with Victor. Afterward she'd go to a new office with new doctors who'd ask her to start from the beginning.

He thought of the cameras high on the walls, and others hidden elsewhere, silently documenting every moment of their lives, every time they muttered to themselves, adjusted their dicks in their pants, picked their noses, or had a quick jack to get sex off the brain for a few hours.

A child's toy. What was the purpose of Maple Grove after all? They never trained in the techniques of spy craft, the clandestine surveillance, encryption, forgery, or interrogations.

He turned away so Jennifer wouldn't see his struggle. He bounced his fists lightly against his head. He wanted to punch his skull open, hurling his brain to the wall with a splat that would obliterate all of his thoughts as far back as he remembered, like his father tearing into his guts, or his mother aiming a needle into her arm. The way they hated him.

He squeezed his eyes, fighting the urge to run somewhere to curl against the world, but there was nowhere to go, no private place. He punched the air, harder and faster, his back to everyone, wanting the song to end more than anything.

Someone tapped his shoulder and he whirled about. Everyone had gone still, looking about with worry, but the song played on, sounding thin without the shouted accompaniment.

"Did you hear that?" Jennifer said.

He gulped down his rage. "What?"

A clear female scream.

The boys looked about, feeling their responsibility to protect a room full of girls, but not knowing what to do.

"Coach?" one boy said.

"They left," another replied.

Another terrified wail knifed the air and ended suddenly, ominously.

He ran to the street, where outside the garage a naked boy named Phil held a girl down with his knee, her dress torn from her shoulders like a wind-ravaged cape.

Her fingers working frantically, uselessly to get a purchase and pull away his tie from her throat. Her face was the color of beets, stuck with eyes as white as eggs. Victor's throat constricted with pity at her helplessness.

He knew the girl's terror and pain. Phil's face morphed into Victor's father's, and Victor was sprawled on the floor, at the mercy of a brutal monster.

He charged as Phil bellowed a stream of fury at the girl. Victor caught the gist, that Phil would teach a lesson to any bitch who slapped him.

Victor slammed into Phil, sending them bouncing and rolling. Ignoring the immediate, shooting pain, Victor sprang to his feet. Phil twisted to rise, his ass facing Victor. Though they were compatible in size, Victor realized his distinct advantage against a naked opponent. As Phil struggled for balance, Victor landed a powerful kick on the back of his balls.

Phil screamed and tipped over, but rolled into a bounce, pushing up.

Victor aimed another kick under Phil's chin that landed square. When Phil's head snapped back, Victor felt the jaw break against his shoe. Phil's mouth crunched, and a bit of flesh flew up, undoubtedly the tip of his tongue. While his injuries were nowhere near fatal, Victor knew Phil was incapacitated, probably for months.

He swiveled to check the girl. She hunched, breathing in great heaves, surrounded by the frills and flounces of the other girls, as they babbled and reached out. The boys hovered, slack-jawed. The girl's face was returning to normal, the red fading, the swelling settling.

Phil moaned, blood spattering his face. A tear split his upper lip, and the corners of his eyes pooled with what looked like raspberry jam. His pupils moved slowly, deliberately. They landed on Victor, and Phil eked out a creaky, sinister smile. Blood slashed the gaps between his teeth.

Victor flashed on his father's teeth, stained brown and separated by dark spaces, a detail he'd forgotten. Rage churned in his chest, and he delivered another swift kick, full in the face.

Phil scrunched and spat. His head thrashed as roared, gurgling and muted, like a starved beast issuing a warning while eating.

Fury blazed through Victor. He lifted him by the armpits, and Phil's head lolled like a broken toy. Victor inhaled, gripped the sweaty torso and slammed Phil against the corner of the garage. A ribbon of blood sailed away.

Phil wailed, modulated by gnashing teeth, staccato and guttural.

The pitiable sound enraged Victor. He used his body to brace Phil against the wall, grasped a fistful of his hair, and pounded Phil's face against the corner until the other boys pulled him away.

Victor caught a glimpse of Phil's floppy corpse. The wreckage of the monster's face, his features shattered, filled him with a triumph so immense he shook himself free and lifted his arms wide, fists clenched, bellowing his victory.

It was time to accept Jennifer's gratitude, his hero's reward, but the girls screamed and pulled back, Jennifer in the middle. Skinny, bangled arms flew protectively in front of her, like the bars of a cage.

For one second their eyes met, and disgust and hatred rocketed through the depths of her terror. She no longer loved him, he saw.

He took two steps in her direction. The girls shrieked into a tighter huddle.

"I love you," he shouted.

The girls gasped in affront and disgust. Jennifer turned away, covering her face with a hand.

The doors from both ends of Maple Grove slammed open. Men pounded down the street. He turned just as four soldiers advanced on him, pointing rifles, screaming orders in Russian. He raised his arms.

The lead soldier twirled his rifle about and smashed the butt against Victor's head.

When Drew returned to the present, he was in the same spot where he'd watched Tom drive off, except Tisha and Althea were now in front of him. They each took an arm and gently led him inside.

16

Limitless Destiny, Fearless Dreams

June–July 1975

Dr. Stein refused to say more about the secret experiment or the mysterious space object. Always polite, he wouldn't even name the astronomer who made the discovery. I restrained my intense impulse to casually ask others at NASA about it, fearful even a vague question to the wrong person might set off alarms. One of my regular sources in Cleveland was a superstar police detective who used to say a good interrogator knows when to go silent.

With the Apollo launch just a few weeks away, the hectic pace made it difficult to land interviews with anyone except politicians who spoke in banalities. In late June, we suddenly realized our taping schedule for the upcoming weekend was unexpectedly free.

Our production schedules were planned on the false assumption space shots had become an interesting routine, but the public was engrossed. Every day we scrambled to meet new deadlines, pushing us farther behind even as launch day loomed.

We were expected to provide two prime-time specials but barely had time to work on them. Tempers flared and arguments escalated. I worried more than I slept, and everyone else looked just as exhausted. I drew faint comfort from the equally dispirited faces of competing network crews also struggling to keep pace. We shared the unspoken, last-ditch hope of people heading for a communal failure, that the totality of the disaster might bestow individual absolution.

I needed a break as much as anyone else, so I shared in the

jubilation when Rick and Colby announced everyone could take the weekend off, even though it seemed an inexcusable indulgence.

I called Arthur in New York, and he happily agreed to make a last-minute trip to Florida. I savored his obvious excitement to see me, tempered by what I might see in his face when I told him I was pregnant. I'd known for weeks.

I was leaning toward an abortion. As I write this from the perspective of the twenty-first century, it's currently fashionable for busybodies to claim even an unmarried man involved in the pregnancy has a right to influence that choice, but the idea is unthinkable, maddening. Pregnancy changes everything for a woman, but a man often skates away. Why should he have input on such a major decision? Can an unmarried mother demand the man have a vasectomy or find a new career?

Marriage to Arthur would change the calculations dramatically, but the timing felt wrong with my career soaring, and I absolutely wouldn't force his hand. Given all this, it might seem hypocritical or even perverse to tell him, but my instinct for honesty was too strong. Plus, I was sure the news would deepen our delicious sense of intimacy. Not for the first time, I wondered why I never seemed to form bonds with women who might provide some direction and advice.

Finding a hotel room in central Florida was impossible with the imminent space mission, so I invited Arthur to stay with me. My coworkers lived in rooms adjoining mine, and I knew they'd gossip, but I felt defiant. The majority of the men on the crew, and they were mostly married men, showed no concern about escorting unfamiliar women about, and the different standards irked me.

Arthur rented a car from the airport and arrived Friday afternoon. Our first moments together in seven weeks crackled with desire. I felt his lust in the firmness of his grip, his snorting growls, his darting hands, and his searching tongue.

"Calm down." I laughed with what I hoped was a wicked gleam. "I made reservations at the only restaurant around worth the name. I had to get their earliest seating since it was so last minute, and we're going to miss our reservation if we don't leave now. There's a movie theater just next door so we can have a real date."

He smiled and grunted as he shook his head. "I feel ready to explode."

I was determined to stick to my plan for the evening: catch up on our lives over dinner, enjoy a movie, and discuss the pregnancy afterward. Only then did I spot my failure to account for sex, but I'd worry about that later.

At the restaurant, people froze and did double takes of recognition as we walked to our table. In Cleveland years before, I learned to look straight ahead when entering a public space, avoiding eye contact. Better to be thought aloof than act like a princess, waving at rooms.

As we ate the acceptable food, my outline for the evening rolled along. "I've already interviewed all the astronauts and project managers, but we're still missing some key players, like engineers. We're way behind schedule. We haven't even started editing our prime-time specials."

"Are you worried?"

"It's rocky. Even basic things like the rundowns and boilerplate scripts aren't finalized. And the network wants live reports almost every night, which pushes everything back even more." I didn't want to fill our date with complaints, so I rushed to add, "But it's exciting. If nothing else, it's exciting."

"I've watched all of your reports. You're doing a great job."

"The public fascination is through the roof. Maybe people are desperate for something to cheer about after Watergate and Vietnam. And you saw the reaction when we arrived. I'm more famous than ever." I didn't add Loren Sanderson was ebullient about a quarter-point jump in the ratings during May sweeps, worth millions in ad rates. I couldn't claim all the credit, but I could claim my share.

"How are things going with your coworkers?"

I flashed on an especially ugly argument in the office trailer a few days before, when producers Rick and Colby announced the title for both prime-time specials: *And So It Begins, Parts One and Two*. I hated it as self-important and nonsensical, especially since the Sunday night installment would air *after* the American and Soviet capsules undocked, an off-key mistake even the most listless viewer would catch. They dismissed my concerns. I fumed, but with so much discord already, I soon dropped my objections.

"There are always personality conflicts," I said with a shrug. I debated telling Arthur about the mysterious object in space and Dr. Stein's secret experiment, but I felt better maintaining my silence.

I asked about his life in New York. He flicked his hand and said, "All is well, except that I feel claustrophobic when I think about how far away you are. I'm hoping you miss me, too."

"I've been busier than ever, but you are always at the top of my mind. It's incredible how much I want to see you, but it's mixed up with my joy that you're in my life." The words flowed as softly as fog over a hilltop. Being so recklessly romantic without fear is one of life's rarest joys.

After dinner we walked to the movie theater to see *Jaws*, already a massive hit in its first week of release. I rested my head on his shoulder while he stroked my arm. On screen, the giant shark tore lazy summer days to bloody chunks. Beachgoers screamed, accusations flew, and panic consumed an entire town in an incoherent hash, since I was focused on feeling him next to me, breathing his scent. When the shark exploded at the movie's climax, it seemed to come from nowhere. We spontaneously giggled while everyone else cheered. We shared a look of happiness for having the same incongruous reaction.

So far, the evening was as close to perfect as I'd ever experienced. I ached to cap it off by closing the door of the hotel room, turning off the lights, and falling into bed with him. I kicked around the tempting idea of delaying the pregnancy discussion. My Midwestern values reared up with indignation, angrily lecturing me about duty before pleasure.

As we entered my room, I steeled myself. He noted the change in my mood. "You seem a bit anxious all of a sudden. Is something wrong?"

"I do have an issue to discuss with you. It's nothing we can't work out."

He sat on the bed, looking concerned while I took a chair. I'd rehearsed a few ways to start the conversation, but spitting it out suddenly seemed the best approach. "I'm pregnant. You're the father. I'm leaning toward an abortion, but I want to hear what you think." I winced inside for asking his opinion after all, but it felt like the right thing to do.

Years of preparation couldn't soften the shock of Arthur's response.

Dazed, he said, "I can't be a father. By all means, I encourage you to go through with the abortion. I'm sorry to be so direct, but I'm mortified at my carelessness and irresponsibility. Fatherhood is out of the question. It's unforgivable on my part."

His blunt indifference to other possibilities scattered my thoughts.

"If you choose to have the child, I will of course provide financial support. I have sufficient resources for whatever you need. But I cannot be an active father, and it would be best for the child if you never mentioned me."

I stuttered and stumbled. "I thought you were in love with me."

"More than I can say," he replied with unhesitating sincerity, shame twisting his face. "And that's why my behavior has been so inexcusable, so inconsiderate. I hope you can forgive me some day." He stood and picked up his weekend travel bag. "I'm sorry, Claudia, but I must be alone. I have many things to think about and consider."

I watched with disbelief as he walked off. He turned back at the door. "Please don't mistake this for abandonment. Rest assured that whatever you need, all you have to do is ask. I'll be waiting on your decision."

"You're leaving?"

Looking haunted, he said, "I'm a trapped man, a zoo animal leaping from an enclosure but crashing into the pit every time." He tore his eyes away and left.

In a short while, my disbelief and despair cleaved into jagged shards of rage. I paced, hammering the bed when my anger demanded release. I swiped away tears of fury, I growled and moaned and hurled a pillow at the walls, marching back and forth to throw it again and again.

"A trapped man," I scoffed aloud. Such mewling self-pity, the enfeebled wail of a lazy narcissist confronted with responsibility. Weak, disreputable, contemptible. Arthur was a coward, and I was a fool for not spotting it before now.

I wouldn't have his child, and I wouldn't ask for his money. The offer was undoubtedly as counterfeit as the man. I'd have the abortion as soon as possible.

It was already very late on Friday night. and despite knowing the crew would hate me, I swelled with ruthless determination. The title *And So It Begins* blotted out the mission's excitement with insufferable pomposity. As the lead anchor, I wanted a new title. We also needed to start work on the rundowns that map the shows, an arduous task that might consume days all by itself. Deadlines loomed for any number of technical and creative decisions.

In today's breakneck media environment, the title of a splashy special is decided well in advance by market researchers and branding specialists, allowing graphic artists, script writers, promo producers, and musicians to integrate the theme for a slick, seamless campaign. Not to mention the social media components, which I know little about. Things were much looser in 1975, when the network submitted TV listings well ahead of time. The generic *Apollo-Soyuz Special Coverage* served as a perfectly fine placeholder.

I reached for the phone to call Ron, my field director who was in a room just down the hall where he no doubt spent hours petting his beard. Without warning, my stomach twisted as if two strong fists were squeezing out a soggy dishrag. The pain took me to my knees, and I broke into a sweat as a tsunami of nausea rose with terrifying speed. Gasping, I struggled to my feet and crouched to the bathroom, a hand over my mouth. The first gush of vomit sprayed between my fingers and splashed to the tiles. I crumpled at the toilet and heaved. The pulses felt powerful enough to purge my organs.

For several minutes, I pumped the mediocre restaurant meal into the water. Even after I expelled every morsel, the involuntary contractions continued as if it was critical nothing remain. Each dry heave grew more painful until it tapered to an occasional retch.

Panting, I leaned against the wall. I pulled a towel from the rack and wiped my face until I felt reasonably recovered, recalling the complaints of other women about the name morning sickness when it attacked at all hours. This was by far the worst bout. After soaking the towel in cold water, I cleaned my face and neck. I remained determined for a new title, and I slouched to the phone.

Ron instantly agreed with me. "You're right. And it's insane to take the weekend off when we're so far behind. I'm calling everyone in tomorrow morning."

The next day, the crew arrived radiating resentment. The techies gathered in the studio with the technical director, while the production staff met in the office trailer, the atmosphere thick with tension. Rick and Colby glared at me with crossed arms, while two associate producers and a team of three writers looked dejectedly at the floor.

At least Ron was on my side.

"Claudia's right," he said, raking his facial hair with his nails. "*And So It Begins* sounds like a sappy television movie about kids and their new stepmom. It doesn't fit this mission. We need excitement. Glamour. Astronauts are as close to demigods as ever walked the earth. It's adventure, it's sexy, it's triumphant."

"It's a fucking title nobody will remember the next day," Rick groused.

I jumped in. "What if Neil Armstrong said, 'gee, it's dusty up here' instead of 'one small step, one giant leap'? Words create history, they set moods, they inspire, and we need to do better than a throwaway title." Their chastened looks were enormously satisfying. "I have two suggestions. The first is *The Star-Spangled Frontier*, which will appeal to the majority of viewers who think the Russians are hitching a ride on American accomplishments, whether it's true or not. The second is more expansive." I had their reluctant attention. "*Limitless Destiny, Fearless Dreams: The Apollo-Soyuz Mission*. We can use it for both shows, but let's drop the *Part One, Part Two* because it won't matter."

After a moment of silence, Ron spoke while stroking his hairy chin. "I like the last one. I like it a lot. Our viewers will automatically think of American manifest destiny. And 'fearless' is magnanimous to the Russians, but people will think of things like American soldiers scaling the cliffs at Omaha Beach." He smiled. "It's really good, Claudia."

"It has a subtitle," Rick muttered. "We aren't public television, for fuck's sake." His expression changed. "But it's pretty good."

Over the next few hours, the resentment in the room dissipated in the unexpected, welcome heat of creative energy. Hammering out the first pages of the scripts fueled an excitement to tackle the rundowns for both shows, a task that accelerated with the spirited clarity of placing the finishing pieces of a jigsaw puzzle. Mid-afternoon, Rick and Colby grabbed two editors and started cutting the interviews into coherent narratives. I worked with Ron to plan the on camera bridges, the writers whipped the voice-over copy into shape, and the techies hummed with purpose. In a single day that began so bleakly, we coalesced into an effective team.

In the following weeks, I managed a few brief calls with Dr. Stein, if only to remind him I wouldn't relent until I knew the results of his experiment. He always assured me I was the only reporter he'd briefed, but about ten days before liftoff, he stopped answering or returning my calls. I figured he was busy and concentrated on the job at hand.

By launch day on July fifteenth, our crew brimmed with optimism. We'd polished our first installment of *Limitless Destiny, Fearless Dreams* into a riveting examination of the mission preparations. Our confidence alarmed the other network crews. They seethed with betrayal, as if we'd broken the unspoken pact to share the failure. They gave me the silent treatment in the press enclosure while the Apollo rocket smoked and rumbled in the distance at the end of the peninsula, impatient for liftoff.

Since that long-ago summer, I've been fortunate to witness vanishingly rare things, such as a field of dozens of lightning bugs pulsing twice in unison. I watched a glacier calve an iceberg the size of a small town. In a submersible on the Atlantic seabed, I held my breath as the prow of the *Titanic* emerged from the darkness like a mythical god from an ancient mist. Nothing ever topped the awe of the Apollo launch that unforgettable day.

We'd all watched the coverage from Russia that morning of the Soyuz launch, giddy because things were under way at last. Thousands of people crowded the viewing stands behind the media enclosure. Mounted on poles high above, a row of speakers hissed and crackled as mission control engineers and the astronauts confirmed settings and readings, speaking as if unaware millions were hanging on their words. It felt strangely intrusive, like we were eavesdropping. A distinct voice often broke in to announce the time to ignition.

At the one minute cue, everyone went still. At thirty seconds, the world seemed to freeze. At ten seconds, people gasped in wonder at being present for the famous countdown. The rocket shook and growled and when the count reached zero, its echo died in an Olympian roar. Huge, roaring flames ripped the rocket from gravity's grip and lifted it like a skyscraper into the sky. The whole world vibrated as the air filled with the piercing chemical scent of rocket fuel, and a slight wave of heat washed over us.

Physicists say the forward momentum of time is an illusion of being trapped in three dimensions. In a five-dimensional space, all of time is visible all at once. Your birth is always happening, as is your death. You can watch your life like a line of video screens displaying every moment, except it's not the playback of a recording. Your life, everyone's life, is an infinite loop that we experience moment by moment because our senses are limited to three dimensions.

We can't travel to the fifth dimension, but the reverse is not true. I wonder if that higher plane sometimes brushes against the fabric of our universe and gently ruffles time's flow. Is that why some moments seem to drag, while others collapse into a crunch?

From liftoff until the American and Soviet capsules decoupled four days later, time raced. Even my memories of those days remain on fast-forward, and I can't arrange them in a logical progression. Live reports, live interviews, rushing to record more footage or another interview, cramming food, changing clothes, brief meetings, removing my makeup and applying more, a quick nap, and then back in front of the camera. I caught snatches of encouragement and praise from Loren and others in New York. I was covering this event, but hardly experiencing it at all.

When I signed off for the Sunday recap of *Limitless Destiny, Fearless Dreams,* the anchor in New York thanked me and the crew for our work and said, "I'm sure I speak for all of our viewers when I say that your coverage has been outstanding, and you've earned some much-needed rest." The red tally light on top of the camera faded.

The Apollo capsule was still high in orbit and the astronauts were still performing experiments, including Dr. Stein's secret study, but our mission was over. Another crew was waiting in Hawaii to cover the splashdown in a few days.

From his spot just off camera, Ron said, "We killed it, Claudia. Speaking for myself, it's the best television I've ever done."

A torrent of dizziness hit me like a personal tornado and forced me to the ground. Suddenly remembering I was pregnant, I puked all over the video cables and audio lines. I don't know how I'd managed to stave off my symptoms for five days.

Ron got me back to the hotel, where I showered and crawled into bed. He returned with a bowl of soup, dry toast, and ginger ale, but I made him leave the tray in the bathroom with the door closed until I could manage to look at or smell food without getting nauseous.

"Do you need a doctor?"

I shook my head, wondering if his suspicious look was real or a figment of my paranoia.

He went on. "It's supposed to be a surprise, but Loren Sanderson will be here in the morning to congratulate us personally." He rubbed his beard. "I think he has another dream assignment for you, but if you want my opinion, you don't look ready to leave that bed for a few weeks at least."

I felt much better when I woke in the morning. In the bathroom, the food Ron delivered sat on the counter. Swirls of fat skimmed the soup, and the toast looked mummified. I drank the ginger ale, flat but still satisfyingly sweet. As usual when I heard or thought the word "ginger," I flashed on the artist Gina Ginger Soda. Choosing that name was a brilliant move, I thought as I slid the tray to the hallway.

I felt rejuvenated. Now that I had time to be more aggressive, I called Dr. Stein. We hadn't talked in nearly two weeks. His phone rang and rang.

An uneasy sensation formed as I hung up. The last time we spoke, Dr. Stein sounded rushed, telling me that scientists are busiest in the lead-up to a space mission. "Once the rocket lifts off, I'll help whenever I can," he'd promised. *Whenever I can.*

"Oh, shit," I muttered, spotting the brush-off two weeks after the fact.

Berating myself, I called a long list of NASA contacts in the media offices as well as other scientists. The few who answered didn't know Dr. Stein's whereabouts. I left a slew of messages with politely unhelpful receptionists.

I was preparing to rush over to his office when someone knocked on my door. I opened it to find Ron and Loren, both casually dressed. I'd never seen Loren in anything but a suit and tie, but he looked just as polished in tan slacks and a polo shirt. I let them inside. "I have to follow up on a story with one of the scientists. I'm sorry to rush off, but it's important."

Beaming, Loren firmly sandwiched my hand between his. "Nonsense. You're going to enjoy your triumph with the best lunch in Florida. I know an exclusive spot that serves a hot buffet with anything you like, including prime rib carved to order."

I imagined a knife slicing bloody strips of meat. Ron rubbed his beard and Loren smiled. I turned away just in time to avoid vomiting on them.

17

Drew picked up the first page of the next chapter. He read the opening lines before setting it down to think.

Grandma didn't have the luxury of the internet. At this point in her story, she had all she needed to realize the full truth about Arthur Brittany, but putting it all together required hours, perhaps days of research at the library.

With a start, Drew realized he hadn't researched Tom. He called up a browser, only to discover Tom used the most restrictive social media privacy settings, with little more than a profile photo on public view. A few popular career networking sites listed only his name, his professional life cloaked. It struck him as a suspicious online strategy for a marketing executive.

The wider internet results were equally threadbare. He found a few mentions of Tom in high school and college, but mostly as part of larger groups and without photos. Tom was quoted a few times in articles from the *Spartan Newsroom*, the Michigan State student news site. He'd also earned a handful of listing in academic awards. It seemed deliberately vague, and Drew felt a niggle of caution.

At the same time, Drew knew his own digital footprint was likely to appear just as ghostly. His own high school years in the East Bay suburb of El Sobrante, as well as four years at Cal State East Bay, provided little insight into Drew Morten. He and Tom apparently shared a disinterest in creating a large internet presence. In theory, he respected Tom's feelings about online discretion, but it was also an undeniable pattern of deception. When combined with Tom's role in his visions, Drew's suspicion thickened to dread.

After he'd had his vision of Maple Grove that morning, he carefully described it to Tisha and Althea, including the way Victor killed Phil after the Homecoming dance. They absorbed the story.

"Why am I seeing Victor's life?" he'd asked Althea.

"I don't know."

"How does Tisha know three people will save the world?"

"If I could tell you, I would. Only you two can pull apart and assemble the details."

"These abilities," Drew said, "the visions, the healing—my grandfather had them as well. Are they genetic?"

"No. All humans are capable of having them, but they must be activated."

"How are they activated?" Tisha said.

"For both of you, it was holding the necklace. That's when the prophecies began."

Drew and Tisha shared an open-mouthed stare. "Prophecies?" Drew said.

"The necklace?"

"Don't become ensnared by biblical words and miraculous names. Your experience is sufficient to understand them without a mystical molasses that will only keep you moribund. Yes, we are sometimes called prophets. And yes, an essence in the necklace is crucial. But you've experienced the burden without the additional weight of fables. It's your life, that's all. Whether people call you prophets or not."

Drew and Tisha argued that the words mattered, and the supernatural element was critical.

"Be as awed as you like," Althea replied. "But this has been my life for much too long for me to care about such things. You have visions of the future. Call them prophecies, call them visions, call them fairy tales, it changes nothing. Something in the necklace, I don't know what, set them off in you. But it isn't confined to the necklace. Whatever it is, is spread across the world. In necklaces, cups, spoons, any number of silver objects. That's all you need to know. Indeed, it's all I know."

"But a lot of other people held that necklace," Drew said. "Why didn't it happen to them?"

"It only happens when necessary."

Drew scoffed with disbelief. "Who decides if it's necessary?"

She gave a faint smile. "For centuries, 'God' was my answer and still serves as the best. Something is approaching, but I don't know all the details and it's getting very close. I've walked this earth for nearly a thousand years, and every year only reveals how little I know."

Somehow, Drew wasn't surprised to learn Althea's true age. Tisha showed no obvious reaction, either.

"My grandma wrote about an object in space NASA was trying to study. Is it connected to all of this?"

"Yes. I don't know how, but yes."

"If you don't know, who does?"

"There is a man." She dipped her head. "If you meet him one day, it will not be soon, so it's best to put him out of your mind."

Despite their best efforts, she refused to say more about the man with the answers.

"Tisha," Althea said, changing the topic with a note of authority. "You are central to whatever is coming next. You must prepare."

Startled, she asked, "How?"

"The memoir," Althea said. "The information is important for you, too."

That was hours ago. In the living room, Tisha set aside another page with a crisp snap.

18

Tania Was a Rolling Stone

August–September 1975

As I'd suspected, the Apollo-Soyuz mission was my audition for the new prime-time program Ron was developing. He and Loren offered me the lead anchor spot the very morning I narrowly avoided puking on them.

With the widespread critical acclaim for *Limitless Destiny, Fearless Dreams*, the network gave us several months to conceptualize the show, which would premiere in November.

Loren sent us to a small home he owned in San Francisco, to focus on the job while reducing expenses. We flew off as soon as we could, allowing Loren to remain in my guest bedroom a while longer.

Lengthy pre-production wasn't uncommon in those days. We had no inkling a new era of television journalism would boil over in the next few years in a slapdash rush to replicate the monster ratings of the news magazine *60 Minutes*. Over the next decades, programs bubbled up and popped out of existence just as quickly. The demand for instant success ignored the way CBS gave *60 Minutes* at least five years to build its reputation and audience, but executive decisions often puzzled me.

Tucked in among taller, lavish Victorian buildings almost flush with the sidewalks, Loren's cute little house looked like it had fallen off a charm bracelet. Resting on the gentle lower slope of Seventeenth Street, it had a lovely small front garden of rosebushes and flowering vines, although nobody had weeded in ages.

About a week after we arrived in San Francisco, I took what was already becoming a routine morning walk along Market Street, a wide boulevard that curved and climbed the hills to the right but marched straight downtown to the left.

Just over the hill was the Haight-Ashbury, the former hippie enclave that had degenerated from free love and marijuana into a dystopian hellscape of heroin addiction. The gay former hippies fled to this side of the hill, an affordable Irish enclave at the intersection of Market and Castro Streets. It was a homey, working-class neighborhood, with houses and small apartment buildings stuffing every available spot, along with shops and diners. An old movie palace offered the chipped and neglected opulence of a former age, so emblematic of the 1970s.

San Francisco's summer fog chilled the morning air, a novelty for anyone used to the dependable mugginess of August. I threw on a pink baseball cap just before I set out, a freebie I found in my bag after buying some expensive cosmetics. It was a simple but effective disguise since people recognized me everywhere lately. I felt vibrant among the bustling workers heading downtown via the underground Muni stop or on lumbering buses. I spotted a pregnant woman waddling in the crowd and placed a hand on the slight bulge at my belly.

While I still burned with anger at Arthur, the euphoria of the Apollo-Soyuz triumph balanced the extremes, providing a bit of clarity. My potential future child was blameless, and I felt a wholly unexpected joy at the thought of being a mother. Of course, I knew the considerable risk. This was fifteen years before Candace Bergen portrayed the television journalist Murphy Brown who gave birth as a single mother, a fictional storyline that provoked real public outrage as well a rebuke from the vice president. I held no illusions about the stakes for my career, but I was still undecided about whether to have the child.

I stopped at a small bookstore where the window display changed daily, and a quick perusal of the titles was always in order. I was fascinated by the number of books written by and for gay men and lesbians. In that bookstore window, I glimpsed an unlikely but gathering cultural wave.

"Save the child!"

A young, filthy man stumbled from a doorway. Startled pedestrians moved aside. He wore a patchwork fur vest and enormous striped bell bottoms as raggedy as a forgotten windsock. A grimy, beaded headband held back his matted hair, and his eyes bulged as if struggling to pop free.

"Save the child!" he screamed again, looking at me. "It's across the street! In the yellow box!"

After a beat, he roared and charged in my direction. I froze in confused disbelief, my mind groping for the logic. He looked enraged.

Feeling a blinding protective urge, I covered my stomach and dove aside just before he reached me. Two men grabbed him and pushed him to the sidewalk, while a third man who I dimly noted was black enfolded me in his arms, using his body to shield me.

On the cement, the tattered man's rage evaporated, leaving fear behind. He hunched against the building and drew up his legs protectively. With a pitiable cry of fright, his eyes frantically searched my saviors for signs of more violence to come.

"The yellow box is across the street," he repeated as an enfeebled explanation. He tapped his head. "I heard them in here. They told me to tell her," he pointed at me, "that she has to save the child, and the yellow box is across the street."

Everyone, including myself, couldn't help but scan the far sidewalk to spot a yellow box. Of course, there was nothing.

I felt dizzy, and the black man who'd protected me with his body steadied me. Others surrounded us, asking if I needed help and angrily muttering to each other about so many heroin addicts living nearby.

The black man and the two others who'd thrown the addict to the sidewalk stayed with me while my heart slowed. I brought my breathing under control and fought off a slight tremor before it escalated to shaking. From the corner of my eye, I saw the heroin addict get up as if nothing unusual had happened and stumble off.

The other pedestrians had moved on by the time I felt confident enough to mumble my thanks to the three men. They escorted me to the corner of Market Street, where I assured them I was fine. They set off for work and were already descending to the Muni stop when I realized I'd failed to convey the depths of my gratitude. Plus, I'd already forgotten their faces. I worried about passing them on the street without so much as a smile of thanks, but it was too late to catch up to them.

As I returned to Loren's house, I reflected on the overpowering instinct to protect my unborn child. Sometimes I momentarily forgot

I was pregnant, for the intense morning sickness had tempered to an occasional bout of nausea, quickly expelled by a retch or two. And yet protecting the fetus was my very first, instinctual response.

I couldn't delay my decision much longer, for my pregnancy would soon become obvious. I felt guilty for concealing the truth from Ron and Loren, who'd placed their trust in me.

When I returned from my walk, Ron was weeding the garden, shirtless even in the cold. His lean, well-shaped frame radiated sex appeal, but he never showed the slightest interest in me or anyone else as far as I could tell. I'd seen both men and women give him looks of desire, but I couldn't decide if he welcomed the attention or was oblivious to it, nor did he show preference for a gender. Maybe he was asexual like Dr. Stein, but I didn't think so.

He stood as I approached, wiping his forehead. He wore heavy work gloves, well-used and deeply stained. He probably found them in the little shed out back, although I wouldn't be surprised if he always carried them in case of need. Sweat matted the light fuzz of his chest and stomach. With his usual solemn expression, he gestured to a pile of weeds as limp as noodles.

"Plants are assholes," he said.

I laughed. "I think clouds are bigger assholes."

He stooped to resume stabbing and digging. "How was your walk?"

I didn't want to talk about the heroin addict. I sat on a small, ornate iron bench and said, "San Francisco is such a city of contrasts. It's so rich in history, but it's fearless about embracing the modern world."

He nodded. "It's determined, too. You belong here, Claudia. You fit in perfectly."

I was flattered to be the subject of his private thoughts. In Florida, he was always crisp and professional, never fluctuating beyond a steady emotional band. After sharing a house for a few days, the totality of his asceticism made a deep impression on me. He looked like a monk tending the garden before morning prayers.

He liked to cook, which suited me fine, and he prepared simple meals such as steamed vegetables paired with a bit of protein, no fancy sauces or spices. He drank only water, splurging now and then with the fizzy variety, but never flavored. His clothes were as plain as a peasant's tunic. His shoes especially seemed chosen for maximum comfort, and the soft leather boots he wore to weed the garden had served him daily in Florida. I'd also seen him wearing the same jeans numerous times.

"Ron, I've been thinking." He stopped to listen. "Developing a new prime-time show gives us an opportunity we may never have again. Of course, we have to cover important news, but can't we elevate our goals a bit? We have the power to inspire America. People love to feel awed."

The dimple on his right cheek, visible through his beard only when he smiled, felt like a reward. "I love that you said that, and I agree. But I'm not going to manipulate people with spooky stories or fake UFO photos."

I paused for a meaningful moment. "What if I have a UFO story from a scientist?"

He asked a few pointed questions and I told him everything I knew about the mysterious star that wasn't a star, since Dr. Stein had cut me off. I lacked the clout to apply pressure at NASA, and if he wouldn't share, nobody else at the space agency would, either. It was a relief to tell somebody.

Ron looked as focused as I'd ever seen him, remarkable for a man who gave full concentration to everything. He asked if I had a copy of the report.

"No. I should have transcribed it, but Dr. Stein seemed so certain about keeping me in the loop that I wasn't worried. I'll never make that mistake again."

"It would be great to kick off our show with a story like that."

Unburdening myself of that secret allowed the next to slip free. "I think I met a man in New York who is more than eight hundred years old." Ron had no visible reaction as I recited the details of Arthur's life. I explained how I did some research at the main branch of the New York Public Library after I returned from Florida, pulling all the strands of his story together. "Obviously, I have no way to prove he was born around 1200, and he was supposed to be the king of England, but I'm certain he was."

"How can you be certain of that?" His tone was curious rather than challenging.

I told him about the shooting and the aftermath. "I saw it with my own eyes. Within ten minutes, it was as if nothing had happened.

I don't know if he's immortal or what, and I can't believe those words are coming out of my mouth."

"Could he have he paid someone to pretend to shoot him?"

"Why would he go to the trouble of faking it?"

"Do you remember how it felt when you had your first on-air job, the way people treated you, looked at you? They'll do anything to get your attention because they think you have influence."

"Arthur wouldn't do that." I dropped my head in self-disgust for automatically defending the man who'd walked out on me. "Not that he's such a great guy. But he wouldn't go to that extreme. And anyway, he's nothing if not logical, and I can't fathom the logic in faking a shooting."

Ron yanked a huge weed from the ground, and the roots snapped deep in the dirt like a muted machine gun volley. He added it to the pile and took a few breaths. "Is he the father?"

Why did I ever wonder if he'd figured it out? "Yes. Does Loren know?"

Ron shrugged and rubbed his beard. "We haven't talked about it, but he's one of the sharpest people I know."

"Will this cause a problem with my job as lead anchor?"

"Not if I can help it. I'm the producer, and I'll stick by you, but I'm not an omnipotent power at the network. Have you decided to have the child?"

"No. I hope it doesn't sound selfish, but I'm worried about what it will mean for my career."

"If it's selfish to worry about how your personal life will affect your professional life, then everyone is selfish." He slipped off a glove and squeezed my hand. "I'm glad to talk about it whenever you like, but I won't impose. From now on, I'll wait for you to raise the topic. And if you need to have an abortion while we're here, I'll be glad to look after you."

Feeling tears, I ducked inside.

For the next few weeks, we pounded the format of the program into shape, painstakingly revisiting every detail. We reviewed set designs, plowed through stacks of resumes, and even spent three full days going over color schemes until I felt I would scream if I saw another little card with subtle variations of the same pigment.

We decided on a quasi-magazine structure, with at least one live studio panel, maybe two. We checked in with Loren regularly, sitting at the kitchen table with both phone extensions. He sounded pleased by our progress.

As the weeks slipped by, I swelled like a water balloon, down to the skin between my toes so that I felt web-footed, waddling like a penguin. I bought stretchy pants and baggy shirts, refusing to browse maternity aisles where frills and ribbons suggested happy women confident about giving birth. Waves of fatigue and bouts of ravenous hunger overwhelmed me. An almost constant urge to urinate drove me to distraction. Ron kept to his promise and never asked about the pregnancy, but I detected his concern and alarm.

In those years, California's abortion laws gave women enormous latitude. Instead of rushing to meet an earlier deadline, I indulged my indecision until my child resolved the matter.

It was a warm, early Saturday morning in September, and I had stopped to scan the bookstore display on my regular walk. Just then, the daughter I'd go on to name Delilah adjusted for a more comfortable position, as casually as if she'd done it a million times. I felt every detail of the move and visualized the way she'd turned and tucked her head closer to her arm. The thrill and amazement didn't sweep away my concerns. Instead, Delilah became a person in that moment, and I was responsible for her care and safety no matter the cost. It was that simple.

All the same, it was a profound and life-altering decision, and I meandered along the nearly deserted sidewalks for much longer than usual. The Victorian buildings filled me with hope, ebullient as they were with bay windows and gabled turrets trimmed with elaborate millwork. Vibrant color palettes highlighted medallions and sunbursts atop doors, floral patterns draped over windows, and egg-and-dart molding parading along façades interspersed with diamonds and squares. I even spotted a playful line of carved dogs cavorting beneath the intricate roof brackets of a house. I suddenly understood why gay people find such places so alluring, the carefree whimsy offering exuberant defiance to utilitarian ugliness. Maybe I could summon the same attitude in the face of scorn for single mothers.

It was almost nine o'clock by the time I headed back, a full hour later than usual. The neighborhood yawned and stretched, slowly wakening to a lazy Saturday. A smattering of customers enjoyed a leisurely meal in the diners before the rush.

Several gay bars in the neighborhood opened at six a.m., and music thumped behind solid doors and covered windows. Just as I passed one of them, a trio of handsome men, two white and one black, spilled outside, rubbery with laughter. They wore tight jeans and T-shirts, clothes for Friday night instead of Saturday morning. I decided they'd been awake all night. They looked tired yet jovial, tipsy but not plastered, and they stopped when they saw me.

I smiled and kept walking until the black man said, "Hey! We stopped that heroin addict from attacking you."

Happy for the opportunity to redeem myself, I greeted them warmly and expressed an appropriate level of gratitude. I studied their faces to give them a thankful smile if I passed them on the street again. Beneath his shaved head, the black man had a kind smile with a set of dimples to rival Ron's. Another had a dark beard and the soft features of a thoroughly huggable man, while the third looked like a disco star, although he kept his hair rather short. "I didn't realize you all knew each other," I said. "I assumed you were strangers."

"Oh, we're strange, honey!" the bearded guy said, setting off another burst of laughter.

They invited me to join them for breakfast. I declined, and after a round of hugs, disco man said, "You just call on the Three Musketeers whenever you need help, sweetheart."

I smiled as they stumbled away while hugging each other about the shoulders. They split off to slap their thighs with unrestrained laughter or to make a spirited point by poking the others in the chest, but they always re-formed into the Three Musketeers.

Back at the house, the warm, delicious scent of an egg and cheese casserole filled the kitchen while Ron prepared a fruit salad. I told him I'd decided to have the child, and he looked pleased. "When are you due?"

"I'm not really sure. Sometime in January, I guess."

"What does your doctor say?"

"I haven't seen a gynecologist yet." He drew back, and I realized how thoughtless I must sound. "I didn't see the point when I wasn't sure if I was going to go through with it or not." He grimaced. I grimaced. "I sound like a fool, don't I?"

He remembered one of his New York friends knew a gynecologist in San Francisco. On Monday morning, he called and booked an appointment for that afternoon. I asked him to come along, and we took a cab to the doctor's office downtown.

We'd been living in Loren's house for a month and had done a bit of San Francisco sightseeing, but we'd never ventured among the skyscrapers. I watched the typical urban landscape of towering buildings and people on the sidewalks when we passed a strange, ornate object on a pedestrian island, so out of place I sat up, filled with the strange conviction I had no excuse for not recognizing it.

It was already well behind us when I asked the driver about it.

"Lotta's Fountain," he said. "Lotta Crabtree was the biggest star of the nineteenth century. She was the toast of Broadway, but she got her start right here in the music halls of San Francisco. After she got rich and famous, she donated that fountain to the city. It's one of our most famous landmarks. Everything in this area was destroyed by the earthquake and fire in 1906, except Lotta's Fountain."

That's why it looked so out of place, a relic stranded in place while the city burned down and re-formed around it. I turned to Ron. "I have the strangest feeling about that fountain. Like I've seen in it some other context."

"You might have seen pictures of it. Like the man said, it's famous."

I didn't think so. It nagged at me for days.

The doctor said the baby and I were doing fine, and I was due the second week of January.

Ron and I formed an unspoken agreement to avoid discussing the major problem of premiering the program in November with a heavily pregnant, unmarried woman as lead anchor. We focused on work and made excellent progress.

A few days after seeing Lotta's Fountain, we sat at the kitchen table reviewing an enormous stack of writing samples when the phone rang. Ron answered. After a few seconds, he covered the mouthpiece. "It's Loren."

A moment later, he bolted upright. His eyes widened. "What?!" He stood, kicking back the chair. It tipped over with a clatter. "Where?" He grabbed a pencil and scribbled furiously. I rose, instantly alert. "We'll be waiting out front!"

He slammed the receiver into the cradle. The bell pinged. "It's Patty Hearst. They arrested her in the Mission District. The local affiliate is sending a crew to pick us up, and they'll be here any minute."

I rushed to my room. Since none of my pants or skirts fit, I didn't change my sweats, but I pulled on a nice top and blazer. Ron urged me to hurry while I gave my hair a quick brush and plastered it with hairspray.

"They're here!"

With a few expert strokes, I applied some mascara and pale lipstick and grabbed the rest of my makeup to finish in the car.

A van waited out front, emblazoned with the logo of the local affiliate, a collapsible microwave dish strapped to the reinforced roof. We hopped in back, nodding to the crew of three men, who scrunched their faces at my clothes.

"You're wearing sweatpants for the network news?" said the man in the passenger seat. He studied my midriff and his expression flashed with the delight of a gossip uncovering a secret. I'd spent some time studying myself in a full-length mirror that morning and concluded I wasn't unmistakably pregnant yet. Seeing his face, I wondered if I was only fooling myself.

"I had about two minutes to get ready," I snapped.

"You'll shoot her from the waist up," Ron replied with the authoritative bark of a network producer. I was annoyed he had to say it. I'd lost count of the number of times I'd seen male anchors and field reporters in jackets and ties up top, and jeans or shorts down below. Everybody treated it as perfectly normal.

As we left, the driver said, "I can't believe Patty Hearst came back to San Francisco. She grew up here. How the hell did she think nobody would recognize her?"

Patty Hearst was just one woman running with a group of dangerous crackpots called the Symbionese Liberation Army, or SLA. Led by a schizophrenic escaped prisoner, they spread mayhem for a scattershot ideology defined mostly by random targets of hatred, including a school superintendent they killed for unfathomable reasons across the bay in Oakland.

But she was also an heiress to the Hearst newspaper fortune, and she'd been kidnapped nineteen months before, dragged screaming from her apartment near UC Berkeley where she was a student. It ignited a national frenzy. The Hearst family abided by the ransom demands to provide free food to poor communities in the Bay Area, but the effort was chaotic and disorganized. The SLA soon saw greater potential in recruiting Hearst to their cause. In less than two months, she'd released a recording announcing she'd changed her name to Tania and joined the outlaw group. A few weeks later, she participated in a San Francisco bank robbery where two people were shot. Security photos showed a slight woman in a long coat and a biker chick wig aiming a rifle and shouting orders. The images of the former society girl shocked America.

About a month after the robbery, the police converged on a house the SLA had commandeered from the terrified residents in a dense Los Angeles neighborhood. The police and SLA exchanged no less than nine thousand rounds of ammunition, making it one of the largest shoot-outs in American history. All the cops survived, but the house burned to the ground and six SLA members lay dead, including the leader.

Investigators picked through the charred rubble, but Patty Hearst was not among the corpses. She and several others were away when the standoff began, and soon she was on "most wanted" posters everywhere. Now she was back in San Francisco and under arrest.

Her saga awakened the world to the Stockholm Syndrome, whereby hostages come to identify with and join their captors. Following her arrest, the public learned she was raped, drugged, and isolated during her first days as a captive. Hearst sought safety by embracing her kidnappers, but all the same she would be sentenced to a seven-year term for her part in the bank robbery. President Carter commuted her sentence after two years. President Clinton wiped her record clean with a presidential pardon.

The impact of her story still echoes. It came amidst a spate of infamous kidnappings and attempts: a wealthy Florida girl named Barbara Mackle who was buried alive in a ventilated fiberglass coffin for four days before being rescued; J. Paul Getty of the famous oil family whose kidnappers sawed off his ear and mailed it to a newspaper to end speculation he faked his abduction to go partying; the botched nighttime attempt to nab Princess Anne near Buckingham Palace when a former English boxer became a national hero for tussling with the would-be kidnapper and shielding the princess with his body. More than the others, Hearst's abduction panicked the elite, who began surrounding themselves with massive security bubbles.

The driver zoomed along until we reached a shambolic neighborhood of narrow streets and small houses at the southern border of San Francisco. Hearst and a companion were arrested without incident, and other than FBI agents swarming in and out of the small clapboard house, there was nothing to see. We shot some B-roll, and I did a few interviews with neighbors and some of the cops guarding the perimeter before we clambered back into the van and set off for the county jail.

Located in the South of Market area, at the time a grim industrial neighborhood of small factories and porno shops, the San Francisco County Jail hunched near an elevated freeway. Fronted by the huge Brutalist Hall of Justice, the jail was barely visible from the main road. We joined a media scrum on the lower steps of the Justice building, but an officer announced Hearst had already been through intake and was locked in a cell. It meant we wouldn't get any pictures of her, and frustrated groans and shouts of anger arose. The most pressing demand on any of us was to obtain a single image of the famous fugitive after her arrest.

"There's no reason to stay here if we can't see her," said a nearby reporter to his crew. "Come on. Let's get some of her old friends to talk." They raced off. Others soon had similar ideas, and the media crowd melted away.

After learning our crew didn't know the location of anyone connected with Patty Hearst, Ron asked if they could get a microwave signal to their station. They confirmed it was close enough. "Tell the engineers to set up the satellite to New York. We need that connection pronto. The national news starts in about forty minutes, and they'll save the top for us." As they went to work, raising the microwave dish to a towering height, he turned to me. "Stay with the crew. I'll call Loren and tell him what to pull from the footage at the arrest location while you throw together some sort of script. Make it generic so we can use the sound bites in any order."

I shook my head. "No way. Other than the fact that she was arrested, I don't have any details. I'll try to find someone who can tell me something."

"Stay here," he ordered, gently grasping my arm. "If you go wandering off, you won't make it back in time. As soon as the crew gets an audio patch, New York can tell you everything from the wires."

"I don't want to lead the national news by reading wire copy."

He looked sympathetic but wasn't swayed. "All the other crews have left. We'll have the only live shot from this location. Looking official is the best we can hope for, especially if we can't even get a picture of her."

He spotted a row of phone booths across the wide street, a glum lineup in front of run-down bail bondsmen offices. With cracked glass and levered push doors broken at slanted angles, the phone booths displayed the remnants of rage from people who placed calls from such a hopeless place. Ron waited for a break in traffic before trotting across.

I watched the crew work for several minutes, edgy about standing around like a stump with Patty Hearst within shouting distance. I took some initiative and stood at the bottom of the steps asking everyone who descended if they knew anything about Patty Hearst. They all shook their heads.

I almost gave up when a trio of men, one black and two white, emerged from the building at the top of the concrete stairs. They wore suits, carried briefcases, and talked in a rapid, jovial patter.

The Three Musketeers! It seemed almost like an omen. I waited on the sidewalk as they descended. All three noticed me at the same time, and their faces lighted with recognition.

"You're that lady from the Apollo-Soyuz show!" the black man said.

I laughed with surprise. They'd only seen me in a camouflaging baseball cap. "I'm also the lady in the pink hat you saved from the heroin addict."

They roared with delight, and I told them I was in town for a few months on assignment and the Patty Hearst story landed in my lap. "Do you guys work here?"

Disco man, who slicked his hair for the office, said, "We're assistant DAs." He popped his eyebrows. "Prosecutors, if you can believe it!"

"Are you working on the Patty Hearst case?"

"The feds have that one," he replied before his eyes widened with conspiracy. He said to the others, "Let's give it to her!" They quickly agreed.

"Give me what?"

"Come on." He took my hand. "Let's go someplace more private."

We ducked behind the balustrade lining the steps, which didn't conceal us from the offices just above our heads, but at least we weren't in view of the entire building. Disco man opened his briefcase and handed me a manila envelope. "We were going to give this to our friend who works at *The Chronicle*. If you don't live here, you probably don't know that *The Chronicle* is the morning paper."

"As opposed to *The Examiner*, which is the afternoon paper owned by the Hearst family, and how's that for a kick in the balls?" the bearded one said.

"But we want you to have it," said the black man. "It's not a really big scoop. Everyone will have it by tomorrow morning, but you'll be the first." I started to open the envelope, but he put a restraining hand on mine. "Give us a few minutes to walk down the street, so nobody will see us with you. My God, Claudia Trenton. It was a pleasure doing business with you. And remember, just call on the Three Musketeers!"

I only waited until they were about twenty feet away. My hands trembled as I undid the metal clasp and pulled the contents free. On top was a black-and-white mug shot, and I gasped at having the most prized scoop in the country at the moment.

I studied both the front and profile photos. Patty Hearst wore a dingy striped T-shirt. Her hair was a mess, her eyes bleary, and her mouth a flat line. She held a sign at a tilted angle with her name in plastic capital letters pressed into corrugated black felt. Despite her cautious expression, I noted the firm set of her shoulders. No sloping resignation for her, as if she'd learned she could survive anything.

Ron was still across the street on the phone when I told the crew we needed to shoot two stills to feed to New York. I held up the photos. They leaped into action, excited and fussing to get the lighting perfect. Immediately afterward, they got the audio patch to New York. I shoved the IFB into my ear and used the microphone to talk to the director.

"I have her mug shots," I said. "They're at the end of the tape the crew is feeding to you right now."

In the digital world where instant photos are taken for granted, it might sound strange to go on about these pictures, but it was extremely rare to have images so quickly. Indeed, many stations still shot with film that required twenty minutes for processing, which was considered lightning speed.

I heard the director shouting to the studio crew about the incoming mug shots, setting off frantic activity in New York that made me smile in San Francisco. He came back, and we worked out the edits from what I remembered of the B-roll and interviews. I formed the ad-libs in my head. We went back and forth until both of us were satisfied we understood the sequence. I listened closely as he relayed it to the editors over his headset, to confirm his instructions matched my understanding.

"The field director is on the phone with Loren right now," I said, watching Ron in the battered phone booth, gesticulating and scribbling and rubbing his beard. "Loren's going to call in a cut sheet any minute for the editors, but we need to go with what we just decided, okay?"

"Got it," he replied.

I was asking the director to ignore the executive producer, and I needed to emphasize my point. "I want to be clear. You need to listen to me. When Loren calls in the time codes for the cut sheet, make sure the editors ignore it. He doesn't know we have the mug shots." He assured me he understood, and I was relieved he wasn't offended by a woman giving orders.

I suddenly realized that in the excitement of having the mug shots, I'd neglected to examine the other papers in the envelope. Juggling the mic, I scanned the pages.

"Oh, my God," I muttered at seeing the booking forms for Patricia Campbell Hearst. As spot news, what she had written down as her occupation was bigger than the end of Vietnam.

The director said, "Three minutes to you, San Francisco," just as Ron returned, oblivious. He started to read the notes from his talk with Loren and I interrupted. "Just stand back."

He gave me a searching look that became a curious smile. "What are you planning?"

I shot my best steely-eyed, determined look and, remembering the mug shots, squared my shoulders. "You're going to have to trust me."

Ron held up his hands in surrender before drifting away to watch the small, black-and-white monitor the crew had set up in the open door of the van. The show opened, and I fixed my eyes on the lens, but in my peripheral vision I saw Ron grab the top of his head with both hands when the mug shots flashed on-screen. I suppressed a giddy smile that would unsettle viewers across America, given the topic. I heard my introduction and nodded soberly at my name.

The director had worked valiantly with the editors to coordinate the sound bites with my ad-libs, and we knocked it out with aplomb despite a few minor glitches. My heart raced at hearing my twenty-second cue and I held up the report for a peerless, on camera *denouement*. "And on a final note, when she was asked for her occupation during booking, Miss Hearst described herself as an 'Urban Guerrilla.'" I paused for America to absorb the head stomp. "That sums up the situation here, where a riveting national story enters a new chapter. This is Claudia Trenton, reporting live from San Francisco."

The tally light went off, and I lowered the microphone while Ron faced me. We shared a long, silent look until he sank to his knees and prostrated himself like I was the queen of Egypt. I laughed, flashing on the Egyptian-style brooch I found in my mother's exquisite jewelry box years before.

Screaming in from the blue, the connection hit me like a bolt. The golden pin with the engraving on the back wasn't a lighthouse. It was Lotta's Fountain.

19

Drew charged into the living room, brandishing the last page.
"Okay, I think I have something!" His heart thumped with the excitement of what felt like a solid clue at last.

Tisha looked up from the couch, still wearing the green caftan and turban, a section of the manuscript in her lap.

"My grandma mentioned the golden pin again. The one she thought was a lighthouse."

"What did she say?"

"It was Lotta's Fountain in San Francisco. I saw Tom next to Lotta's Fountain in my vision this morning, looking up at that tornado. Althea said we'd find clues, and that has to be one!"

She set the pages aside and stood. "You've looked everywhere for that jewelry box?"

"I think so."

"We need to find that pin. If your grandmother stashed it away, and her mother hid it for years before then, it has to be important. It's almost as if they felt the need to protect it. They were saving it for us to find, even if they weren't aware of it. Are you sure it wasn't in the safe deposit box?"

"Positive."

"And you looked everywhere for the jewelry box?"

"Yeah. I was looking for the necklace, and I kept my eye out for both of them." He paused, remembering the publicity still of Delilah Fuller wearing the necklace. "Wait a minute. I didn't check the boxes in the garage."

Moments later, in the sterile glare of LED lights on concrete, he pulled the box marked "Delilah" to an empty spot on the floor. Of the dozens of boxes, it seemed like the logical place to start.

Kneeling, they removed piles of his grandmother's old news scripts with Delilah's handwritten notes, stacks of publicity photos of her as a young girl reporter, and what seemed like hundreds of envelopes addressed to "Claudia."

"Delilah really was in love with your grandma," Tisha muttered with melancholic wonder.

The scale dazed him, too. The isolated bits of Delilah's unrequited, unspoken, and quiet devotion screamed in despair when seen all at once. It was as touching as it was desolating; love without hope, safe in the closet but living only in darkness.

At the bottom, Drew found a padded envelope addressed to Grandma in New York City. It held something bulky, but it didn't feel heavy enough to be the jewelry box. Carefully, he reached inside and removed an early VHS tape, with sturdy plastic screwed together tightly. On top was a folded, neatly written note:

Claudia—When I called the night Delilah Fuller died on the set, I mentioned she said some stuff right before she passed away. What I didn't say was the cameras were rolling, and she was talking about you. It was just senile rambling that didn't make any sense, and I didn't want to upset you. But for several years now, it's been bothering me you didn't know her final words were meant for you.

The station is moving to that new VHS format, and we got some new decks that make it really easy to transfer our one-inch reels. I hope you don't think it's too gruesome, but I made a copy of what happened in the studio that day. I've watched this a hundred times, and I still don't know what she was talking about, so I want to give you the option to watch it or not. Maybe it will make sense to you.

I watch Perspectives every week. You've certainly hit the big time. Take Care, Betty.

Tisha asked, "Did your grandma mention this video in her memoir?"

"No. It looks like Betty sent it a few years after Delilah died."

Tisha examined the tape like an ancient relic. "We shouldn't get sidetracked from searching for that jewelry box, but finding this tape feels important, too. We need to watch it, but I haven't seen a VHS machine in years." She looked about. "She must have had one at some point. Maybe it's still here."

Drew didn't relish watching an old lady die on camera, but he trusted Tisha's instincts. They needed to know what Delilah said in her final moments.

They searched the shelves, pushing things aside. "Aha!" Tisha said, pulling an old box free, with a picture of a VHS player on the front. She lifted the flaps and rummaged around. "It even has those old cables."

They carried it inside to the small, high-definition television next to the sofa, and after fumbling with the unfamiliar cords, they got a connection. Gingerly, Drew pushed the tape into the slot and the machine swallowed it greedily, chunking and whirring. The tape crinkled, and they scrunched their faces, fearing it would snap.

The screen went gray and flickered until fuzzy color bars popped on, accompanied by a steady whine. Drew pressed the fast-forward button, and the whine rose to a screech until the screen went black and silent. He hit play, and moments later at regular speed, they saw an older woman sitting at a news set.

Delilah's orange hair flowed like waves of fancy mango buttercream. She wore a blue dress with a voluminous matching boa that smothered her shoulders in cascades of feathers. As indistinct voices talked offscreen, the lengthy steadiness of her gaze softened her expression. Drew realized she wasn't angry as much as lost in thought.

It was eerie knowing that at around the time this was being recorded, his grandma was hiding in her New York apartment with a new baby in the other room, terrified out of her wits about something the memoir hadn't revealed yet.

A man's voice called out. "Okay, Delilah, let's do the cutaways. Look camera right and give us a few nods."

Delilah followed his instructions without any change in expression.

The man raised his voice. "You were interviewing the lady from the zoo about the new giraffe exhibit. Can you give us a little smile?"

Delilah's mouth briefly curled up. The man reminded her to look friendly, and he prompted her for a few uh-huhs followed by a bright, sudden smile that required four takes.

He asked her for a chuckle when, without warning, her head drooped.

"This is it," Tisha whispered, grasping his hand tight. He squeezed back.

The man jokingly said, "You still with us, Delilah?" Nervous titters came from others offscreen.

"Delilah?" A hiss. "Delilah?"

Her head snapped up; she looked straight into the camera and with perfect lucidity said, "Tell Claudia Trenton. Tell her the child must be saved. And the yellow box is across the street."

She took a few gasping breaths and slumped forward. Her orange wig came loose at the back, barely managing to hang on as it sank into blue feathers that grabbed at it like fingers.

Remembering the heroin addict shouting the same words at his grandma, Drew stood. He watched the screen but hardly noticed as the studio crew called out, approaching Delilah cautiously. They tried to nudge her awake and grew alarmed when she didn't respond.

"Oh, shit," someone said.

"Stop recording!" the man shouted, and the screen went black.

20

Something Bold, Something Crude, Something Borrowed, Something Shrewd

September–November 1975

A jubilant Loren arrived in San Francisco the day after my Patty Hearst scoop. He took a cab to the house and marched inside with a cheery greeting and a joyful smile. Carrying a folded travel bag, he raised his arm and merrily shouted, "Let me see the best reporter I've ever hired!"

Reassuring myself I wasn't visibly pregnant, I stood.

His face popped with alarm as he cried out.

Thirty minutes later, as he and Ron and I drank tea at the table, Loren said, "Not everyone would know you're expecting, but my wife bore three children and the overall effect is unmistakable. Sorry to be so direct, but you look plump everywhere."

Loren had brought scones from a New York deli famous for its bakery. They looked delicious, calling to me on a plate in the center, but I resisted with the absurd impulse that eating would highlight my pregnancy.

"Let's get back to the real issue," Ron said. "If we push the premiere to January, we'll have nothing to worry about."

"Maybe you won't," I replied, "but I'll have just given birth. Even if I feel ready to be on the air, I'll have an infant to care for."

"And," Loren added, "it still doesn't solve the issue of having an unmarried mother in such a prominent broadcast position. Like it or not, journalists are becoming celebrities, and people will be curious about Claudia's personal life. It's bound to get out."

Ron started to argue, but Loren held up his hand. "Before you launch yet another lecture about defying priggish hypocrisy, let me repeat that we can't redirect the tide of public opinion all by ourselves."

Ron scoffed. "It makes me sick. They call women sluts when they have an abortion and sluts when they have a baby."

"Only if they're unmarried," I muttered.

And you're unmarried hung in the air. We went silent, stuck again at this impossible roadblock we'd hit numerous times already, until Loren cleared his throat, shifted, and said, "You're unmarried...*for now*."

I gave a mirthless laugh. "Unless you can wish my ideal man into existence in the next few weeks, I'm going to be single when the show premieres."

"You'll never meet an ideal man," Loren said softly, his eyes glistening with what looked like hope and fear. His intentions formed in front of my eyes, seeming to surprise him as much as me. "Even if you fall madly in love, you'll discover irritations and letdowns, disappointments and even betrayals. I speak from experience. The best marriages I've ever known were based on compromises."

"And lies," Ron added. "Not just little white lies, although those are important. Even big lies are necessary at times, as long as they're told for the sake of being kind, not to get your ass out of a scrape."

"Forgetfulness, too," Loren said. "Pretending you didn't see something, didn't hear something. You must recognize the other person is only human after all."

The words knocked around in my head like pinballs: irritation, letdowns, lies, forgetfulness. Betrayal. Neither mentioned love other than to discount its importance. "Why do people get married?" I said.

They chuckled as I tipped the spout of the porcelain teapot over my cup but got only a splash. I rose to get the kettle boiling just when my daughter decided to explore her world with a quick flutter of her fingertips against my skin. I froze and placed my hand on the spot.

"Did the child just land an uppercut?" Loren asked happily.

I nodded.

He clapped and rubbed his hands. "I love this stage, when the baby begins to explore. I'd keep my hands on my wife's belly for hours, thinking about that new life. At the risk of sounding hopelessly corny, I was amazed I'd helped create a new human that possessed curiosity, its own thoughts. It's as close to godhood as we will ever get."

Ron sat back with an ironic smile while petting his beard. In a plain T-shirt, sweaty and stained from a morning landscaping in the medium-sized backyard, he never looked more handsome. "Only until we start making robots, artificial intelligence, drones."

"Drones?" Loren repeated with a laugh and a good-natured, dismissive wave. "Your veins run with a serum cooked up in a lab. Wait until it's your baby wondering about the world for the first time. Fatherhood changes a man."

I grunted, remembering Arthur's self-absorbed look just before he walked out. "It didn't change this child's father."

They went dour. "Excuse me," I said.

I went out front and sat on the iron bench in the garden, wondering how two men, even if I respected them, could understand my turmoil. The San Francisco summer fog filled the sky and skittered past, shredding in the brisk, cool wind.

The easy answer beckoned: bow out of the lead anchor spot. I had my choice of two other prominent openings on the show, as the lead correspondent or the permanent moderator for the discussion panel. Either would make me the regular fill-in for lead anchor.

Unless the program failed. Or it was reformatted to eliminate my segments. Or my Q-Rating cooled. Or one of a million other things intervened.

A few weeks before, I'd read a sad article about an actress in the British series *Upstairs, Downstairs*, a crown jewel of 1970s television that enjoyed critical acclaim and immense popularity on both sides of the Atlantic. Despite a starring role as one of the leading characters, the actress found the demanding schedule irritating and left the show, instantly rejoining the herd of unemployed actors desperate for a vehicle with even a fraction of its popularity. She was filled with immediate, searing regret for indulging little more than a passing mood. Years later, I was dejected to learn she never overcame her remorse.

Sometimes television journalists, especially men, age into the amber emeritus glow of wise elders, but few do. Even fewer deserve their reputation for wisdom. Famous reporters and anchors regularly fade, getting lower-profile assignments placed farther back in the rundown as the public changes the channel looking for fresh faces. The stalwarts give a false sense of inevitability.

I wanted the lead anchor spot for many reasons, but most of all, I knew I'd never get another chance at a national show.

Just as the chilly day nearly drove me inside, Ron emerged from the house wearing a fleece-lined corduroy jacket, carrying a heavy windbreaker for me. I slipped it on with a brief smile of gratitude.

"Let's take a waddle up to Twin Peaks," he suggested, with a painfully cute smile.

I chuckled and immediately felt brighter.

We walked to Market Street and turned right, heading uphill along the bustling road lined with small houses and apartment buildings. The Pacific gales blew in from the other side of the tall hills, steady and cold, and for a long while we said nothing until I couldn't hold back any longer. "I'll withdraw as lead anchor and take one of the other on-air slots."

At a switchback halfway up the hill, he led me off the busy street into a quiet neighborhood. "Why are you giving up the lead anchor position?"

I sighed. "It's not fair women have to deal with double standards, but I'm not in charge of sorting out what's fair or not. It will be easier on everyone if I bow out gracefully."

"Do you think you can do the job as a single mother?"

I ticked my tongue. "How does being a single mother mean I can't report the news?"

"Then you're bowing out just for my sake and Loren's. You're making it easy for us, not yourself. Don't give up yet."

We slowed to a thoughtful plod. He steered us up a narrow concrete walkway between two apartment buildings, taking us past the residential zoning limit. It ended at a field of waist-high weeds rising to the double summit, dissolving in the fog. The determined Pacific wind smelled of the ocean and rushed down the hillside, making the field look like an exuberant dance floor.

Pregnant or not, I relished the moderate challenge and we climbed, keeping close to each other. "What do you suggest I do?" I said. He didn't reply, so halfway up, I repeated the question.

"Get married," he said. With immense effort, I kept a spark of unexpected hope from my face. "As soon as you do, your private life won't matter."

"Who do you suggest I marry?"

"Loren's in love with you."

Naturally, Ron had seen the same thing in Loren's eyes. The man missed nothing. "Did Loren ask you to say something to me?"

"No, he'd never discuss anything personal with a guy like me. He's the kind of man who's only comfortable with women. Nothing wrong with that, and he's obviously crazy about you. That doesn't mean you're obligated to marry him, but it will solve your problem. There are worse ways to go through life than putting up with a spouse who is madly in love with you. And he's an ethical man, a good guy. I wouldn't say that if it wasn't true."

The slope steepened, and Ron took my hand with brotherly concern until we reached the crest, where the fog bank pouring in from the ocean fringed into foamy curls twisting into the vast sky above the city. We made our way to a viewing platform where the cloudy flows gave us flashes of the breathtaking panorama stretching to the Berkeley Hills across the bay. Elongated shadows textured the city like a mountain scree.

He asked what I was thinking.

"What if I marry him, and then I fall in love with someone else?"

"You'd run that risk with anyone."

"He's my boss. People will say I slept my way to the top."

He snorted. "They'll say that anyway, Claudia."

"What's the point of any of this?"

"Are you asking the meaning of life? I think I know."

I smiled and nudged him with my elbow. "Go on, tell me the meaning of life. This should be good."

"Life means whatever you want it to mean."

It was too sensible to tease about. We went silent for a long while before I said, "I know what you meant when you said Loren would never discuss anything personal with you. I feel funny saying this, but I think Loren is intimidated by men like you. He'd never hike up a steep hill, and certainly not with a pregnant woman. I think he wishes he could be more like you. Dig up a garden, fix a faucet, or," I paused, but pressed on with what felt like an important point, "project an image of knowing how to have good sex." Ron listened respectfully without reacting, proving my point, I suppose. "He feels inadequate when he measures himself against that. You're right about Loren being a good man, but I feel more comfortable with men like you." I scarcely believed I'd found the courage to say such things, but I didn't feel the least bit awkward.

"Thanks, but by now you must know I have no interest in a relationship with anyone."

I nodded, neither uncomfortable nor defensive, although I was mad with curiosity. "I know. I'm just glad we're friends."

He grinned and squeezed my hand. "Me, too."

About an hour later back at the house, Ron announced his plans to make a gourmet lamb stew for dinner. He needed to shop for ingredients, and he gave me a meaningful look before leaving me and Loren at the table. The atmosphere grew heavy with silence.

I never craved love, and I knew I wouldn't pine for it, even in a marriage. Still, in a world filled with tempting and intriguing strangers, sexual fidelity without the anchor of love could easily become unbearable. Also, using Loren as a temporary solution was monumentally unfair to him, at least without complete honesty.

"Claudia, I feel certain we're thinking about the same thing, a solution to our problem."

Loren was undeniably handsome, but not unlike how men's expensive dress shoes are attractive—perfectly stitched and polished. He'd showered and changed while Ron and I were out walking, and for a casual day about the house, he'd pulled on slacks and a polo shirt, an outfit that would do for a breakfast buffet at a country club. Ron had gone off to shop wearing the same jeans, T-shirt, and boots he'd worn in the garden that morning as well as for our hike up Twin Peaks. I knew which man I felt more comfortable with.

"Loren, before we say another word, you need to know I don't love you."

"But you are fond of me, I hope."

"Of course."

He reached for my hand but hesitated just before they met. I closed the gap myself, and he smiled. His happiness for my simple gesture both pleased and saddened me.

"Claudia, I'm many things but I'm no kind of fool. I know you don't love me. But I love you, and I promise I'll do whatever you say to make you happy. If you get tired of me, I'll understand and make myself scarce for as long as you need."

"I'm going to have another man's child. Will that bother you?"

He looked horrified. "Never. I have no patience for men who wound innocents for the sake of their own egos. I will treat your child just like I treated my own, or any others we may have."

The idea had never occurred to me, and I was grateful he had the good sense to raise it at such an early stage. "I don't know how I feel about that."

"I'm fifty-four years old, but that's not too old to raise a child. I do so love my children, and I miss those early years. There's no sweeter sound in the world than a child's laughter. I feel sure even my soon-to-be ex-wife would agree I was a good father. But we needn't decide now."

We discussed his financial and legal situations. Born into an old New York family, he inherited a considerable estate that included a grand home with a coveted address on Seventy-Seventh Street on the Upper East Side. "Of course, my wife will take the family home and half of the money, and I'll support my children until they've graduated from university. That will take another five or six years, during which I'll be stony broke, as my uncle James used to say. But afterward my finances will improve considerably and all I have will be yours."

In those days before no-fault divorce, the law required one spouse to accuse the other from a list of specific wrongdoings. If the accused contested the allegations or countersued, the court assigned blame in a process that only benefited the lawyers, often lavishly. Loren had freely accepted fault, and the final papers were nearly finalized. "I'll be free to marry as soon as I sign. As soon as next week, possibly."

"Hold on. You're my boss and that's a big deal."

"I've already considered that, and it's easily solved. As much as I love the bustle of the newsroom, I'll resign as executive producer." His voice went melancholic, and I watched as he overcame painful regret for walking away from a job he loved. He was so easy to read, so trusting. Or he was unaware of how his true feelings showed. "I have a standing invitation to join corporate, and the executive suite has been anxious for me to take over the television division for at least a year."

"That only puts you higher up on the food chain."

He patted my hand. "It's well out of nepotism range. It's a matter of a single phone call."

I thought of Barry in Cleveland, and all the other men who would never consider such a sacrifice. I thought of the actress from *Upstairs, Downstairs*. Combined with everything else, the enormity of his offer clinched it for me, but a huge oversight rocked me. "You haven't even asked me."

He smiled and slid off the chair heading for the floor, but I gripped his arm with something close to panic and said, "Do not get on bended knee!"

His smile grew. "Fine. The words are the same seated."

He asked. After powering past my hesitation, I agreed. "This doesn't mean I'll have more children with you. My answer may be a firm no."

Ours was the most unromantic proposal since medieval kings sent ambassadors to ask for the hands of distant princesses sight unseen, but Loren seemed joyful. When Ron returned laden with grocery bags, he congratulated us with an appropriate gravity for the strange circumstances, before making a lamb stew worthy of a top-tier French restaurant.

Loren looked hopeful when I said I was going to bed, but I gave him a kiss on the cheek and closed the door. Ron went to the other bedroom and Loren slept on the sofa in the living room of his own house.

The next day, Loren booked a flight to New York, anxious to finalize his divorce. He would return to San Francisco as soon as possible for a private, civil ceremony.

We waved as a grinning Loren climbed into a cab and left for the airport. Ron said, "He's really happy."

"He was probably happy before his first marriage, too."

"Not that happy. Not ever in his life. When a man goes around with a dopey smile like that, it's because he feels young again."

We went inside. "I'm worried I'll make the poor man miserable. I'm grateful to him, and he is a nice guy, but I can't pretend I love him. I just can't be dishonest in such a basic way."

"You'd better learn how if you're going to anchor a national news program."

Ron brought the writing samples we'd been reviewing when we got the call about Patty Hearst. We resumed work as if nothing happened. Over the next few weeks, we filled all five on-air and production jobs, choosing only current employees with track records at the network. We also finalized and sent our design and graphic suggestions to New York.

Loren returned a few weeks later, carrying his signed divorce papers like a presidential pardon. We got our blood tests, a horribly invasive procedure left over from the days when syphilis was deadly and respectable people advocated sterilization to halt the spread of deformities and mental illness. Most states allowed people to ignore the results, so in addition to being slightly sinister, they were pointless and were eliminated almost everywhere in the years since.

Loren invited his children to our wedding, but they declined. "Out of allegiance to their mother, not spite for us," he assured me. I suspected he was shielding me from the truth, but I didn't press for details because the scene must have been unbearable for him, even in the best of circumstances. Also, glares from his children would spoil the day, and if I couldn't have a joyous wedding, I'd settle for calm. I'd have to face them eventually, but I'd worry about that when necessary.

For our wedding day, I splurged on a ravishing, full-length maternity dress that flowed with dark cherry tulle with a silk bow at the ruffled neckline, and I carried a sweet nosegay of baby roses. Loren wore a dark blue evening suit with a matching boutonniere, while Ron looked dashing in a sport coat and tie, a single white rose pinned to his lapel.

After we got the license mid-morning, a judge married us in a brief ceremony beneath a coffered, gilded arch near the dramatic steps pouring into the ornate rotunda of San Francisco City Hall. Before noon, we strolled happily outside, both me and Loren wearing plain gold wedding bands.

We went to the fancy Fairmont hotel, where the three of us enjoyed a wedding feast of multiple courses, finishing with a tidy white wedding cake fluffy with whole, candied rose blossoms. Even though I was a responsible mother for all of my pregnancies, I took occasional, dainty sips of a rosé that tasted like sunrise.

Loren had booked a room for the night, so we said goodbye to Ron and went upstairs to a spacious, elegant suite where I curled on a white sofa. The baby seemed transported by the sumptuous meal, throwing her limbs about. Loren asked to join me, and I gladly hefted aside to make room. He put an arm about my shoulders and, smiling broadly, asked for permission to put his hand on my swollen belly. I was both pleased and relieved he didn't think my body belonged to him now. I was beginning to understand the depths of his thoughtfulness and consideration, and I thought we made a fine little family.

Loren returned to New York soon after, where he'd already taken on his new position. He asked for my permission to share the news, and I didn't see any reason to keep our marriage secret. Indeed, the whole point was to let others know. Of course, people would gossip, saying my pregnancy caused Loren's divorce, but I decided to worry about that only if necessary.

Loren's replacement as executive producer was named Paul Balek, and Ron knew him from a previous job. "He's going to make a lot of people miserable. When I worked with him, everyone above him thought he was a golden boy, and everyone below him hated his guts. There are an awful lot of people who think they're doing something right if the workers are on edge all the time, but they're fools. If people think they're disposable, they won't care about anything. They'll sabotage equipment, throw important things away, screw with the assignment boards, you name it."

"Does he think journalism is all about the money?"

"He thinks it's all about show biz. People like him are taking over the industry. He's not going to give us any time to build an audience for our new program, so let's just cross our fingers and jump."

My mouth went dry, but he looked placid. I asked him why he seemed so calm.

"I've been dreaming about buying a VW bus or a van and hitting the road. If the show fails, I know what I'll do. Camp, hike, explore. When I run out of money, I can get a job at a little television or radio station somewhere. Or maybe I'll be a hiking guide or a rafting instructor." His eyes gleamed.

For the first time, I felt irritated with Ron for being thoughtless. I wished I could be so blasé about the possibility of the show being canceled and finding myself unemployed, but I'd gotten married for the sake of the program, and I was about to have a child. Years later, I understood his wisdom with crystalline precision. Why worry when you can dream?

In late October, we said goodbye to the little two-bedroom house in San Francisco. I'd grown to love it, as well as the neighborhood. New York is an exciting town, and it offers the best of the world's culture, but you almost always scuttle along in skyscraper shadows, and people live their whole lives piled on top of each other. San Francisco feels like a collection of sunny villages, places to linger and stroll and chat. Much has changed over the years, but those are my fixed impressions.

Back in New York, we learned the new boss changed the title we'd chosen for the program, *Home for the Night*, to the facile and off-putting *Perspectives*. I was deeply disappointed. *Home for the Night* felt warm and welcoming, all of us gathered together instead of being out on the town.

I was sure viewers would respond to the comfy feel, but the publicist who led us to the studio to see the new set remarked, "Paul thinks that title is too old-fashioned, like people are pulling taffy and listening to the radio." He snorted in agreement, looking like a little bird, all bony angles. "Paul thinks *Perspectives* will make people feel important, like they're not actually lazy slobs sitting on their asses, shoveling down cheese puffs and sucking on beer." He cast concerned glances at my belly, which looked large enough to pop with a sewing needle.

For the set, Ron and I had suggested simple sofas and end tables in muted colors to make it fade into the background. Instead, the anchor desk zoomed out from a fake wall like a race car, sleek and streamlined, striped in firehouse red and a strange deep teal. I despaired as I imagined myself seated there. "I'm going to look like Liberace in a biker bar," I said to Ron. He gave me a "what can you do?" expression.

"Hey, hey, hey!" shouted an older man who I knew at once was Paul Balek. He strode into the studio wearing a slick blue suit, his hair permed into precise gray curls. His features pinched to the center of his face almost prettily, which could easily be appealing if handled correctly. Instead, it created an unnerving contrast with his shark persona. He reared back when he saw my belly.

"Holy fuck! You're *pregnant*?" It sounded like an accusation of treachery.

Ron stepped forward and extended his hand. "I don't know if you remember me, but we worked together on the Super Bowl a few years back. I was the second director, and I plotted a few camera angles that everyone else has been copying ever since."

"I remember," Paul replied, shaking Ron's hand like he was pumping water. "You did a fantastic job, too. I was happy to see you on this project, but for fuck's sake, Ron." Scorn tilted his voice. "*Home for the Night*? A set that looks like a local library? A pregnant lead anchor? What are we running here, a county fair?"

The publicist gave a loud, grating laugh. Ron said, "Her pregnancy has no effect on the show. And when she's behind that desk, nobody will even notice for the glare."

Paul led us to Loren's old office. As I stepped into the newsroom, I could hardly believe my first day had only been seven months before. So much had changed for me. I smiled and nodded at everyone I recognized. They did double takes and leaned together to chatter even though it was clear I could see everything. I wasn't sure if they knew about my marriage to Loren, but they damn sure knew I was pregnant.

Paul had turned Loren's office into a glitzy shrine to himself. I didn't know much about his background, but his walls and shelves featured photos with celebrities, chic decorative items like intricate macramé hangings, and cascading ferns and spider plants. In a brief scan of his framed television awards and certificates, I saw nothing that mentioned journalism.

He started talking about the show, and my alarm grew as he savaged two months of work. "We aren't going to copy *60 Minutes*," he said emphatically.

"We specifically avoided that," I countered. "We have live interviews and panel discussions, along with packages and pacers. Nobody will think we're copying."

"I don't care if they think that, I just don't want a single topic dragging on for twenty minutes." He sorted through some papers on his desk to pick up what I recognized as the *précis* we wrote at the table in San Francisco. It took nearly a week to refine and polish that half-page description. Holding it high, he gave it a shake. "I'm putting the kibosh on this stupid plan right now." He crumpled and tossed it without aim. "The world is changing. Everything's faster. We're going to have computers in a few years. We need to position this news operation as on the cutting edge, and long-format journalism is as dead as Marilyn Monroe."

I shook slightly as we rode the elevator to our production offices, a little warren with two small rooms and a larger common area, already filled with battered furniture. As we looked around, I said, "He's going to hate everything we do. He's only waiting for an excuse to fire us both."

"He won't fire you because you're a star. But you won't be if you don't get back on the air stat, so let's give him what he wants."

"He doesn't know what he wants."

"I know what he wants."

"You do? What do you mean?"

"Let me think about it overnight."

Loren had moved into my apartment, filling it with fancy furniture I didn't dislike enough to make a fuss about. After our meeting with Paul, I trudged inside quietly, hoping Loren was working late, but no such luck. I mentioned I felt terrible about being responsible for the terrifying disruption to the lives of everyone in the newsroom.

"He even fired all the people we hired. There were only five positions, and we hired in-house, so they'll keep their old jobs, but I feel awful."

Loren responded with a diplomatic, dignified, and sympathetic silence. I realized I'd pushed too far, and again I let him feel the baby exploring.

The next morning, Ron showed me a ludicrously overblown rundown he'd whipped up for the first show. "Broadway superstars, complete with musical clips? Race car testing in the Nevada desert? Interviews with household employees of Howard Hughes? We don't have the time or contacts for any of this. Not to mention we'd blow our budget for the whole year in the first show."

He used his fingers to shape the end of his beard to a point, which I recognized as his most absorbed gesture. "This will get Paul Balek off our backs until the premiere, and we can produce whatever we want." He described his real plan for the first broadcast. I loved it and feared it in equal measures.

Paul went euphoric when he saw the fraudulent rundown. "This is exactly what I want! Let's get some promo producers on this, and we'll start running them as soon as we can."

Ron didn't flinch at this unexpected curveball, but I felt a clutch of fear. It was one thing to pleasantly surprise viewers with an interesting show, but it was a serious breach to entice millions to watch with false promises. I felt panic rising.

"No content promos," Ron said firmly. "After Watergate and Vietnam, people are suspicious of big promises. Let's run some generic promos that feature Claudia. She's a known quantity, and people will tune in to watch her. Then we'll spring this incredible show on them. It's all anyone will talk about the next day, and if you can take control of the water cooler talk, you can take control of the country. It'll be like the premiere of a big Hollywood movie with an incredible ending, a huge twist that will blow away everyone. That's how you take America by storm."

It was the most garish speech I'd ever heard from him, and I doubted anyone who rose to be executive producer of news at a major network would buy it. Paul did.

On Monday, the new production staff arrived, all men since Paul had hired them. We passed out assignments based on our real plans. It was risky, but we couldn't do all the work by ourselves. We gambled we could hum along quietly if we kept out of Paul's line of sight, and we won that bet.

Three days before our premiere, Paul put my generic promos for *Perspectives* into heavy rotation. I'd asked for a fairly tight shot to conceal the obnoxious set, so my face filled the screen twice an hour. The day before the premiere, he added a third promo every sixty minutes. It guaranteed a huge audience at the top of the first show.

Five hours before the premiere, Paul summoned Ron and me to his office. The refined older lady who worked for Loren had moved with him to corporate, and Paul's assistant wasn't at her desk, so we knocked on the door and he yelled "Come in!"

He was on the phone and waved us to chairs without looking up, having a rapid conversation I eventually deduced was with a congressional aide complaining about our coverage of some issue. While he was distracted, I surreptitiously studied Paul's awards and certificates and confirmed none commended him for his work in journalism.

"Tell that cocksucker I don't give a shit what he puts in the *Congressional Record*! Just makes sure he spells my name right."

A year later, Paddy Chayefsky's brilliant movie *Network* was released. It was marketed as a satire of network television news, but I don't think I took a breath the entire film. The audience laughed at what they thought was an outrageous, over-the-top, cartoony send-up, but it contained an urgent warning about a malevolent spirit already afoot. Amoral executives shed their weighty responsibilities to the public in favor of backroom accolades and ruthless victories. The spirit of fictional executives Frank Hackett and Diane Christensen animated real people like Paul Balek, who were already in charge.

Paul slammed the phone down and instantly launched into a tirade directed at us, like a tornado changing course. "I'm having a shindig at my place tonight for the *Perspectives* premiere. My wife knows some mucky-muck at the opera and we think Pavarotti or one of those fat fucks will make it." He crossed his fingers. "Maybe even Jackie O. A lot of top brass will be there, too.

"But I think you've been lying your asses off," he said, "and you bit off more than you can chew. You haven't shown me shit for tonight." His voice dropped with menace. "If you two make me look like dog shit in my own home in front of my wife and important guests," he pointed at Ron, "I'm going to tell everyone you're a faggot that got caught taking it up the ass from a mail boy and," he pointed at me, "I'll say you take it up the ass for any man who can do you favors. I'll ruin both of you, and you'll never work in television again."

Ron and I shared a look before leaving without a word. I shook with rage.

Fifteen minutes before air, I greeted our guests in the green room and walked to the studio. Ron was waiting at the door and asked how I felt.

"I'm ready to puke, if you want the truth." My baby must have sensed my anxiety and seemed as immovable as a rock, huddled in terror. I took my chair at the race car set and let the audio tech mic me up while I shoved the IFB into my ear. My hands shook.

Ron noticed and put a hand on my shoulder. "Here's the thing. If Jackie O and Pavarotti come to Paul's party, they'll love the show. It's interesting, and it assumes the audience is intelligent, and they'll gush about it late into the night. Just do the show as if only Jackie O is watching."

Serenity washed over me like a warm bath. "That's brilliant, Ron." I smiled with relief. "Thank you." My baby stirred, and I gently willed her to settle down for the next hour.

He gave me a thumbs-up and stood aside as I heard the open

music. I smiled and when the tally light came on and the stage manager threw his finger at me, I spoke with bright confidence to Jackie O.

"Good evening, I'm Claudia Trenton, and welcome to *Perspectives*. Tonight, we're devoting our first show to the future, but not the predictions of astrologers and gypsies with crystal balls. Instead, we'll explore the fascinating new world of futurists, people who examine current trends and predict where they will take us. We'll talk to scientists and engineers to explain how some of this new technology will work. And we'll learn about the changes coming to your home, your family, and to our country. You'll be surprised to learn how far along many of these innovations already are." I gave Jackie a huge smile. "I promise you will be amazed. Please stay with us."

After the first commercial break, I welcomed an engineer from Harvard to the set. Personable, warm, and interesting, he discussed robotics and drone technology. The conversation grew animated when he talked about miniaturization, and I said, "You're telling me that we'll have tiny transistors everywhere?"

"Yes, and it will revolutionize our lives, probably in twenty-five years or less. Imagine everyone will be able to hold all the computing power in the world right now in their own hands. It will make everyday communication ridiculously easy. These devices will become the focus of personal power and be useful for thousands of things. And as their power increases, they'll become smaller, which is when the danger arrives. We think that's a fairly obvious trend line, that danger will follow usefulness."

"What sort of danger?"

"The smaller the machines become, the more powerful they get. Imagine, for example, drones the size of bees. They might have cameras. They might shoot fatal projectiles. And they could self-regenerate, like von Neumann probes."

"Von Neumann probes?" I hadn't gone over any of this with him beforehand, and I worried it was too disturbing, but Jackie would find it fascinating. I decided to learn about it along with her, right on national television.

"They're named after a physicist named John von Neumann. He theorized about self-replicating machines built by an advanced, alien civilization using raw material they find in space, and spreading throughout the galaxy. But with advances in miniaturization, there's no reason humans can't invent them as well. But if they are used for warfare or some other devious purpose, they may well be more destructive than nuclear weapons."

In 1975, this was very radical and shocking stuff and we had a riveting conversation that went three minutes over, until the first commercial break. When we came back, I threw to a lively package about a dawning age of digital technology poised to radicalize everything from television viewing to school lessons. After that, we followed with a panel of two scientists who explained the unmistakable and shocking trendlines of technological advancement, and a recent spike that revealed we were already at the start of a dizzying climb.

From the control room, Ron allowed the interesting conversation to go on an extra two minutes, which meant I'd only have time to show some graphics we'd ordered from the art department, drawings that imagined how some of this technology might look. I wish I still had those pictures. I remember some of them as remarkably accurate.

I said goodbye to the viewers and closed the show. The crew buzzed as I unclipped my mic. "That was really interesting," someone said.

Ron walked up. "It felt good," I said to him. "What do you think?"

"It was good, but we'll see what happens tomorrow. There's no point in worrying." With a smile, he added, "After all, we can't predict the future," and we chuckled.

The next day, we heard that both Jackie O and Pavarotti came to the party, and both raved.

21

When Drew woke in the morning, even while still in bed, he was filled with the conviction he'd forgotten something crucial. After thinking about it for a moment and shoving it aside, he got up.

He made it to the kitchen before the random knowledge began to unfurl in his mind like an endless scroll, bristling and sparkling with countless things he hadn't known when he went to sleep.

He knew a fad for Victorian stoneware would sweep the interior design world in six years, the prices escalating until the madness collapsed under the weight of a massive number of forgeries.

He knew silent, vast clouds of methane escaping the thawing Siberian tundra would catch fire sometime in the coming decades, igniting a flash inferno that would roar across hundreds of square miles in a matter of minutes, incinerating thousands of people in the greatest firestorm since the meteor that set the world ablaze sixty-five million years ago.

He saw huge metallic objects undulating like jellyfish high above the clouds, filtering the atmosphere to collect gases that belonged underground.

He saw fireworks bursting into beautiful and intricate patterns, like a school of tropical fish that swam for several strokes, red heart shapes that beat a few times, flowers that bloomed, before blinking out to the roars of an approving crowd.

He saw a raging inferno across a vast sweep of what he knew was Northern California, probably the same fire he'd seen devouring Althea's house.

He saw a sleek rocket propped at a forty-five-degree angle at the very moment a ring of light pulsed from the rear. The rocket shot across the vast horizon at dizzying speed until the earth curved away, and the rocket speared the atmosphere. It left a trail of what looked like donuts across the sky, growing smaller and slowly fading.

He saw Victor again, walking across the vast asphalt expanse surrounding the GRU compound.

❖

About a month after the homecoming dance, when he had recovered from the rifle butt to his head, Victor joined regular training at the GRU compound, despite being younger than even the youngest recruits. Someone must have pulled strings, but nobody explained anything. He was told where to go and never thought to question why, moving into another of the huge buildings on site. Thus, he became the youngest GRU analyst ever, before beginning his formal training as an operative, where he excelled. The bloody scene with Phil went unmentioned. The other boys from Maple Grove vanished.

In time, he realized the absurdity of his situation and decided to learn more. No matter who he asked, how persistent he was, or how patiently he explained why it was important, everyone refused to talk about Maple Grove.

For many years, he lacked the security clearance to enter the building with the little replica of America. It was the most secretive place on the compound. He finally gained limited access but found not a trace, not even their first-year barracks. Suggestions from supervisors and instructors to drop the subject got firmer and angrier until Victor realized he would never learn the truth. He let it go.

He wondered how much of his life really happened. Both Tolyatti and Maple Grove were like old chalk marks on the blackboard not fully erased, still slightly visible under newer layers.

A few years before his assignment in the USA, while doing a standard review of digital protocols, he stumbled across a security oversight in an old electronic form, long out of use, still connected to the internal databases. The box at the top of the form only gave instructions for filling it out. Since it didn't collect information, nobody at the time saw the need to clamp it with digital locks. The unsecure box sat unnoticed for years. As soon as he discovered it, Victor crawled inside and quietly rummaged his way to classified documents. After many months, the first page of a report popped on his screen:

Maple Grove
Stressors on Pubescent Males from Psychopathological and Deviant Sociosexual Environments

A study about stress. That's all it was. Instead of preparing for the life of an undercover spy in America, the boys had been studied to help develop diversionary programs for schoolchildren. Millions of young Russians were coming of age in the severe destitution of economic and political collapse, and the government and military commissioned numerous studies that flouted basic ethics to deal with an urgent crisis of widespread cultural destabilization. If some pubescent boys suffered psychological distress as guinea pigs, it was regrettable but necessary. Maple Grove was by no means the only study to skirt ethical guidelines.

Pages of theory explained how giving the boys the impression of preparing for an exciting future, entirely alien to all, was ideal for weakening the social stratification that inevitably forms in groups of adolescent males. It was only a theory, but Victor studied the research and couldn't fault the reasoning. The equalizing storyline produced the purest raw data, all of it captured by secret cameras, confirming his suspicions. In a way, the videos were the whole point.

The boys were selected according to a matrix of family sexual and substance abuse pathologies, in addition to extreme economic hardship. Despite their age, some of the subjects entered Maple Grove with violent criminal records, with Subject Phil identified as a highly dangerous psychosexual sadist.

The unnamed leader of a secret political intelligence unit, undoubtedly "Mr. Thompson," caught wind of the plans for Maple Grove and demanded influence in selecting some of the participants. A handful of the boys, he argued, might show aptitude for the training and grow into valuable intelligence resources.

"Not planning for that possibility is a disgraceful waste of a such a rare, premium opportunity," he thundered in an unsigned memo. He was granted permission to select two participants, on the condition they came from environments with the targeted stressors. He also insisted on posing as the leader of the project for the sake of his two participants, which was permitted with the firm understanding he had no actual power.

Unable to find another portal into the deeper classified files, Victor's search ended. He wondered which of the other boys shared the distinction of being selected by Mr. Thompson.

Just before he left for the U.S., he returned to his apartment in the compound one night to find Mr. Thompson sitting at his table, wearing a long coat and looking much older.

Victor smiled. "I only have one door and designed the security myself. I don't want to know how you bypassed it. I'll imagine you walked through the wall. I've thought of you that way most of my life."

Mr. Thompson looked embarrassed for the compliment as Victor sat across from him. Silence fell, supplanting an unwanted conversation about their ambivalence at seeing each other again.

Mr. Thompson finally spoke. "I've kept my eye on you all these years. I heard you are being activated, and I wanted to congratulate you in person. You are finally going to put all that Maple Grove learning to work, in America no less. And your American voice is as strong as ever. Well done."

Victor gave a nod.

"I know you can't tell me specifics, but does your mission have targets and objectives?"

"No. Strictly informational. I've been told your foresight gives me a believable digital biography in the U.S. They tell me you had my name salted in American records. Few would have thought to do that when it was easier."

"Digital security was severely neglected at that time, all across the world. I planted many names everywhere, just in case. Employment, school records, voting rolls, even local newsletters, and campus articles." He shook his head. "The world seems to be spinning out of control, Victor. I'm hopeful I'll be dead before it all falls apart. I've begun to worry all this technology will lengthen human life before I can die in peace. I know GRU has files on the Prophets. I assume you've heard the reports about the people who live for hundreds of years and can predict the future?"

"I have. It strikes me as a legend."

"Most likely, and yet I've seen some reports that would make you doubt. Their existence has been known across the globe for centuries. They heal very quickly as long as the injury is not too severe. I read a detailed study of one such person. She was found after World War Two, an old lady from East Berlin who was born into one of those tin-pot kingdoms that made sixteenth-century Germany look like a broken pot.

"Stalin ordered that poor woman tortured, infecting her with deadly pathogens, burning her, cutting her. She always recovered, but she never wavered. She didn't know where her powers came from. She claimed to have met others who sought her out, suggesting the existence of a loose organization that doesn't seem to have a central objective. She eventually died from severe head trauma, so she was not immortal." He shook his head, raised a hand. "I'm glad Stalin never found the source of her powers. It spares me the worry of living much longer. The world can be a terrible place."

"It can."

"Do you hate me?" Mr. Thompson said.

"No, but I understand why you might wonder."

"Have you read the files on Maple Grove?"

"They're above my security level."

"Does that matter?"

"I have read some of them."

"Possibly I can get the rest, if you want. Or I can answer any of your most pressing questions now."

"Was Maple Grove a successful study?"

Mr. Thompson shrugged. "One study leads to another, as they say. In that sense, they are all successful. But it was successful with respect to you. It gave us a highly intelligent operative who can be invisible in the U.S."

A beat. "When you asked me if I wanted to kill my parents, and I said no? Would you have left me in Tolyatti if I'd said yes?"

"Either answer was fine. I just wanted to know how your mind worked."

"And would you have let me kill them?"

"Certainly. I'm sure you know your father was already dead by the time I made the offer, but I would have handed you the pistol if you had wanted to kill your mother. When we were considering you for Maple

Grove, we sent several undercover agents to that filthy den by the old port. She talked freely to all of them. She knew your father was abusing you. She witnessed it many times. Did you know that?"

He shook his head.

"Her most basic inhibitions were eroded by the chronic, irreversible nature of her addiction. Permitting abuse of your own child is no different than social opprobrium, mere kindling in the inferno of heroin. The next dose was the entirety of her life's purpose. Killing her would have been merciful. You are aware she died several years after you left Tolyatti?"

"Yes. Do you know what happened to the other boys from Maple Grove?"

"One of them works for me, and I won't say more. The rest, scattered. I know several overdosed from heroin. Well, drug addiction was inevitable for all of you, according to the research. For all the wrong I've done, I saved you from that."

In the coffee shop in San Francisco, Victor checked his phone. It was forty minutes until launch.

He returned to the sidewalk and crossed Market Street, passing the pedestrian island that surrounded Lotta's Fountain. The reliefs showed California's frontier days, doubtless romanticized depictions, but he found them fascinating and wished he'd lived back then.

When he arrived in the U.S. with a new beard, along with GRU orders to burrow as deeply as possible into Silicon Valley's high-tech mysteries, he discarded the option of ostentatious wealth.

Victor chose a more complex role: someone without the obvious appearance of money while always seeming to have it, an irresistible draw for the people he wanted to attract. He rented an office at a well-known Palo Alto address, an unremarkable building from the outside but well-known in the right circles, where receptionists served a handful of private executives, juggling different company names for calls and emails. He bought two condos, one in suburban Menlo Park, the other in a San Francisco tower, both chosen for their location in red-hot markets.

He made a show of handing out business cards, always hesitating so that takers clutched them with hope, feeling lucky to get one. He said, "I'm looking for some investments, but I'm only interested in taking a substantial share." It dissuaded those who dreaded a nosy investor, and he planned to be nosy.

Victor avoided the sleek superstars of Silicon Valley. Their hunger for publicity made him leery. Some even hired private publicists, eager for notoriety in a way that disgusted him. He planned to track down promising rumors himself.

In his first weeks of appearing in the audience at conferences, asking questions after presentations, and socializing at popular bars and large parties, the first inquiries started arriving from people desperate for start-up funds.

Two months later, he invested fifty thousand dollars in ten different start-ups he'd selected for their small staffs and quirky product goals. The amount made barely a ripple in the churning money torrent of Silicon Valley. He gave the companies the same firm instructions not to reveal his investment to anybody, all the while knowing lower level employees with off-the-wall ideas, goofball friends, or both, would whisper anyway.

Just as he'd planned, the proposals soon tumbled in. Victor reviewed them all, placing the ambitious ones with lofty but feasible goals into a special pile.

One of the first proposals that caught his attention was for a company called DemoDrones. It proposed a system of self-replicating nanobots to dismantle unwanted metal in a fraction of normal demolition time. The bots would shred old ships or structural skeletons into billions of pieces in a matter of minutes. A central device would guide the microdrones to re-solidify into whatever shape was required. Victor recognized the basic idea as von Neumann probes.

Other potential candidates materialized, but he always returned to DemoDrones. He called the company to request a meeting. He talked to the CEO for a few minutes and asked for the names of the cross-functional team leaders. "Just to get an idea of what kind of talent you're bringing to the table." He scribbled them down.

An hour later, after running the names through a GRU database he accessed from the untraceable Tor browser, he found what he wanted.

He arranged a lunch meeting with the CEO, undoubtedly a recent graduate who'd argued with his friends until they agreed to give him the top title. They met at a hip, crowded, and pricey restaurant in San

Francisco, with old farm equipment on walls paneled in bleached rough wood.

The nervous CEO stood as he approached. Victor figured him for perhaps twenty-five, wearing a new suit that was a bit too conservative.

Victor let him ramble. Although Victor was just five years older, the CEO seemed like a kid. When he was done, Victor said, "Do you have photos of your team?"

As if worried Victor was springing a trap, he apologized and said no.

"I like to see the people I'm investing with. You must have some. On your phone?"

Hesitant, he pulled his phone from his pocket and Victor said, "Don't worry. I'm not interested in your dick pics and porn." The kid melted with a loud laugh, telling him not to wince if they came across something racy.

The CEO showed photos of one girl and three guys, but Victor was only interested in the last one. "And this is our mechanical engineer. Allen. He calls himself Buce, as in Bucephalus."

"Alexander the Great's horse," Victor said, smiling.

"Yeah. Buce is a little odd, but he's an expert on robotic movement efficiency, which is really tricky."

The photo showed an unsmiling young man, and in his eyes, Victor saw exactly who he was looking for. With stringy, unkempt hair and a thin face tilted at an indignant angle, Buce knew someone was taking his picture, but he refused to look at the camera. Victor recognized the despair of Tolyatti, the confusion of Maple Grove, and the alienation and anger of both.

"I want to meet your team," Victor said.

"But see, we need that initial investment to get our office together."

"You have your initial investment. I want to meet your team to discuss the funding for the first two years of development."

A month later, greeted as a hero in the new offices of DemoDrones in a trendy San Francisco neighborhood, Victor gave a speech to the staff, now grown to seven, stressing the massive commercial appeal of the product. "Yeah, it's environmentally sound and will help with really dangerous stuff like clearing land mines, but people will pay whatever we ask." He talked of his expectation of reaping an enormous return for himself, and Buce's downcast reaction was exactly what he'd hoped for. He piled it on some more.

Buce lived in an old apartment building in a gentrified San Francisco neighborhood. Victor arrived one night unannounced, identifying himself through the door pad speaker. He heard fear in Buce's voice before he buzzed Victor inside.

Although freshened with new paint and carpets, the sharp stink of ancient cigarettes and poverty lingered in the old building. He pushed the elevator button, smiling at the same, no-chip elevator technology he remembered from Tolyatti.

Buce was already waiting with his door open, wearing shorts and a T-shirt hanging indifferently over his thin frame, his hair to his shoulders. He stepped back to let Victor inside his apartment, a large room with a tiny kitchen and bathroom with old, sturdy fixtures.

In the main room, filled with the unapologetic Maple Grove smell of an unwashed male, a mattress sat on the floor with clothes scattered about. A large desk held an incongruously high-tech computer system, with three monitors plus a smaller laptop.

In an empty spot on the desk, a small mirror and a razor blade sat next to a neat line of white powder. It elated Victor, validating his instincts. At the same time, he wanted to slap the stupid shithead to the floor.

Buce inhaled with wide-eyed fear when he realized he'd left it in view.

Victor didn't like cocaine, but to neutralize the situation he laughed, picked up a stunted straw, and snorted the line. Buce looked cautiously relieved.

"Your personal life is your own, Buce. I don't care what you do." Even after they sat, Victor still towered over him. "I'm sorry for barging in like this. I hope it's not inconvenient."

"It's okay," Buce muttered resentfully. "I don't bring my work home, so I can't show you anything from DemoDrones."

"That's going to have to change. I want to make a proposal to you."

"What do you mean?"

"I saw the way you responded to my speech about making money. You looked disgusted. Tell me what you were thinking. There's no need to bullshit me."

Loosened by the assurance, Buce looked up fearlessly and Victor knew this would go well. "I didn't like it. We're developing something that could really help people, and all you care about is the money."

"You're not the kind of guy who doesn't like to make money, Buce. You're just offended that I'm getting rich while guys like you do all the work."

"Fuck, yes," he barked, slicing the air with an emphatic gesture. Victor wanted to congratulate him and slit his throat in equal measure. "We slave away, and you make millions."

"I know how that feels. I was..."

"You don't know jack. Look at you. Some asshole who spends all his time at the gym and wears those expensive clothes. You don't even need more money. You've always had enough. It's just a fucking game to you."

"I grew up in poverty that makes this place look like a palace. By fifth grade, I used to get drunk on my way to school in the morning." Victor carefully slipped Tolyatti into his voice. "My father molested me, and my mother died of a heroin overdose. I spent years as a guinea pig for a government experiment." His voice went down the abyss. "I killed a friend who went crazy on a girl one night. That was my life for years."

Looking terrified, Buce muttered a wavering "Bullshit," but Victor knew he believed every word.

Reverting to his American voice, Victor said, "If you shut your fucking mouth and listen to me, Buce, I'll tell you how you can make more money than you ever dreamed."

Two and a half years later, Victor left the coffee house, passed Lotta's Fountain, and entered an office building on Market Street for a meeting with an advertising firm.

Opened recently by two exiles from New York, the firm was anxious to land a client like DemoDrones, an unknown company with an exciting new product and, more importantly, dangling a budget proposal worth tens of millions of dollars.

The firm set up a lunch meeting on an outside veranda, with exterior walls shaped like the decorative turrets of an English country manor. The building was much shorter than the others in the immediate area, and skyscrapers towered all about.

"This is a surprise," Victor said, stepping out to the large patio, lined with beautiful ceramic tiles. Heavy furniture with soft but industrial-strength padding sat about, and in the center, a dining table had been arranged with the meticulous and expensive care required to make it look casual. Large, potted plants added an element of luxury and comfort, almost decadent so high up, surrounded by all that glass. And metal.

Victor had asked for the entire staff to attend, assistants and computer specialists as well. "I really like getting to know everyone involved. I'm going to be spending a lot of money, and I want to meet the people who make your office tick."

It was a bit of a squeeze, but they managed to fit at the table. He asked for introductions from everyone. All thirteen said hello, including the computer expert, Jen. With a pretty smile, she said, "I'm really excited to be in such a creative environment."

Victor had caught glimpses of her over the past two years in San Francisco. Recently, she'd had her hair cut into a boyish style. It enraged him, and he burned to order her to grow it back the way she wore it at the dance.

He beamed. "Where is that accent from, Jen?"

"Oh, a place much colder than here!"

Everyone laughed, nobody louder than Victor.

As servers bustled about, one of the partners asked Victor to describe the DemoDrones product. "It sounds amazing," she said. "But it's a little difficult to grasp, so take it slow for those of us with an artistic sensibility."

"Of course." He wiped his mouth, took a sip of water, and noted the time. Fifteen minutes to launch. "We're going to revolutionize construction and demolition. Our nanobot technology will save huge amounts of time and money. It's based on the von Neumann probe concept. Say you have a space probe the size of one of these little quinoa grains." He pinched one from his salad plate for display.

"It travels through space searching the galaxy. This little probe would take countless years to explore even a tiny corner, so all by itself, it's pretty worthless. But you can program this little guy to seek out asteroids made of metal. It lands on the asteroid and uses those metals to build a replica of itself. Suddenly, you have two probes, and you've cut your exploration time in half. But now you have two probes that can reproduce, then four, then eight. Growth is exponential, and soon you'd have swarms of these little guys, searching everywhere."

❖

"You fucking psycho!" Buce had screamed the other night in Victor's high-rise condo. "Do you know how dangerous this is?"

"Listen to me, Buce, I'm the reason you have a fancy mansion in Pacific Heights, your own driver, and a beach house in Maui. I'm the reason a beautiful woman married a skinny shit like you who still looks and smells like you haven't showered in a week."

"I don't give a shit! Take it all back, take everything!" Tears streaked his face. "You're gambling with the whole world!"

❖

On the patio, the other advertising partner said, "You're not planning on sending your microdrones into space, are you?"

"No. Flying technology for nanobots is an entirely different matter, almost an industry to itself. Early on, we realized it would delay our release date by years and explode our budget." He gave a conspiratorial smile. "Candidly, that technology does exist, but it was developed in other labs, mostly for the military. It's a closely guarded secret, but we know it's possible."

❖

"Those fuckers are programmed to fly!" Buce screamed, his voice cracking, clutching his hair. "Have you calculated the potential destruction, you asshole? It will take two weeks for the bots to cover the earth, eating every piece of metal they find!"

"You stole that technology yourself, Buce, from a friend at another lab. I paid you to do it."

Buce's chest heaved, honking on each inhale. "I didn't know you were a psychopath!"

❖

"But there's something I still don't understand," the first partner said. "Metals have different compositions, alloys, mixes. I'm not sure how to phrase this…"

"I know exactly what you're asking. You want to know if every bot works on every kind of metal. The answer is no, but there are enough bots in every square inch for every kind of metal. Alloys are mixes, but we've developed alloy bots."

"How do you turn them on?"

"DemoDronesPaste. It's just what it sounds like, a paste that's a little thicker than oil paint. For many reasons, the color is bright blue. The nanobots are solar powered, so you just slather a bit of the paste somewhere with light, and it takes about a minute for the bots to power up and get to work. The replication process is very complex, and I don't understand it myself, but it's amazing to see. At first it looks like the metal is dissolving, but the speed increases exponentially as more bots come online, so the metal starts falling away like powder in no time at all."

"But if the new drones are created inside in the dark, how do they get power?"

"They're programmed to work as teams. They share their energy. As long as you have nanobots in the light, they send power to those in the dark. They store energy, too. They go dormant at night, but they're back at work once the morning sun rises. Once you set them free, they're unstoppable."

A concerned silence fell. "If they're unstoppable," said the partner, "how do you turn them off?"

"We have a central control source, a big panel that looks like something NASA might use. But obsolescence is also programmed into the software. Put another way, if they didn't die, they wouldn't power up in the first place."

Buce kicked a table, and the expensive lamp shattered. "Not only did you turn off the obsolescence, you shut down the security on the start-up program! If you're so fucking innocent, why did you turn off the *alarms*? Because you're a deranged sack of shit, that's why! You didn't want anyone to know what you were doing!"

Buce went limp, exhausted. Victor had given him whisky without being asked, knowing that cocaine addicts always appreciate a little alcohol to take the edge off. Buce drank the last of it and set the glass down, flopping to a cushioned white chair. He stared out the wall of windows at the nighttime San Francisco skyline, dashes of light rising.

"Maybe this is how it was always going to end," Buce muttered. "Religious wars, political conflicts, racial tension, and the whole time the clock was ticking down to one unstable lunatic."

"Have you heard of the nuclear app?" Victor said.

Buce didn't respond.

"It's one of those game theory riddles. Imagine an app appearing on every smartphone on earth at the same time, turning every phone into a nuclear bomb. You set it off with one tap."

"Big riddle. It would take about fifteen seconds for the first explosion."

"Six seconds seems to be the consensus."

Buce buried his face in his hands, convulsed by a wave of sobs. He sniffed and wiped his nose. "Look at me, the stupid motherfucker who helped make it happen." He bolted upright with ironic glee. "Holy shit, I'm Igor! I'm fucking Igor!" He fell back with manic laughter.

"You're working yourself into a state for no reason. I've had the sample for a week and nothing's happened. It's in a perfectly safe place. If I was the madman you say I am, I'd have used it already."

Buce sucked in a big snort of snot. "I bought a gun recently. In the back of my mind, I always thought that if the apocalypse comes, I'd put a bullet in my head before somebody else does it, or before I starve. But the bots will eat my gun."

"Why not stockpile a cocaine apocalypse kit? Go out on a bender, high as a kite."

Buce's head turned slowly. "You fucking asshole."

❖

"But let's say you're taking apart an old ship, so you have billions of drones, but just one of those little guys decides it doesn't want to die?"

"The bots are pretty fragile on their own or in small groups. Let's say we have ten thousand next to my plate." He gave a light tap. "I've just destroyed them all. If a swarm started getting out of hand, we could send a variety of signals, and we'd send all of them, just to be extra cautious. The last resort is to send an EMP, an electromagnetic pulse. It disables anything that uses power. Obviously, that's a last resort but it will never come to that. Here." He wiped his mouth and stood. "Come with me, all of you, down to the street."

A few people stood while the rest looked to the partners for guidance. The woman partner said, "Okay, let's go!" and they headed downstairs.

❖

Buce came in close, his face splotchy and wet. Victor hadn't seen such despair since he came upon his mother in the kitchen after his father left.

Buce said, "It's easy for a guy who looks like you to fool everyone, but you're a sick and twisted fuck. All that shit that happened to you in Russia, your parents, that dumb little fake America, losing your shit and killing someone, it screwed with your head. You're the most fucked-up person I've ever met. If your emotional state showed on your face, you'd be the ugliest motherfucker around."

"Go home and get some rest, Buce. You look like shit."

Buce sniffed. "You don't have the emotional maturity to recognize your own feelings, and that's why you don't even know how much you hate everyone on the planet."

"Try not to do any more lines tonight. And if you can't help yourself, pop a few benzos afterward. You really need to get some sleep."

"Do you even know what emotions feel like? Hate? Or love?"

A face flashed in Victor's mind.

"I could report you to the FBI. Somebody needs to stop you. I'll lose everything, but I don't care. I was happier when I was just a regular schlub."

Victor pushed a button and his door slid open. "I wasn't. Now good night, Buce, and don't make any unnecessary trouble."

Buce shuffled off with a glare.

Victor grabbed a thick plastic bag and a towel and headed for the empty whisky glass. Halfway across the room, he realized it didn't matter and left it sitting in plain sight.

Buce didn't live far, so he'd make it home in time to set up a few lines of white powder. With any luck, he'd slump on the table with the coke in plain sight. They'd schedule an autopsy, but with his cause of death so obvious, they wouldn't rush. There'd be no reason to suspect another poison.

❖

Victor led all thirteen employees of the advertising firm to the island holding Lotta's Fountain. He checked his phone. One minute away.

Victor had snapped up a warehouse and shipping company a few weeks back when formulating today's plan. He'd visited the previous night, and a few hours ago gave one of the moving crew supervisors half of a hefty tip.

The worker was certainly standing by, remembering Victor's promise to pay the other half if he was exactly on time. Just then, the time changed. Two twenty p.m. Victor pictured the man leaping into action and smiled.

He took a spot in front of Lotta's Fountain. The senior staff looked game to indulge a wealthy new client, but the others seemed unnerved, including Jen, the computer expert with a cold climate accent.

Victor raised his voice over the traffic. "Let me explain why we have so many safety features on the nanobots. Look around you." They craned their heads. "If DemoDrones could fly and if they weren't controlled by a central device, imagine what would happen if we let some loose right now." He swiveled and pointed to a building. "Now there you see nothing but mirrored glass, but metal provides the structural support for the glazing. DemoDrones will work their way through every crack, every tiny opening. The nanobots eat the metal supports, and the windows fall, like the building has decided to give us a strip show!"

It drew a few smiles.

"And DemoDrones keep going, now hugely multiplied, and start eating away at the steel structure. The new bots are powered by the ones still outside in full daylight, like all the gorgeous sunshine we have this afternoon. They're amassing into huge swarms, and the structural integrity of the building starts to fail, and when that happens in even a few places, it won't take any time at all until the whole thing collapses. Probably less than a minute."

He glanced down the street, a typical work afternoon, nothing amiss.

"As I've said, the nanobots are programmed for efficient, synchronized demolition, but just like your car's GPS calculates a new direction when you miss a turn, DemoDrones will search for the next answer to the only problem they will ever try to solve: *Where can I find metal to make more copies of myself?* When a critical mass finds a rich new source, all the drones in that vicinity will congregate to, let's say the building with the light granite façade. But the swarm that blew to this side of the street when the first structure fell will coordinate separately when a critical mass forms on this building here."

He swept his hand across a slender, silver-colored office tower. "Other swarms will go in the other two directions, so just a few minutes after the original building collapses, four more will come down."

A commotion erupted down the street, cars screeching when suddenly changing direction, horns honking, and a worried little crowd forming, barely visible through the traffic. Alarm grew among people on the far sidewalk, but the employees at the advertising firm focused only on Victor, uncertainty driving off their phony enthusiasm.

He made huge sweeping gestures, letting a bit of Tolyatti into his voice. His heart pumped a hot rush. "As DemoDrones multiply exponentially, so does their power. If five buildings fall in the first several minutes, up to forty will fall in the next few. Smaller packs will form and race along the streets, eating cars and buses, flying through cracks in the pavement to the underground trains."

Screams came from down the street as a dark, smoky cloud swirled up.

He raised his voice. "They'll eat gold rings and necklaces, platinum watches, keys inside your pockets, loose change. They'll detect the trace metals in our bodies, and burrow through our skin to our blood vessels, and when we breathe them in, our lungs will fill with metallic dust." They shrank back and stepped away. "Ten minutes after their release, all you see around us will be falling away. Within a day, all the West Coast. Within a week…"

With a horrified look, Jen recognized him and screamed, "Victor!" The others paid no attention, drawn to the disturbance down the street. Jen rushed up screaming, "Stop this!" She slapped his face.

The sting filled him with delirious joy. He spun her around, holding her tight. Her coworkers backed away, their stricken eyes fixed into the distance.

"Look!" A dusty tornado grew thicker and darker by the moment, wrapping a tall office building in a mechanical, mesmerizing swirl that rose thousands of feet in the sky. A car raced past and more followed. Two crashed halfway down the block, one rising to expose its underside before it fell to the pavement. It melted until it puffed into powder that separated into streams zooming to nearby vehicles. People jumped from their cars to race blindly, slapping all about as if fighting off mosquitos. In a flash, their skin seemed to turn inside out, and they staggered a few steps before falling.

"Make this stop, Victor!" Jen screamed, squirming uselessly. Her muscles loosened, and she slumped. He squeezed tighter.

Windows up and down the building tipped free, and soon great hunks of the skyscraper's exterior sheered off and plunged to the sidewalk below.

Many people fell as their legs gave out from terror, tripping those behind. Writhing mounds grew as more scrambled over and became trapped. People shoved the elderly and slower aside. They crashed to the cement, and their screams joined the others filling the air, the horns, the tires, sirens, and a world-shaking buzz. Breaking through the cacophony, enormous metallic tearing and snaps rang clear.

Victor resisted the instinct to flee and roared into Jen's ear, "I saved that girl! I did something good!"

Coughing and gagging and sobbing, the pretty girl who danced with such innocent freshness slapped his arms, weakly repeating his name.

It took longer than he predicted for the first building to fall, but not as long for the next. It seemed synchronized, for when the first plummeted, three more followed in seconds. Even as the debris surge bore down on them, two more skyscrapers sank into the clouds. High in the sky, others tilted and swayed, groaning.

The dust clouds reached Victor and Jennifer, carrying swarms of nanobots. Instantly engulfed by pain as searing as flames, he saw the skin on his arm shred to a bloody rag before he went blind. His chest filled with what felt like cement. This close, the buzzing sounded monotonous and mundane, like a leaf blower.

Tisha had arrived and led Drew to the sofa, where they sat with her arm about his shoulders.

Drew also knew the drones would spread faster than Victor imagined, for they wouldn't stall at night but keep working, sluggishly, with massive quantities of stored solar energy.

Tisha shook him gently. "When you're ready, I'm here. Just tell me what your vision revealed."

A minute later, staring wide-eyed at the ground, he started.

22

The Third Warning

November 1975–January 1976

The heavy promo rotation delivered a sizable audience for the premiere of *Perspectives*, and the viewers stayed the full hour. The overnights promised a strong splash in the ratings, and Paul Balek couldn't argue with success. He groused about our deception with the rundown but knew which side his bread was buttered on. "Somehow you found an audience that likes intellectual shit, so keep them happy and don't fuck it up."

In my head, my mother admonished me to be gracious in victory, but I ignored her pleas from the beyond. I was professional with Paul when required but ignored him otherwise, even when passing each other in the newsroom or hallways. My rising Q-Rating and the show's success gave me the luxury to openly demonstrate my dislike in front of everyone, a privilege few others enjoyed. I like to think many people took vicarious revenge.

Our viewers returned for three subsequent weeks, conclusive proof of a solid hit with staying power. We weren't at the top of the ratings, but any show would envy such a strong beginning. A focus group agreed the race car set was silly. Ron ordered it painted in soft pastels, a vast improvement.

As I reached the last month of pregnancy, it was as if a firm hand held me down at all times. The extra weight robbed me of effortless coordination, my joints ached and became unreliable, and I floundered to rise from a chair or to get out of bed. As the two-week holiday break approached, I bowed to reality and let our secondary anchor take the lead spot until after I gave birth.

Loren's children insisted on spending the holiday season with their mother. He tried to interest me in staying a few days with some of his old friends on Long Island, but I declined. "I can't be a guest in someone's house in this condition. You go have fun with your friends. I'll be fine on my own." He put up a considerate fuss until it became cloying and I snapped. "I miss the solitude of living alone. I'll be perfectly fine by myself, and a little peace and quiet would be a relief."

He looked hurt, and I apologized for sounding insensitive and ungrateful. "I haven't had to consider another person's opinion about how to spend my time in a very long time. But you'd be doing me a favor by going."

"I can't leave you alone in your condition, on our first holiday together no less. Aside from what my friends would rightly think of me, I'd never forgive myself."

I scoffed and rolled my eyes, necessitating another apology.

We attended a few parties in elegant homes and apartments. I met a lot of network brass for the first time, having spent most of the past nine months on the road. I also chatted with famous writers, Broadway stars, and familiar television faces. I loved watching their expressions flash with delighted recognition at seeing me.

Loren rushed around to various shops, hovering as painters and delivery men transformed the guest room into a nursery. We spent Christmas and New Year's Eve alone. Since my building came cable ready, we had the unimaginable luxury of twenty-six channels to watch, along with reading, making dinner, and preparing for the baby's arrival.

Late on the evening of January fifth, I was curled on the sofa reading when it felt as if a pair of invisible hands decided to yank me apart. I inhaled with as much disbelief as pain. Loren drove me to the hospital and just a few hours later, early in the morning of January sixth, I gave birth to my baby girl.

I felt my daughter slip free, and her first exhale was an unwavering, glass-shattering, icepick pierce of a screech. The crew in masks and scrubs laughed in appreciation.

After the doctor fussed for a bit, a nurse swooped in with a blanket, gathered up my baby, and hurried away. I caught a glimpse of a tiny fist glistening with slime.

"What are you doing with her?" I said, frantically trying to keep my child in sight.

"They're just going to clean her up," another nurse said, taking the doctor's spot and giving me a quick wash. "We'll get you all set and take you back to your room. They'll bring the baby to you there."

They wheeled me to my room where Loren waited. He looked ecstatic, and I was touched by his enthusiasm for a child that wasn't his.

"Here she is," a nurse sang out, walking in with a screaming bundle.

Loren gingerly took the blanket. He laughed and carefully nestled her into my arms.

Babies always looked identical to me. My whole life, I feigned agreement as parents and grandparents pointed out distinct features on a new infant the way sweet little girls excitedly describe their woodland fairy-tale friends. My daughter changed all that.

She was tiny and beautiful. Mottled with already-fading red splotches, she radiated fresh life so potent she sparkled. Awed, I whispered, "Hello, my baby girl," and she sighed contentedly and settled, her face softening. I thrilled at having the power to soothe her anger with a few words. At the corner of her mouth, a bubble popped into a viscous flow. As I wiped it away with my finger, I was filled with a blinding determination to protect her, along with an overpowering and all-consuming love. I wished I could share this feeling with my mother.

A few hours later, as I recorded the extraordinary details in my journal, I struggled to remember how long Loren and I stared wordlessly at my daughter, and it was some time before we shared a smile.

"You should settle on a name," he said.

"I was hoping the perfect name would come to me when I saw her for the first time. I'll just call her 'beautiful' until I'm absolutely certain."

"There's something I need to tell you." He sounded serious. "I tried to get out of it, but there's an emergency division meeting in Los Angeles. I must leave as soon as possible."

"What's the emergency?"

"It's the entertainment schedule, nothing that would interest you. But as head of television, I don't have the luxury of ignoring it."

I squeezed his hand. "Thank you for taking a job you didn't want for my sake."

He kissed my forehead.

As was routine in 1976, I was scheduled to spend up to five days in the hospital after giving birth. By day three, Loren was gone. I wanted to go home, but every nurse warned me I didn't realize how tired I was. Although I loved holding and spending time with my daughter, the relief I felt in handing her over to the nursery staff for the night convinced me to stay.

I slept in the bed closest to the window and the other was empty, so I had a private room. I woke up very early on my fourth day. Outside, dawn looked hours away with only a few scattered office lights dotting the distant towers. I watched a gentle and hypnotic snowfall in the tin-colored sky and imagined I was rushing through a tunnel of stars.

I turned to check the wall clock above the door, but I couldn't read it in the dark. The large door was open to the corridor with dim overnight lighting. Crisp footsteps echoed somewhere far down the hall, growing fainter.

Needing to use the bathroom, I threw aside the blanket and sat up when something stirred at the foot of the bed. I realized someone was seated in the shadows, and I recoiled with a gasp.

The silhouette revealed the slight form of an old woman. "Don't fret, dear," she said in the soft, disarming voice of a schoolmarm. "I'm sorry to startle you, but it was imperative that I come."

My heart hammering, my shock blazed to anger. "What are you doing in my room?"

She stepped into a hazy shaft of hallway light. Doughy and capped with silver curls, she laid a large object on the bed, wrapped with what looked like a shawl. "I brought a gift for your child. You must tell her the truth about her father."

"What do you know about her father?"

"Your daughter is destined for a crucial role. The child must be saved."

In just a matter of hours, Delilah Fuller would send me the same warning right before she died on the set in Cleveland, but I wouldn't learn about Delilah's message for several years. At that moment in the hospital room, I flashed on the heroin addict in San Francisco screaming the same warning. Bizarrely, I felt an irrational relief because the old woman failed to deliver the rest of the message.

"Also, my dear, the yellow box is across the street."

I drew in a deep breath. "Who are you?"

"An ancient, wandering soul. There are many more of us than you suspect. I felt drawn to see you. Rarely do we bring new life into the world, for we are destined to lose all those we love, and children are the bitterest loss. Your daughter is a rare and special gift. Arthur of Brittany is the luckiest man alive, but only for now. The loss of his daughter will be exponentially worse than the loss of his throne."

With a smile, she turned and walked off. I scooted off the bed and followed her to the hallway. With people sleeping, I kept my voice low. "How did you find out about me and my daughter? Did Arthur Brittany send you?"

"No, and don't be alarmed, dear. Nobody means you any harm." She raised an eyebrow. "Quite the contrary. We are your greatest allies."

She walked away, and I watched until she turned a corner. I returned to my room, flipped on the light, and unwrapped the shawl. I felt a sour twist in my heart when I saw the title, *The Royal Lineage.*

It felt like an accusation. Somehow, I'd managed to drive Arthur from my mind, but the implications suddenly forced themselves to the front of my consciousness. It was just a little after four o'clock in the morning, but I needed to talk to someone. I called Ron.

He answered, and I apologized for waking him. "I know it's early, but I really need to discuss something with you. It's important. They're pretty lax about enforcing visiting hours in the maternity ward, so come as soon as you can."

"Give me an hour."

As I hung up, I decided to check on my baby. The nursery was down the hallway and around a corner. The infants were displayed in a large room holding rows of cribs behind a glass wall. It was dark, but two large openings to the fully lighted nurses' station let in just enough light to see.

My daughter was in the second row, but reflections obscured my view. I got close, shaded my eyes and squinted.

The crib was empty.

My heart fluttered with alarm as I scanned the other cribs, although I knew the nurses wouldn't change her spot without telling me. With only a handful of babies scattered in the rows, I quickly realized she was gone. I let loose with a cry of shock.

I pushed my way through a swinging door to the side, ignoring the stern warning "Hospital Staff Only." The short corridor opened to a disorganized nurses' station, which was empty.

I raced into the glass-fronted crib room, but my daughter wasn't there. I saw her shape on the soft lining.

A sharp rap on the glass drew my attention. A nurse in the hallway was furiously gesturing for me to leave. I rushed to the back room as her voice rose with anger. My heart raced, and my breath came in shallow gasps. A roar filled my head.

From this side of the room, I noticed another short hallway along the left wall with three open doors. I heard voices and ran. The first two rooms were empty, but the last held three nurses, chatting in starched uniforms. My baby was on a changing table, kicking her legs as a nurse pinned on a fresh diaper.

I cried out with relief and their heads snapped up. "Ma'am, you aren't allowed back here," one barked. Her white cap bore the silver insignia of the head nurse.

I rushed to pick up my baby, but the nurse closest to me stepped in front. "Ma'am, you need to leave!"

"Call security," the head nurse snapped.

The baby turned her head in my direction. At seeing her serene expression, my panic evaporated. It left behind a yawning emptiness that made me weak. I stumbled to a chair, desperately needing oxygen but breathing too rapidly to get enough. It's a strange and terrifying feeling to lose control of something as basic as breathing.

"She's hyperventilating," a nurse said as a pair of strong hands grabbed my shoulders. Vertigo swept in and carried me along, and I felt as helpless as a leaf sliding over a waterfall. I surrendered to the unexpectedly soothing sensation of free fall.

When I woke up back in the hospital room, the sun had risen on a gray winter morning. The snow had stopped.

I shot up, seized by the conviction my baby needed me.

"Whoa!" Ron said, suddenly appearing and holding me down. "Don't move. You have nowhere to go, and the baby is perfectly fine. I saw her ten minutes ago."

"Are you sure? I need to see her."

His hair was tousled in the way I remembered from San Francisco, before he showered and dressed for the day. It was nice to see him so disheveled again. "Claudia, you're scaring the nurses, you're scaring me, and there's no reason to scare the baby."

I gave in and melted back. "I had a bad morning." I gave a bitter laugh at my own understatement. "I should go apologize to the nurses."

"Don't worry about it. I already talked to them, and they said it's not unusual for a new mother to have a panic attack." He sat next to the bed. "Did something happen?"

I told him about the heroin addict in San Francisco, then I explained about my visitor early that morning. "They both said the same thing. The child must be saved, and the yellow box is across the street. It can't be a coincidence. It means something. And the lady this morning left a book..." I looked around.

"Is this it?" He picked it up from beneath his chair. "I've been looking through it. I think it's a genuine medieval masterpiece."

I was glad to see it, for it was concrete proof my morning visitor wasn't a delusion. Ron opened the front cover and handed me a slip of paper embossed with the name of the antique shop and a New York City address. Someone had written the dates of England's Plantagenet dynasty.

A patient and her husband shuffled past my open door, and I lowered my voice. "This proves I'm not insane for imagining Arthur Brittany's real identity."

"I thought we knew that because you watched him survive a bullet to the stomach."

I held up the paper. "But this proves other people made the same connection. Ron, we're the producer and lead anchor for a national news show. We could be sitting on the biggest story of all time, and we're not doing anything to investigate what, or how, or why this is happening."

"Claudia, come on!"

"I know we don't have proof..."

"We don't have *anything*. If you go on the air with this, you'll sound like a crazy woman, and you'll make me look like the biggest huckster in television. You'll destroy both of us. It's not going to happen on my program."

In the mid-1970s, he was correct. We never imagined the immense profitability and rewards for the battiest, shabbiest, and most ill-informed lunacy of online platforms. Anyone with a convincing rant, shameless ambition, and a little bit of luck could land a windfall.

I wasn't ready to concede. "Look, Arthur Brittany works at Columbia University. Maybe we can send somebody undercover."

"He resigned in July."

I blinked, my mouth open.

"I checked out your story when you told me about it in San Francisco. I also contacted a few people at NASA about the secret radiation study, too. Nobody knew anything."

"I'm telling you the truth."

"I know, but that's not the issue. Let me ask you this—will you tell your daughter the truth about her father?"

My voice went defensive and weak. "I haven't thought about it."

"If you can't figure out how to tell your own child, how can you possibly explain it to a national television audience?"

I knew he was right, and I nodded.

He gave me a quick peck on the cheek. "I have to go, but I'll come back later." He patted the book. "Be careful with this. It's a pretty special book."

"There's no need to come back. I'm fine now."

"I want to check in on you, so I'll be back."

I was pleased and touched by his concern. "Okay."

When I wasn't spending time with my daughter, I spent the day drifting in and out of sleep, looking out the window, and flipping the pages of *The Royal Lineage*. My thoughts always returned to Arthur Brittany. He'd promised to support the baby, and I was freshly annoyed at him. He'd given me no notice about how to reach him.

The maternity ward was quiet. Only two women had arrived to give birth all day, and with the three departures in the afternoon, only six new mothers were scattered in rooms up and down the hallway. When the afternoon nurse arrived to take my temperature and blood pressure, I mentioned the sleepy pace.

"It's always like this in the dead of winter," she said with a sly smile. "This time of year, people are busy making babies, not giving birth. Half of the nurses are on vacation, and one called in sick, so we're down to three."

"I know you just came on duty, but I'm sure you heard about my little meltdown this morning. I'm really sorry. The last thing I want is to make trouble for the nurses. I'm sure your jobs are difficult enough without new mothers going crazy on you."

"We've seen it all on this ward. There's always an emergency. I just hope we don't have a big one with so many nurses out."

Half an hour later, I heard a loud commotion in the hallway, alarming enough to get up and investigate. Other mothers stood at their doors, craning to see. Far down, past the nursery, something was happening that involved a gurney, two doctors, a passel of nurses, and a screaming woman.

"Sounds serious," said a very young-looking new mother a few doors away. The rest of us mumbled our assent.

The nurse who took my vitals rushed out from the nursery hallway and raced to help. She reached the scene of the emergency and after consulting with a doctor, ran back and shouted a list of things to someone we couldn't see before doubling back. A few moments later, another nurse rushed from the hallway with an armful of supplies.

After a frantic but well-choreographed series of moves, they pushed the gurney into a room. The whole team followed, leaving the hallway empty.

"Is anyone watching the babies?" the young mother asked.

"I'm sure someone must be," said another. "There's always four nurses on duty."

The woman closest to the nursery said, "I saw the head nurse leave a few minutes ago, so there's one nurse left."

"One of the nurses called in sick," I said. The realization dawned on us the infants were alone.

All of us headed for the nursery. One of the mothers was ahead of me, and after she turned the corner, she cried, "Hey! What are you doing?"

The rest of us hadn't yet turned the corner, and we speeded up.

"You!" she cried again. "Get away from that baby!"

We broke into runs, slapping the linoleum with our hospital slippers. It sounded like a heavy rain.

I rounded the corner just as the first woman pushed through the swinging door. I rushed after her, and I caught a glimpse of adults standing in the second row, near my daughter's crib.

My panic returned in a flash, accompanied by a terrifying

calculation about the odds of a satisfactory outcome twice in one day. I slammed down the short corridor, but I took the turn to the crib room too tightly and bumped into the wall. Gripping the edge, I flung myself into the nursery.

An older couple stood above my daughter's crib, watching us as we entered. "We mean no harm," the man said. The woman nodded earnestly. "No harm at all."

I charged into the row but stopped halfway down, nervous about spooking the strangers. "Please go away!" I cried. They repeated their good intentions but didn't move.

The other mothers gathered up their babies and fled, leaving me alone with the couple looming above my daughter. When I reflect on that moment today, I can muster sympathy and understanding for those women. Getting their children to safety was their sole concern, as well it should have been, but it took many years to feel anything but rage at how they abandoned me.

I felt helpless and terrified. The couple looked harmless, as benign as an elderly pair strolling in the park, dressed nicely in warm clothes.

"Your daughter is a rare and special gift," the woman said. "We only wanted to see her. She gives one such hope."

I pushed my way to the crib, and they moved aside. My baby was sleeping. I scooped her up and shouldered my way past the unwelcome visitors. Before I left the room, I stopped. "You need to leave us alone. Tell all of your crazy friends the same thing. I don't want your help." I turned away.

"The fate of the world rests on that little baby," the man said, bringing me to a halt. The woman grabbed his arm, nodding furiously. "All is lost without her. You have nothing to fear. Someone will always be watching her, keeping her safe."

"Leave us alone!" I screamed. Crying, I raced off, nearly stumbling as I left through the swinging door.

Ron was waiting in my room as I rushed inside. "Thank God you're here! I need you to take me home right now." I carefully handed the baby to him and grabbed my overnight bag.

"Claudia, what happened?"

I stuffed my things inside carelessly. I threw on a thick winter jacket over the hospital robe and considered changing out of the slippers but decided I couldn't wait. "Come on, let's go."

"You didn't get everything."

I flung the bag over my shoulder and took the baby from him. "I'm leaving this instant. You can stay if you want to get the rest." He grabbed the book and followed me. We got a few odd looks as we left the hospital, but nobody stopped us.

In the car, Ron let me shake and cry until I felt strong enough to talk. "I need to call Loren. He needs to come back as soon as possible."

"The first thing we need to do is call the hospital and tell them both you and the baby are safe. And then afterward you can explain why we rushed out of there like we were trying to skip out on the bill."

"Just take me home. I need to get my baby in a safe place. And I need you to spend the night."

"Did the lady from this morning come back?"

"Please don't ask any more questions. I just want to get home." I hugged my baby tight.

Ron helped me inside, and I heard him call the hospital as I put the baby in the crib. After I put a blanket over her, I ran room to room, drawing the blinds.

As I was lowering the last one, Ron said, "The hospital wants you to come back. They're worried about you and the baby."

"I don't care what they want. I'm going to make some coffee for us."

"Claudia, I have to leave for a few hours…"

"No! Ron, I need you to stay with me. Please." I grabbed his hands.

"I promised my neighbor I'd pick up her prescriptions from the drugstore. She's an elderly lady, and I was supposed to do it this morning, but I had to cancel because you needed me at the hospital. She's counting on me, and I can't let her down. Besides, if I'm going to spend the night here, it will give me a chance to pick up a change of clothes and some things I'll need in the morning."

I felt panicky. "Have a cup of coffee first."

"The sooner I leave, the sooner I'll be back." He gave me a hug. "You'll be fine. Skip the coffee and try to get some rest."

After he was gone, the silence felt familiar and comfortable, and soon I was fighting fatigue. I didn't dare lie down on the bed or sofa, for I'd fall asleep in no time, so I turned off the lights and stretched on the floor.

The fate of the world rests on that little baby. All is lost without her. Someone will always be watching her.

My shakes returned, wondering how I ever imagined I could escape the looming shadow of Arthur Brittany. I had no idea what I was up against, what centuries-long puzzle or scheme he'd brought into my life, sealed now by a daughter in the next room. The tears came as my helpless situation crystalized.

That's when Betty from Cleveland called to tell me that Delilah had died, leaving out the message Delilah sent the moment before her death. It was also when I settled on the perfect name for my little girl.

23

The fate of the world rests on that little baby. All is lost without her. Someone will always be watching her.

Those warnings came from people urging Drew's grandmother to protect his mother.

The child must be saved.

"That part of the warning was about *me*," he said to Tisha as they sat at the kitchen table. "I had to be saved because you and me have to stop Victor from releasing the bots."

"That's one way to look at it," she agreed, "but remember my prophecy specified three people."

He felt a faint shiver. "It feels weird. Sixteen years before I was born, people were warning my grandmother I needed protection."

Surprised, she said, "I guess I never put it together your mom was only sixteen when she had you."

"She and my dad were in high school."

"I'm dying to talk to you about it, but let's get back to the topic at hand. We know Victor plans to release the bots at two twenty in the afternoon. But we need a date and the exact location."

"The location is about a block west of Lotta's Fountain."

"Yeah, but if it only takes a minute for the bots to power up in the sun, we need to know exactly where the yellow box will be. We won't have time to go looking. And we need a date. I keep going back to that Lotta's Fountain pin. Your grandma wrote about a date engraved on the back. I mean, come on. Lotta's Fountain and a date. It has to be the date he's going to release the bots."

"We were looking for the jewelry box when we got sidetracked with the VHS tape. We never did a thorough search of all the boxes in the garage."

It was dark outside, so Drew opened the garage door and flipped on the light. They tore through everything, but the jewelry box was nowhere to be found. After a while, they returned to the house.

The memoir was strewn on the coffee table. Tisha flipped through the pages until she found what she was looking for. "Here's the key sentence: 'On the reverse I found the engraving, *To my dearest* followed by a date that meant nothing to me.'" She shook the page. "That has to be the date we need. Where did she hide that jewelry box?"

They'd opened every cupboard, rifled every box, examined every drawer, and squeezed around every piece of furniture. Only the yard was unexplored, a small patch of grass in front, and a fenced-in deck out back, but Drew couldn't imagine Grandma digging a hole.

Tisha released a huge sigh. "I'm wiped. I also haven't showered or changed since yesterday morning, so I'm heading home. I'll take the memoir with me. Give me everything you've already read."

He separated the last chapter and gave her the rest. She kissed his cheek and squeezed his shoulder. "Get some rest. I'll come over soon. Maybe tomorrow night."

After she left, he couldn't focus enough to read. He went to the kitchen table and opened his laptop. He searched for Lotta's Fountain and scanned the links, finally clicking on the map.

A large red drop pin marked the location of the fountain in the triangular angle formed by Market and Geary Streets. Smaller drop pins showed nearby restaurants, art galleries, gyms, and other places of interest.

In his vision, the bots had been released somewhere to the west. He clicked on the street view and manipulated the image, but he couldn't get a precise match with his memory.

He swore under his breath. He'd passed through this section of Market Street countless times but never studied the details. He clicked his way up and down the street, opening several business links. It occurred to him that the yellow box might be a semipermanent object, and he studied the sidewalk scenes, looking for an architectural feature or a utility container but nothing jumped out.

He clicked a link for nearby events, and a list popped on his screen. His eyes landed on the second one down: *Gina Ginger Soda returns to SF*. He sat up, remembering his grandmother went to Gina Ginger Soda's first gallery show in New York City in 1975.

He opened the article. "Oh, my God," he muttered aloud.

Gina Ginger Soda's new exhibit was opening this coming weekend at an art space about a block west of Lotta's Fountain. The show was called *The Prophets: Gina Ginger Soda Explores an Unspoken World.*

The listing included a recent video interview with Gina Ginger Soda. She sat on a small stage wearing a fashionable outfit and jewelry, her white hair cropped short. Drew recognized her as the woman from his vision who was walking down the sidewalk in a long coat.

Gina seemed relaxed and engaging while a man asked questions. "Your new exhibit is called *The Prophets*," he said. "I understand there's an interesting genesis for that name."

"There are multiple geneses, muses from all areas of my life, but some are more profound than others. In particular, I met a woman named Kaya who claims she was born in Sendia, Japan, more than four hundred years ago. She doesn't look a day over twenty. I'm not claiming to know the truth, but back in the seventeenth century, on a day of little note otherwise, she saw a towering silhouette gliding on the Pacific close to shore, unimaginably huge. It was centuries before she realized it was an aircraft carrier. Kaya had other visions of the future, and in a few more years, she realized she wasn't getting any older."

"How did she explain that to the people around her?"

"Thankfully she was alone for her first vision. It gave her time to realize the importance of discretion. She also didn't tell anyone when the normal cuts and abrasions of life starting healing in minutes." Gina leaned forward. "But Kaya is adamant about her normalcy and rejects any claim to being immortal or supernatural. She will die someday. But the collision of the magical and the mundane causes horrendous pain."

Sounding amused, the man said, "Four centuries of being twenty years old doesn't sound too bad."

Gina raised an eyebrow. "Have you ever heard of a happy prophet?" The audience laughed. "There's a reason prophets are unpopular. People worry about the things you're not saying, especially if you're a woman. Kaya knew she'd be accused of witchery and tortured. She spent the centuries wandering, never getting too close to anyone. She fell in love several times. She even married and gave birth. She nursed her son for one day before abandoning him to her husband's family, slipping away in the night. She couldn't bear the thought of watching him grow into adulthood only to watch him age and die. All the while, she would live on and on."

His voice now reflective, the man said, "It explains why prophets find solace being alone in the wilderness."

"They don't find solace," she corrected sharply. "Never. It's an unimaginably lonely existence."

"You're using the plural. Are there other prophets?"

"Yes, that's what I'm trying to show with this exhibit. There aren't many, probably no more than several hundred."

"How can you know that?"

"Kaya once met a woman who seemed to have some sort of leadership role, who helped other prophets when she could. She was born in England in the eleventh century, but even that lady didn't know everything."

"Althea," Drew muttered aloud.

He looked out the window. Althea's house was dark.

He closed his laptop and drifted off to sleep on the couch.

In the morning, he was jolted awake by someone furiously banging on his door. He recognized Tisha's muffled voice. He flung open the door and she charged inside, revelation on her face.

"The jewelry box is under her bed! It's tied to her box spring the way her mother did it."

He berated himself for not realizing it sooner.

They bounded up the stairs. Tisha reached the bed first and knelt, using the light from her phone to search underneath. She stood. "There's something wrapped in a towel. Let's get the mattress off." They pushed it away, revealing a rope tied about the box frame. Drew untied the knot and Tisha pulled the object free.

Carefully, she unwrapped the jewelry box, which was as beautiful as his grandmother described. They shared a look filled with the enormity of their responsibility, the sudden weight of their lives. If the Lotta's Fountain pin revealed the date Victor planned to release the bots, it also gave the exact date that standard evolutionary life on earth would crash into human technology, demolishing both.

She lifted the lid, found the golden Lotta's Fountain pin and turned it about. The engraved date read, *February 23*.

Tisha inhaled while Drew shouted, "It's today!"

In just over six hours, an unwitting worker would open a yellow box and release the bots while Victor watched, a block away, with the employees of the advertising firm in front of Lotta's Fountain.

In minutes, they were heading for San Francisco in Drew's car.

"Slow down!" Tisha ordered.

Drew tried. It was hard.

By tonight, millions of people would be dead. By tomorrow, terror and panic would erupt across the globe.

The response options would swiftly narrow to nuclear weapons, and vast regions of the world would be incinerated and radiated only a few days from now. The explosions would sterilize the blast zones of nanobots and disable billions more with the electromagnetic pulses that cut all power, but it wouldn't matter. The massive energy of nuclear explosions would accelerate the destruction by hurling unscathed bots on the margins faster than they could fly. As long as one nanobot survived, as insubstantial as a speck of dust, the pitiless cycle would kick back to life within hours. Minutes.

Destroying the bots before they powered up in the light was the only way to prevent worldwide destruction. Any caustic agent would kill the tiny robots on contact, while they were still inert in the blue DemoDronesPaste. Charcoal fluid and a lighter would annihilate them in seconds.

Drew tried to focus on the theoretical ease of their task. It required finding a yellow box and destroying a streak of blue paint. Simple.

His mind raced to the enormous consequences of failure and, according to Tisha's vision, the need to find a third person to help.

They settled on a plan to fill a spray bottle with flammable liquid, spritz it on the blue paint, and set it on fire.

Traffic in downtown San Francisco crept along on a workday. Drew and Tisha skirted the Market Street corridor and found a spot in a parking garage a block down from the art gallery.

At a department store across the street, they found charcoal fluid and a fireplace lighter with a long, tapering tip. After buying a plastic spray bottle, they tested the lighter, assembled their kit, and carried it up to Market Street in a paper bag.

The yellow box is across the street.

It sounded easy enough.

A flatbed truck was pulling away from the intersection, leaving behind a battered shipping container that took three parking spots. Although banged up and scratched, it was painted yellow, locked up tight with a padlock and heavy bars.

"That shipping container is yellow," Drew said. "Nobody said the box wasn't the size of a shipping container."

"Look over there." Tisha pointed across the street. A rack of three yellow metal boxes offered free tourist brochures.

A courier walked past wearing a company uniform, carrying a gold-colored box with white stripes.

A man in a stained, full-length white apron turned the corner, pushing a dolly with three plastic bins, two blue with green lids, the bottom one yellow with a red lid.

And suddenly, he saw yellow everywhere, boxes everywhere, variations of yellow boxes at every turn.

As if echoing his thoughts, Tisha said, "Let's remember we're looking for a yellow box. Not stripes, not yellow lids, not half and half. A yellow box. Let's trust the warnings. You're right that the shipping container is a possibility, but remember, the yellow box is *across the street*. Those tourist brochure boxes are across the street."

"But anyone can open those brochure boxes at any time. There's no reason for Victor to pay somebody to open one at precisely twenty past two."

As if to prove his point, a large group of tourists arrived just then, opening them all to rifle the brochures, presumably looking for their language.

"There's something about them that draws me," Tisha said. "Are you feeling the same tug from the shipping container?"

"No, but I have the strong feeling it's not those brochure boxes."

They spent some time looking around the neighborhood. They shaded their eyes to see into the art gallery. It was closed, the interior cleared to make way for the Gina Ginger Soda exhibit.

With a few hours to go, they set off for Lotta's Fountain.

"Save the child!"

A young, filthy man came stumbling, zeroing in on Tisha. She cringed, and Drew stepped in front.

"Save the child!" the man screamed at Tisha.

Drew took note of his filthy patchwork vest and a dated, beaded headband keeping his matted hair from his face. It was exactly as his grandmother described in her memoir, when a heroin addict shouted the same thing at her in 1975.

"You!" Drew shouted, and the man looked at him, his bloodshot eyes crinkled in amazement that someone was talking to him. "How old are you?" Drew said, his heart racing.

The guy looked skyward. "The clock just keeps ticking, man. I don't think people are people anymore. It's like everyone's gone crazy, talking into these little walkie-talkies or something. Nobody looks at each other." He went awed. "Poster boards at the bus stop move around, and they *glow*, man. They fucking *glow*." He waved Drew closer to share a secret. "I see a UFO, man. Crazy thing. It's way off in space and talks to me. Sending me messages. It tells me when I gotta say to a lady," he nodded at Tisha, "that she has to save the child."

"What child?"

"They never say, man."

"What year were you born?"

The guy smiled slowly. His teeth looked like pebbles scraped from the dirt. "I was born the day Hitler died, man. He liked junk, too. The last time I saw my mama, she said Hitler musta found a new body to inhabit when I was born. She was wrong, man. I'm nothing like him."

He stumbled off. They watched him weave down the sidewalk, threading through people talking into their phones.

"My grandma met him in 1975. He's now around seventy years old."

"People freeze into their current state when the visions start," Tisha noted. "He's been high from the last time he shot up, what, fifty years ago?"

The pitiless nature of the prophecies struck him then. The bedraggled man's retreating back was the clearest evidence of indifference about who received the visions. What did that say about their ability to manage the events of the day to come?

"If a heroin addict was chosen, are we sure we have the mettle?"

"Yes," she replied instantly. "He's playing his part in delivering messages to the right people. We're playing our parts by recognizing them. Don't lose heart, Drew. We need to keep each other strong."

A woman passed, pushing a stroller with a serene child bouncing inside. The baby was bundled up on a warm, sunny morning, shielded by a canopy, looking as safe as any baby ever did. Drew admired the expression of the protective mother, who masked her sharp-eyed alertness with apparent disinterest.

The child must be saved.

At the next intersection, Lotta's Fountain sat squat on the pedestrian island on the other side of Market Street. They stopped, but only for a moment. When they turned back, Drew recognized the entrance to Victor's fancy condo building.

"Victor lives on the fourteenth floor." Directly across the street was a bustling, stylish establishment. "And that's the coffee house where he's going to stop before his meeting at the advertising company."

"We might as well wait for him," Tisha suggested.

The coffee shop had a huge seating area, filled with people having quick meetings and discussing work. Drew and Tisha ordered and carried their drinks to a table at the very back of the room. After a long while and two refills, Victor entered.

"That's him," Drew whispered.

After getting his coffee, Victor took an empty seat in the middle of the room, paying scant attention to the surroundings. Drew knew Victor was thinking about his parents and life in Tolyatti while casually sizing up people he sincerely believed he didn't hate, even though he planned to kill them all.

"I just had a thought," Tisha said. "What if Victor has a second set of bots, in case this attack fails?"

The idea numbed him. "I didn't see anything like that in my vision."

"We need to consider that possibility. If he's planned everything so carefully, it doesn't seem like a stretch he might have a backup plan."

Drew wondered why he'd been selected for this mission when something so obvious had never crossed his mind. If Tisha was right, the challenge mushroomed to the insurmountable difficulty of getting Victor to confess he had more bots. He'd already killed to hide his secret. How could they hope to gain Victor's trust or threaten him when he was happy to destroy everything anyway? Finding and destroying the bots seemed almost easy in comparison.

Tom walked into the coffee shop, wearing jeans and a light sweater.

Drew gawked, scarcely believing how the day was becoming more complex by the moment.

Tisha gasped and gripped his arm.

"I already saw him." They huddled to hide their faces. Even though they were well in back of a large, crowded room, Tom was almost certain to spot them if he looked their way.

As Tom waited in line, he looked at his phone or at the chalk menu high above the counter, anywhere but inside the room and the people at the tables.

"He knows Victor is here," Tisha said.

Drew had the same impression. Tom's indifference to the other customers was too deliberate.

Tom walked to the seating area with a cup of coffee and a pastry plate. He passed Victor without a look and found a seat close behind him. When he sat, Tom dropped his pretense and watched Victor closely.

"What's he doing here, and why is he looking at Victor?" Drew said.

"Tom obviously knows something about Victor."

Drew's battering heart filled his mind, remembering his vision of Tom staring up at the bot swarm swirling in the sky.

After a while, Victor stood and headed for the door. With only forty minutes to launch, Drew knew Victor was leaving for his lunch meeting at the advertising company where Jen worked.

Tom followed, the final confirmation he was shadowing Victor.

"Okay, party time," Tisha said, rising. "Let's go." He grabbed the bag with the charcoal fluid and lighter.

Outside, Victor was already across Market Street. Tom observed him closely just outside the coffee house door.

Even though Tom might be the third person in Tisha's prophecy, Drew wanted to slip away. Tisha marched right up to him and said, "Tom," as if pleasantly surprised.

Tom turned. He went wide-eyed.

"What are you doing here?" she said.

He flashed a sickly smile, struggling to speak. "I-I'm supposed to meet up with an old high school buddy." His attempt to sound breezy and lighthearted failed. He gave Drew a manic smile a quick peck on the lips. "What are you two doing here?"

"It was a spur-of-the-moment thing," Drew said, his anxiety

rising. A block away, a yellow box waited, and he was trapped by banal chitchat. Tom looked equally anxious to be off. "We don't want to hold you up if you're meeting up with your old friend."

"Yeah, I should go look for him. He's probably lost in the big city. It's easy for a guy from Maple Grove, Michigan, to get lost in San Francisco."

In his unsettled state, Tom didn't seem to notice Drew's shock.

"We have to get going, too," Tisha said.

Abrupt as it was, the desire to be rid of each other was palpable to all of them. After a quick round of relieved goodbyes and a promise to be in touch soon, they set off.

Halfway down the block, Drew looked back. Tom was gone. *Did we just lose the third person in Tisha's prophecy?*

His vision of Tom going to the pavement, tracked by rifles, suddenly made sense. After Victor killed Phil, all the boys must have been rounded up.

"Tom must be the other spy who grew up in Maple Grove," Drew said, "the one who went to work directly for Mr. Thompson. They were teenagers the last time they saw each other, so Victor didn't recognize him. Somebody in Russia must be suspicious of Victor to send Tom to keep an eye on him."

"He's here for a reason, but he obviously doesn't know it. How did you meet him?"

"My friend Broderick pointed him out to me at the Guerneville Resort."

"That can't be a coincidence."

They arrived at the intersection with the art gallery and looked about. To Drew's eyes, the yellow shipping container was the only possible answer.

It sat placidly, still padlocked.

He checked the time. 2:14. Trembles rippled his legs and shoulders. At this moment, Victor was regaling the employees of the advertising company at lunch with the details of his amazing new product.

Somebody was going to open a yellow box in only six minutes and set off the apocalypse.

"The yellow box is across the street," Tisha muttered, looking at the tourist boxes.

"The yellow box is the shipping container."

"Drew, you're ignoring a critical point. *Across the street*. All the warnings specified it was across the street."

He was certain the bots were in the shipping container, but with a sinking sense of dread, he realized she was right. "Let's run across and take a look around," he said.

When they got the walk signal, they sprinted. They hopped up to the sidewalk. His fear rose and threatened to overwhelm him. He gripped the bag.

Tisha walked to the tourist brochure boxes, her body tightly compressed. She gave all three a quick inspection.

"Nothing," she said. "No blue paint."

He turned around. From this side, the shipping container was across the street.

His sense of failure opened like a sinkhole. *The yellow box is across the street*. Only in the final moments did the simple instruction reveal itself as a diabolical riddle.

And where was the third person?

The art gallery door opened, and workers in orange vests marched for the container.

Suddenly, Gina Ginger Soda appeared on the sidewalk, walking crisply, dressed in a long coat, like he remembered from his vision. She gave the container a protective pat.

Drew instantly understood. "It's her art show," he said, his voice rising. "In the shipping container!" His voice rose to a shout. "They're going to unload it!"

"Drew!" Tisha shouted.

"Come on!"

The light changed just as he reached the crosswalk. The heavy Market Street traffic surged to life.

With a start, he realized Tisha wasn't at his side. In disbelief, he saw her racing up to someone, talking frantically.

What is she doing?

In front of the container, a worker checked his phone. He shouted something and another responded, rustling a set of keys as he approached the padlock.

He couldn't wait for Tisha or the traffic. He dashed into the street with only a faint impression of the speed and location of moving cars. Vehicles braked and erupted with angry honks. Voices raged.

To Drew's right, a car screeched to a skidding halt with just enough force to knock him to the street. He stopped his fall, but sharp pain exploded from his wrists.

The driver got out and raced up to him, but Drew watched as the worker inserted a key in the padlock. A second later, it snapped open. With a clang, the others twisted away the protective bars. The hinges screamed as the double doors opened. Inside, rows of canvas paintings sat rigid in wooden support slats.

With a roar, Drew pushed up and brushed aside the worried driver. Alarms filled his head.

Two workers pulled the first painting free. It was covered by a sheet, and they propped it against the door frame. Gina Ginger Soda arrived, pointing and issuing orders. She pulled the sheet away.

He focused through the pain, his heart hammering. A dizzying wave overtook him, and he staggered to the sidewalk.

He was still too far away to see details inside the container. Inhaling like he'd just emerged from water, he forced himself to stumble forward.

Gina shot a blistering look at the workers. They responded with indifference. She issued a stream of angry words. Drew ignored her as he stumbled past to the container opening. Panting, he grasped the side and scanned the shadowy interior.

"This is pure vandalism!" Gina cried.

He whipped around. Gina was gesturing to a painting with precise red and yellow forms, cut with a diagonal slash of blue.

The blue paint began to boil.

"We just move the stuff, lady!" one of the workers shouted.

"It's your warehouse!"

Drew pushed through them. Already primed by Gina's outburst, the workers bristled with anger and one pushed back. Drew shrugged him off.

He reached the painting and froze when he realized his hands were empty. He'd dropped the bag.

The bots squirmed like maggots. *Smash them!* He could easily pulverize them with a swipe of his hand.

He paused when he realized the danger. If he dislodged so much as one nanobot, sweeping it aside while crushing the rest, it would delay the inevitable by only a few minutes. Without some sort of caustic agent, nothing would destroy all the bots.

"Help me!" he screamed at the workers.

Seeing the writhing blue paint, Gina and the workers backed away, aghast and freaked. Growing stronger by the moment, the bots sizzled like the fizz of volcanic mud.

Drew lacked an effective way to destroy them. His failure cleaved his mind. Stunned, he couldn't move.

He roared, willing his mind to reform. The bots were helpless. He still had the upper hand. At this moment, his only mission was to start destroying them. He'd worry about stray bots when necessary.

Three men pushed him aside. One of them screamed, "Go!" Another sprayed the blue paint using the same plastic bottle Drew dropped. An African American man stood to the side, ready with the fireplace lighter.

The man with the charcoal fluid made efficient work of it, misting the entire streak in seconds.

"Now!" he yelled.

Drew spotted the first nanobot emerge and start to rise. The man clicked the lighter.

Flames raced across the canvas, consuming the flying nanobot midair. It fell as a spark.

The man with the bottle unscrewed the spray top and flung the charcoal fluid on the fire. The flames streaked to his hand, which he batted it against his leg.

The fire raged, consuming the entire painting. None of the bots could have survived.

The men turned to him, smiling. Three of them, like Tisha's prophecy said.

"You're the Three Musketeers," Drew said.

The guy who must have been disco man wore his hair short these days. "We were looking for you and Tisha on the other side of the street. She spotted us right as you took off running. When you dropped the bag in the middle of the street, she told us your plan."

The African American man jumped in. "Congratulations on

choosing a strategy that only required a few seconds to explain. We ran after you, picked up the bag, and here we are!"

The sequence explained why the warnings specified *across the street*. Somehow, the prophecy and warnings factored in the critical role of the Three Musketeers, who would be across the street.

"You should leave before the police get here," the bearded man said. Drew noted emergency sirens growing louder. "Can you move? You took a pretty hard tumble when that car hit you."

The pain was fading to dull aches. Drew nodded.

Gina and the workers stood mesmerized.

"Go!" disco man shouted as the sirens wailed. "They're almost here."

Drew turned about. The fire had drawn a thin crowd. A few people gave him curious looks, trying to work out his role in the strange scene.

Tisha raced up to him. She gave him a brief, ecstatic hug. "We have to learn if Victor has more bots."

Suddenly feeling triumphant and invincible, Drew took her hand, and they raced to Market Street.

Screaming police cars whizzed past and screeched to a halt.

"Hello, Drew."

They stopped and Drew was surprised to see Broderick, who'd pointed Tom out at the Guerneville Resort. He stood next to a beautiful blond woman, smiling with a knowing intensity.

Tisha gave them a piercing look. "They're prophets, too."

"Many of us came today," the woman said. "The final pieces are moving into place."

Drew swiveled to take in the view, spotting individuals or pairs fixed on them. At least twenty people watched from across the street, down the block, at bus stops, and beside doors. All races, ages, shapes. A few feet away stood a man who stroked his beard, smiling.

"There's still more for you to do," Broderick said.

Without warning, Victor strode into view, looking concerned. He must have left the puzzled staff of the advertising firm at Lotta's Fountain when he realized his plan had failed.

Startled, Drew took a step back, and Tisha gripped his arm. Victor walked on, oblivious to prophecies and visions and children that needed to be saved.

"Don't let us get in the way," Broderick said. "Go."

He and Tisha followed Victor to the edge the crowd, growing larger now that police had arrived. The workers in orange vests gestured and shouted at one of the cops. The Three Musketeers stood next to Gina, talking to another officer with more control.

Agitated, Victor ran his hand over his buzzed head. With an angry glare, he twisted about and headed back to Lotta's Fountain. Drew and Tisha kept several strides behind.

Victor set a slanting path to the right, toward the building where he lived on the fourteenth floor. They couldn't allow him to get safely inside, where he might have more bots to release.

Drew communicated all those thoughts to Tisha with a look. She understood and nodded her agreement.

Confident, Drew trotted to Victor's side, matching his pace. "Do you know a good coffee shop around here?" Drew asked cheerfully.

"Fuck off."

"You look like a guy who knows where to find a powerful shot of espresso."

Victor stopped abruptly, snorting with rage. "Get the fuck away from me, or I'll knock you out cold."

"I'll bet you take four shots," Drew said breezily.

Suddenly wary, Victor trotted off. Drew kept abreast. Victor tapped his wallet against a pad, unlocking the building's door and pushing inside.

"Having a weak shot of espresso is like having half a tit."

Victor froze. His face went slack, his mouth open.

Tisha arrived. "We have a message from Mr. Thompson that you need to hear."

Victor glanced at Tisha as he returned outside. "I don't know a Mr. Thompson. You have me confused with someone else."

"You must remember Mr. Thompson. You knew him in Maple Grove. He has a message for you about Phil. You know, that time after the homecoming dance when you taught Phil a lesson about how to treat a girl? A girl like Jennifer?"

Drew saw Victor's intricate thoughts with perfect clarity, like examining a patterned block of marble. Amid the terror and confusion ran a strong vein of admiration and envy.

In the aftermath of Victor's failed plot to destroy the world, two strangers arrived, knowing his most private secrets. Drew knew Victor burned to be them, to have the power to stop a man in his tracks, the way he longed his whole life to be somebody other than Viktor Alexeev of Tolyatti, Russia. The desire formed at the center of his being the first time his father lay on top of him and his mother put a needle in her arm, but he couldn't kill that frightened little boy without destroying himself. His only option was to destroy everything else, a task too important to fail.

He had more bots.

"Give us the other sample of DemoDronesPaste, and we'll leave you alone," Drew offered.

Victor stared.

"There are other options for you," Drew went on. "You don't have to report to GRU. With your skills, you can vanish into a thousand places in America. You can be a new person."

"That's right," Tisha said. "Anything you want. Without a tie to Russia, you'll be a whole new man. Free."

"Are you with the U.S. government? The FBI?"

Their spontaneous laughter comforted him.

"Then who are you?"

"We're prophets. You've heard of us."

Victor started to speak, but Tisha held up a hand. "We won't tell you anything else. We can't. But we'll vanish soon enough. We always do."

Victor shrank with surrender. He seemed to morph into that little boy who was afraid to comfort his mother.

"We'll always be two steps ahead of you, Victor. You'll never get rid of us, so you might as well work with us."

The afternoon bustled around them, people worrying about an assignment at work, the new scratch on their car, their credit card debt. They hurried along, as unknowing as Stone Age humans just minutes after an asteroid had skimmed past.

"The other sample is secure," Victor said at last. "They won't escape for ten thousand years."

"Give them to us, and you'll be free." Tisha said with a warm smile. "I promise."

Drew ached to see the hope in his eyes. Victor was a deeply deranged man who still had the means to destroy the planet, but his eager, childlike desire to believe them stirred Drew's sympathy, for a moment at least.

Victor's decision was obvious even before he spoke. "Come with me. I'll give you the sample."

Drew was suspicious. Victor had another plan.

Drew stole a glance at Tisha, and she nodded, silently understanding and agreeing.

Victor led them to a garage behind his condo, muttering constantly. His sleek silver car was parked in a prime, first floor spot in an out-of-the-way cove. He hit a button on a fob and the car unlocked. He mumbled on, disjointed, as if the words were in no particular order.

Just out of his earshot, Tisha whispered, "He's losing it."

She was right. In a way, Victor's whole life had led him to this moment. Mr. Thompson promised him a new identity and took him to Maple Grove. He emerged stronger, immeasurably more capable, possessed of rare skills, and with a purpose. For all of that, he remained Viktor Alexeev of Tolyatti.

The trunk popped open, and Victor removed a small leather case. "Here's the other sample. It's an airtight cobalt container. They'll stay dormant as long as they stay inside." He handed the case to Tisha before he bent over the trunk to remove something else. He turned around holding a pistol, pointing it somewhere between them.

"Victor," Drew said, shaken to see a gun pointed at him no matter how quickly he would heal. "It's pointless to shoot us."

"Even prophets die. If I shoot you in the head, you'll die. But I won't shoot you if you take me with you."

"We have nowhere to go," Drew said. "We don't know what comes next."

He snorted. "You're prophets."

"It doesn't work like that."

"That's right," Tisha said. "We can't give you a life worth living. You have to make your own."

"I gave you my last sample of nanobots," he raged with quiet, compressed fury. The pistol shook slightly. "It's only fair you give something back."

"You've killed two people," Drew said. "We're being more than generous by letting you go."

With a sudden intake of breath and a rustle of clothing, Victor looked to his left and swung about. Drew grabbed Tisha just as Victor fired at something to the side.

The dry pop of the gun echoed like a cannon in the concrete surroundings. A split second later, Drew heard a volley too rapid to be anything other than two pistols firing at almost the same moment.

Drew looked just in time to see Victor's head snap back. A fine red mist flew off behind. Victor fell to the ground like a puppet with a cut string, crumpling into a bent pose only a dead man would make.

The echoes of the shots raced and bounced to every corner of the garage. People would come looking, and soon.

Tom was on the ground, clutching his side and hollering. His pistol dangled uselessly from a finger.

They rushed up and fell to their knees beside him. Pain distorted Tom's face.

"Tom!" Drew yelled. It earned him a fleeting look.

Suddenly, another man arrived with thatch-like hair and a craggy face. He nudged Drew and Tisha back. He cradled Tom and quickly located his wound. He shook his head. "He needs urgent medical attention."

Mesmerized, Drew saw the truth about the stranger.

Distant shouts came from somewhere in the garage.

"You two must leave," the man snapped. "Now!"

"Who are you?" Tisha said.

The handsome man waited for Drew to respond.

"He's my grandfather," Drew said.

"Go!" Arthur Brittany yelled. "The police will be here soon."

Drew helped Tisha to her feet. "Will Tom be okay?"

"Unless you've coordinated a believable story for the police, they'll pick your lies apart. Hurry!"

The shouts closed in. With a last look at his grandfather and Tom, Drew and Tisha fled.

Later that night, Drew and Tisha made a small bonfire on San Francisco's Ocean Beach. When the fire was raging, they filled it with rocks. Drew set the cobalt jar on the sand and opened the lid. Quickly, Tisha filled it with acid. They sealed and shook it rapidly. After they were certain the acid had destroyed the nanobots, they stood back. Drew hurled the jar to the rocks. It exploded with brilliant pinks, violets, and greens.

24

How Pizza and West Side Story *Saved My Life*

1976–present

At the beginning of this memoir, I said I would write about a particularly eventful year in my life, both professionally and personally. I trust you believe me now.

A year after Delilah was born, I gave birth to another daughter, Vivian. My son, Dennis, came along three years after that.

Loren's relationship with his children and his first wife improved considerably a few years after our marriage, when his ex-wife invited the whole family to the Upper East Side mansion for a big announcement. I was amazed to be included, and even more so by her welcoming, friendly attitude. She publicly forgave Loren for his lapse and introduced a woman named Wanda as her life partner to her blindsided family. They made a lively couple, and blending the families for holidays and special occasions became enjoyable.

In 1976, Barbara Walters became the first television journalist to command a salary of one million dollars. ABC installed her as co-anchor of the national news with Harry Reasoner. They bombed because they had the chemistry of cinder blocks plopped into anchor chairs, but the huge salary broke a psychological barrier.

By the late 1970s, the trappings of celebrity culture swamped national and major market television journalists. To me, it felt like a violation of our public trust. Agents became necessary to negotiate complicated contracts, along with publicists and marketing specialists. These professionals do difficult, essential jobs, but building trust as a journalist should come from a solid track record for accuracy, not superior branding.

Loren insisted I sign with an agent. When I dallied, he found one for me, causing a mini-scandal at work. Was he putting the network's interest first, or his wife's? The controversy caused major headaches for me, leading to our only patch of serious marital discord. After things quieted down, Loren apologized. He couldn't understand why I'd put up such a fuss. I explained I'd walked into my first television job literally off the street, and it was becoming impossible for new generations to do the same.

Similar barriers rose across the professional world. It wasn't intentional, but over time entry-level positions in prestigious careers became vanishingly rare for children of the working class, like me. Even middle-class students find themselves shut out because most creative environments now demand free labor dressed up as internships, in cities that grow ever more expensive. It reserves exciting opportunities for children of the wealthy elite and accelerates our widening class divisions. It also degrades creativity. The visionaries are hard at work somewhere, creating amazing art and lifting their voices, but not in the major cities where stagnation grows ever more pungent over American culture.

I worry about people like my grandson, Drew, who will read this memoir first. He's handsome, an undeniable advantage, especially when combined with his intelligence. But his courage and fortitude remain unforged because he's never had the chance to be tested by the fiery heat of pressure. I marvel to imagine what he's capable of once that happens.

I enjoyed *Perspectives* and loved working with Ron. The show was popular enough to withstand some risk. Several times a year, Ron and I put our considerable weight behind a controversial segment, like a look at the growing visibility of homosexuality, prompted by my memories of that bookstore window in San Francisco. We also covered the findings of the Church Commission, the Senate report on abuses in America's intelligence community. These and other segments drew fire, and we endured intense criticism from people who, most of the time, hadn't seen the report in question.

In the five years we were on the air, we never cracked the top ten in ratings, but millions of Americans watched every week, and I look back on our work with pride. We had our share of fluff, but I insisted every show have a segment produced with Jackie O in mind.

After my son Dennis was born in 1980, the presidential campaign was in full swing, and Ronald Reagan's victory seemed inevitable. I unexpectedly found myself dreading the end of maternity leave. Over the two previous years, my Q-Rating drifted down until it took unmistakable plunges, with a corresponding drop in our ratings. A new and unfamiliar anxiety overwhelmed me. I became obsessed with a graphic revamp and a new set, irrationally certain cosmetics could power us back. Ron argued it would make little difference, and rightly so.

Soon after I returned from maternity leave in the summer of 1980, seventeen thousand workers went on strike at the Lenin Shipyard in Gdansk, Poland, a thrilling roar of defiance against their Soviet overlords. The work stoppage spread and threatened to expand to other Soviet satellite countries. Within a few weeks, the panicked Kremlin ordered the Polish government to recognize the Solidarity federation of trade unions.

Americans cheered for union workers in Poland at the same time they cheered the anti-union rhetoric of Ronald Reagan in the U.S. I pitched a segment idea to Ron about the contradiction.

"It's a great idea," he said, "but no way. We'll piss off the advertisers, and many of our viewers will think we're making fun of them."

"Challenging them to think through their ideas isn't mocking them. Look, we always get our way when we stick to our guns."

He sagged. "Yeah, we'll get the segment on the air and then what? I'll have to listen to a bunch of lectures from brass about showing liberal bias. Then the union people will chew our heads off because we said something that proves we're corporate lackeys. And then the hordes will arrive with flaming torches because they heard you inflect a certain syllable or emphasize a certain word, or you made a little gesture that revealed our hidden agenda to destroy their community. A community they hate anyway, by all the available evidence. And all for a four-minute segment. I'm so sick of it, Claudia."

I was, too. Exhausted.

So, even before the 1980 election, both Ron and I resigned. They changed the title of the show and redesigned the graphics and the set.

It chugged on for another year, but their ratings sank from sight, and it was canceled.

When I told Loren I decided to resign, I also told him I wanted to be a full-time mother to our three children under five. "I'm only going to be a mom once, and I want to get it right."

At that moment, Loren decided to resign as well, to devote himself to fatherhood. With my savings, and Loren's alimony and child support behind him, we had plenty to live on without working.

I also told him I wanted to leave New York City. "It's a great place, but I'm tired of everyone living on top of each other. Why don't we move to your house in San Francisco?"

"We have three children and the house only has two bedrooms."

"Let's add another bedroom or two in back. There won't be much left of the yard, but we'll have enough to grow a vegetable garden and still have a patch of lawn."

I never regretted leaving television or New York, and I loved our years in San Francisco.

My oldest daughter, Delilah, was determined to set an individual path from the moment she took her first steps. When she was around ten years old, she cross-checked the math with the calendar and asked if Loren was her real father. I told her the truth. I'd had a brief but passionate fling with a man named Arthur Brittany, but I didn't know where to find him.

"Do I remind you of him?"

"Only in the best ways."

She was stunned, but also gleeful about having such a dramatic beginning. I delighted in imagining her reaction to learning she was a genuine royal princess. I know royal titles only pass through married parents, but if ever a case deserved some leeway... In the silliest errand of my life, I walked to the huge library across from San Francisco's city hall to study the line of succession for the English throne. I told myself it was a lark. I was the only mother on earth with a genuine reason to research the topic for my child's sake, and I should embrace such a singular opportunity. I was somewhat crushed to learn a law passed in 1701 to prevent Roman Catholics from taking the throne also cut off my daughter.

Delilah was a junior in high school when she and her boyfriend, Carl, nervously told us she was pregnant. We handled it as well as any parents could, I believe. When I was alone with Delilah later that night, I assured her I would support any decision she made.

"Do you mean an abortion?"

"Yes. But I'll be equally glad to support you as a mother."

She put on a brave face, but her eyes flashed with terror. "I love Carl, and we want to start a family."

Loren and I rented an apartment for them nearby. I enjoyed babysitting all my grandchildren, but in those first years with Delilah and Carl so young and living so close, I poured myself into caring for my grandson Drew until they moved across the bay to El Sobrante.

Loren was a solid husband, and I grew to love him in a fond, affectionate way. It lacked passion but eventually that proved a minor difficulty. He died in 1997, and I still think about and miss him every day.

In his will, Loren carved out a significant sum with instructions for me to do something with it for myself, whatever extravagant wish it could grant. I used it for an extremely pricey hour at the bottom of the Atlantic, looking out a tiny porthole at the wreckage of the *Titanic*.

In 2005, my son, Dennis, married, the last of my children to tie the knot. I still loved my neighborhood, a gay wonderland awash in rainbow flags by that time, but I grew impatient with city noise and bustle. With all three of my kids thriving in their own homes with their own families, I sold the San Francisco house and moved to Guerneville. I'd always lived in cities, and I longed for mornings full of birdsong.

Just before I left San Francisco, on my regular morning walk, I spotted the Three Musketeers down the sidewalk, heading in my direction. They wore new hairstyles and clothes, but they hadn't aged in thirty years. I suddenly understood Loren's shock at the Met's fundraising gala, when his eyes landed on his ageless prep school teacher.

I stepped into a storefront before they spotted me. I held my breath as they passed. I returned to the sidewalk to watch their backs until they turned a distant corner.

A few months after I settled into my lovely little cottage, a woman named Althea moved in across the street. We became friendly, but I detected a massive undercurrent in her interest about me and my family.

She frequently invited me for tea, and one day, a question popped into my head and came out of my mouth almost instantly. "Did Arthur Brittany send you to watch over me?"

"No. I've met him, but I have my own reasons for moving here."

"Do you know what's in the yellow box?"

"It holds a sense of raging injustice in the form of massive destruction. I wish I could be more precise, but that's all I know."

I plowed ahead. "Is Delilah out of danger?"

"None of us is ever out of danger."

"You know what I mean. They told me, 'the child must be saved.'"

"They weren't talking only about Delilah."

I never anticipated that possibility, and the implications loomed. Terrified, I stopped asking questions.

A few years later, Delilah and her husband were killed in a car accident at the bottom of my road. They were both thirty-six years old. It sent me reeling, and it took me a year to work up the courage to ask Althea if she could get a message to Arthur Brittany. "Please tell him I know why he left. He wasn't afraid of having a child, he was afraid of losing one. I understand now. It makes you feel unworthy of life, like you're stealing every breath. I don't need to see him. Just tell him I understand."

She nodded. "I'll try."

Months later, I was on one of my regular strolls in downtown Guerneville, such as it is. With only a few blocks, I walked back and forth many times on both sides of the street. I chatted with shop owners and locals, enjoying the sense of community.

I also loved looking in the windows, especially the antique store where an old, small mirror offered a smoky, speckled reflection inside a gloriously carved frame. A little paper tag read *Antwerp, 1590*, an age when mirrors were so rare and magical, they starred in fairy tales.

A man with thatched hair and a crooked smile stepped into the dim reflection. I gasped. I was an old, gray, and wrinkled woman, next to a vigorous and handsome man in his eternal prime. In four centuries, that mirror never cast a reflection more misbegotten and hopeless, revealing for all to see the impossibility of my only passionate love affair.

"Arthur!" I flushed with a pulse of enchantment that dissipated into a long thrum of loss. "Oh, my God, Arthur. I'm so old, and you're still so beautiful."

He gently took my hands. "I got your message about our daughter. Thank you."

I blinked back tears. "I hated you for so long, but that's in the past. I'm worried about our grandson. You have to protect him because I can't."

"I've been looking after Drew for years. I always will."

It was comforting. "I realized the whole truth about you soon after you left me in Florida. I can't tell him, so you must."

"Tell him what?"

"That his grandfather was heir to the English throne. He needs to know how special he is. He needs to hear it from someone other than me." Feeling off balance and short of breath, I took a step back. "I don't think I can talk to you much longer. I'm afraid I'm going to faint."

He gripped my shoulders. After forty years, his touch still filled me with a thrilling and delicious warmth. "Do you need to sit down?"

"No. I need you to listen to me. Before Drew was born, even before his *mother* was born, people warned me he's in danger. I absolutely do not want the details because I'll worry myself into an early grave, but please keep my grandson safe until I die. Let me go first, I'm begging you."

"I can't promise that, Claudia. It's not up to me."

Damn his dignified honesty. "Why did this destiny fall on Drew? Is it because you're his grandfather?"

"No. And it's not destiny. None of this is preordained. The pieces move, players leave their spots, others take them. It's all coincidental. Accidental."

"But what's the reason for all of this?"

"It hasn't come into focus yet, at least not for me. Something is approaching." He glanced into the sky and I knew it involved that mysterious object in space somehow. "It's been coming for so long, the journey must be a measurable fraction of eternity."

I placed a hand on his chest. "Please don't say any more. I'm going to walk away in just a second here. Promise not to follow me or to contact me again."

"Of course. But before you go, I must tell you Drew needs to be alert for a man named Victor. You need to tell him, but only at the right time."

"How will I know when it's the right time?"

"You'll know. That's how it always works. And finally, you must write your life story down for our grandson. It will save his life one day. I don't know how, but I know it will."

It was a radiant promise, a chance to redeem my mistakes, to repent for my stupidity. "Are you certain my story will save his life?"

"I promise."

His promise was golden. I squeezed his arm. "I'm so grateful I met you. Goodbye, Arthur."

It seemed a pitifully deficient way to bid farewell to Arthur Brittany for the last time, after the turbulent and magnificent way he disrupted my life. I walked off in tears.

I asked Althea what I should write, what part of my story would save Drew from danger, but she didn't know. "Write whatever feels appropriate, Claudia. Write what comes to your mind."

Over my life, I've learned just enough to realize how little I know. At times when I explore my woody, hilly neighborhood, I see a fern shake for no apparent reason deep in the stillness of the redwoods. I sit by the stream and hear conversations in a language I don't understand. I catch an unexplainable flash of ravishing color and light high in the trees.

So, at the risk of sounding like a superstitious old fool, before I started this memoir, I went into the forest and begged a muse to take pity on me. I explained my immense responsibility to write a story that was crucial for my grandson, but I didn't know what to say. I felt a compassionate and diligent spirit arrive a moment later, and she floated alongside as I returned home. Lately, I feel her restlessness, her yearning for the redwoods. I'm going to miss her.

My old producer Ron visits me when he's in Northern California, which isn't often. Of course, he hasn't aged a day, but you saw that coming from a mile away. For the past few years, he's been working as a landscape designer specializing in vertical gardens. He was here a few weeks ago, and I asked how it feels to go on living while everything changes.

"Change is easy," he said. "Humans adjust to anything, except the death of people you love. You learn to accept it, but it's never easy."

The old saying goes that money can't buy happiness but neither can fame make you happy. Love doesn't bring happiness either, which many of us seem to forget despite the overwhelming evidence from our own lives.

I hear my grandson pulling into my driveway for the weekend. Tonight, we're going to be adventurous and make a pizza from scratch, tomato sauce and all. Tomorrow we have tickets to see a community theatre production of *West Side Story*. We've seen some of the players in other productions, and the woman who plays Maria has a sweet, innocent voice.

I'm so happy when he's here.

25

After five days in the hospital, Tom was released with a cracked rib and without a spleen, frozen like a statue in a wheelchair. Drew carried Tom's medication and personal things in a plastic bag and pushed him to the parking garage. Next to his car, Drew locked the chair. He set Tom's cell phone on top of a concrete barrier and pulled out a hammer.

"I know all about Maple Grove," Drew said. Tom's eyes went wide. "If you want to recuperate in Guerneville, you can't bring your phone. Or you can keep your phone, and I'll drop you off wherever you want, but you can't call or visit me again. I don't want Russian intelligence showing up at my door in the middle of the night."

"My phone is untraceable. You can track individual towers, but it doesn't have any GPS features."

"Maybe that's true or maybe that's just what they told you. Either way, I'm not taking any chances."

"You're telling me to give up my life. To be a traitor."

"I'm only telling you to make a decision about where you want to recover."

Tom took a heavy breath followed by a wince of pain. "Do you want me around?"

Drew nodded. "Yeah. I do. I think we have as much of a chance to make it work as any two guys ever had. It's worth a try. How do you feel about it?"

A slow smile spread across Tom's face. "Smash it."

Drew raised the hammer, and Tom winced and chuckled through the slaughter.

Back at Drew's house, after positioning Tom upright on the couch, Drew pulled a chair to his side.

"Why were you tailing Victor?"

"GRU has been nervous about Victor for a while. Aside from him, your average GRU agent is fairly distinctive. They didn't want to send one of their own, so I got the assignment."

"Weren't you afraid he'd recognize you?"

"We were teenagers in Maple Grove. We've both changed. Why were you following him?"

"I'll tell you some day. For now, I want to know if you've ever heard of the prophets."

Tom went cautious. "Every intelligence agency on earth knows about them. It's one of those legends nobody really believes, but everyone has a story about. You know, they heard something from an old teacher, who heard a story from one of their old teachers."

Drew explained about himself and Tisha. When he was finished, Tom looked at the wall in silence for a long while.

Drew squeezed his hand. "We can talk about this later."

Tom remained upright and immobile most of the time. They tapered the meds, and Drew admired his stoic resistance against pain, a scrunched, quiet face. Tom's sexual desires sometimes overpowered the discomfort, and they developed inventive ways of working on each other, most of which required Drew to do all the work, but he didn't mind. At all.

Tisha turned inward after they thwarted Victor, becoming solemn. She dropped out of school and quit the hospice. Drew asked why, but she put him off, telling him she'd explain when the time was right.

Althea invited Drew and Tisha to her house. She'd been steadfast in her refusal to answer their questions, but Drew's need to know felt less urgent. Aside from his burning curiosity about the spaceship, he knew he'd have any information when he needed it, just as Althea always promised.

They sat at her kitchen table. "I'm leaving," Althea said, stopping their protests with a hand. "I'm needed elsewhere. Whatever is to come, you'll be able to handle it without my help."

She explained that she filed a quitclaim deed, giving ownership of her house and its contents to Tisha.

"It's important for you to keep close to each other. Someone will be here soon who will need your guidance and protection. The visions will start again when necessary."

"And who decides when it's necessary?" Drew said. "The aliens in that spaceship?"

"Ultimately, the answers spring from your own mind. For this next phase, they are in this very room." Her voice dropped to a whisper. "The child must be saved."

Drew sat up. "I was the child who must be saved, to stop Victor from releasing the nanobots."

"Tisha?" Althea said. "Do you have something to tell us?"

Tisha squirmed. "I haven't told anybody, but I'm not surprised you know."

"What are you talking about?"

"I'm pregnant," Tisha said.

"Tisha's child *must* be saved," Althea said. "Both of you are integral as we flip the page to the final chapter. I've been waiting a thousand years for what is coming. It will be more spectacular and terrifying than anything so far."

Althea left two days later. Drew returned her necklace before she left.

Drew helped Tisha move into Althea's old house. With her frugal nature and the limits of a small apartment, it only took a few hours. After a hug and a kiss, Drew left her to settle into her new home.

Drew walked into the street, looking at his cottage. Tom was inside, propped up on pillows. Sometimes, Tom's eyes sank into despair so deep Drew began to suspect Tom would slip away as soon as he felt better. He wouldn't blame him. What did it mean to become involved with someone like Drew who never aged and who lived at the mercy of visions?

For that matter, what did it mean for Drew? He had family and friends scattered around. He didn't see much of them, but he kept in touch sporadically on social media and with texts. How could he do that now? Wasn't it better to slink away silently?

It was dusk. He walked down the lane to the redwood forest,

where the light dimmed by the moment. He stepped into the stillness of the woods and looked about.

Suddenly, the woodland filled with pure white light. Unlike streaming shafts of sunlight, this white light exposed everything, squeezing the shadows into sketch lines.

The change was too rapid to be anything but a vision. He looked up, expecting to see the alien spaceship.

It wasn't alien, but it filled him with terror.

About the Author

Bud Gundy is a Lambda Literary Award Finalist. He's won two Emmy Awards and is an executive producer at KQED, San Francisco's PBS and NPR affiliate. Born and raised near Cleveland, Ohio, he started his television career in 1983 and has lived in San Francisco since 1988. He is one-half of a popular on-air fundraising team and you can see and hear him on the air, asking for support during those annoying pledge drives. He's a history and science buff and lives with his boyfriend, Chris. Visit his website at budgundy.com.

Books Available From Bold Strokes Books

Accidental Prophet by Bud Gundy. Days after his grandmother dies, Drew Morten learns his true identity and finds himself racing against time to save civilization from the apocalypse. (978-1-63555-452-6)

In Case You Forgot by Fredrick Smith and Chaz Lamar. Zaire and Kenny, two newly single, Black, queer, and socially aware men, start again—in love, career, and life—in the West Hollywood neighborhood of LA. (978-1-63555-493-9)

Counting for Thunder by Phillip Irwin Cooper. A struggling actor returns to the Deep South to manage a family crisis but finds love and ultimately his own voice as his mother is regaining hers for possibly the last time. (978-1-63555-450-2)

Survivor's Guilt and Other Stories by Greg Herren. Award-winning author Greg Herren's short stories are finally pulled together into a single collection, including the Macavity Award–nominated title story and the first-ever Chanse MacLeod short story. (978-1-63555-413-7)

Saints + Sinners Anthology 2019, edited by Tracy Cunningham and Paul Willis. An anthology of short fiction featuring the finalist selections from the 2019 Saints + Sinners Literary Festival. (978-1-63555-447-2)

The Shape of the Earth by Gary Garth McCann. After appearing in *Best Gay Love Stories*, *HarringtonGMFQ*, *Q Review*, and *Off the Rocks*, Lenny and his partner Dave return in a hotbed of manhood and jealousy. (978-1-63555-391-8)

Exit Plans for Teenage Freaks by 'Nathan Burgoine. Cole always has a plan—especially for escaping his small-town reputation as "that kid who was kidnapped when he was four"—but when he teleports to a museum, it's time to face facts: it's possible he's a total freak after all. (978-1-163555-098-6)

Death Checks In by David S. Pederson. Despite Heath's promises to Alan to not get involved, Heath can't resist investigating a shopkeeper's murder in Chicago, which dashes their plans for a romantic weekend getaway. (978-1-163555-329-1)

Of Echoes Born by 'Nathan Burgoine. A collection of queer fantasy short stories set in Canada from Lambda Literary Award finalist 'Nathan Burgoine. (978-1-63555-096-2)

The Lurid Sea by Tom Cardamone. Cursed to spend eternity on his knees, Nerites is having the time of his life. (978-1-62639-911-2)

Sinister Justice by Steve Pickens. When a vigilante targets citizens of Jake Finnigan's hometown, Jake and his partner Sam fall under suspicion themselves as they investigate the murders. (978-1-63555-094-8)

Club Arcana: Operation Janus by Jon Wilson. Wizards, demons, Elder Gods: Who knew the universe was so crowded, and that they'd all be out to get Angus McAslan? (978-1-62639-969-3)

Triad Soul by 'Nathan Burgoine. Luc, Anders, and Curtis—vampire, demon, and wizard—must use their powers of blood, soul, and magic to defeat a murderer determined to turn their city into a battlefield. (978-1-62639-863-4)

Gatecrasher by Stephen Graham King. Aided by a high-tech thief, the Maverick Heart crew race against time to prevent a cadre of savage corporate mercenaries from seizing control of a revolutionary wormhole technology. (978-1-62639-936-5)

Wicked Frat Boy Ways by Todd Gregory. Beta Kappa brothers Brandon Benson and Phil Connor play an increasingly dangerous game of love, seduction, and emotional manipulation. (978-1-62639-671-5)

Death Goes Overboard by David S. Pederson. Heath Barrington and Alan Keyes are two sides of a steamy love triangle as they encounter gangsters, con men, murder, and more aboard an old lake steamer. (978-1-62639-907-5)

A Careful Heart by Ralph Josiah Bardsley. Be careful what you wish for…love changes everything. (978-1-62639-887-0)

Worms of Sin by Lyle Blake Smythers. A haunted mental asylum turned drug treatment facility exposes supernatural detective Finn M'Coul to an outbreak of murderous insanity, a strange parasite, and ghosts that seek sex with the living. (978-1-62639-823-8)

Tartarus by Eric Andrews-Katz. When Echidna, Mother of all Monsters, escapes from Tartarus and into the modern world, only an Olympian has the power to oppose her. (978-1-62639-746-0)

Rank by Richard Compson Sater. Rank means nothing to the heart, but the Air Force isn't as impartial. Every airman learns that rank has its privileges. What about love? (978-1-62639-845-0)

The Grim Reaper's Calling Card by Donald Webb. When Katsuro Tanaka begins investigating the disappearance of a young nurse, he discovers more missing persons, and they all have one thing in common: The Grim Reaper Tarot Card. (978-1-62639-748-4)

Smoldering Desires by C.E. Knipes. Evan McGarrity has found the man of his dreams in Sebastian Tantalos. When an old boyfriend from Sebastian's past enters the picture, Evan must fight for the man he loves. (978-1-62639-714-9)

www.ingramcontent.com/pod-product-compliance
Lightning Source LLC
Chambersburg PA
CBHW032209030726
47494CB00020B/934